Stay with Me

Center Point
Large Print

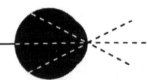

**This Large Print Book carries the
Seal of Approval of N.A.V.H.**

Stay with Me

Ayobami Adebayo

CENTER POINT LARGE PRINT
THORNDIKE, MAINE

This Center Point Large Print edition is published in the year 2017 by arrangement with Alfred A. Knopf, an imprint of The Knopf Doubleday Publishing Group, a division of Penguin Random House LLC.

This is a work of fiction.
Names, characters, places, and incidents either are the product of the author's imagination or are used fictitiously. Any resemblance to actual persons, living or dead, events, or locales is entirely coincidental.

The text of this Large Print edition is unabridged. In other aspects, this book may vary from the original edition. Printed in the United States of America on permanent paper. Set in 16-point Times New Roman type.

ISBN: 978-1-68324-570-4

Library of Congress Cataloging-in-Publication Data

Names: Adebayo, Ayobami, 1988- author.
Title: Stay with me / Ayobami Adebayo.
Description: Center Point Large Print edition. | Thorndike, Maine : Center Point Large Print, 2017.
Identifiers: LCCN 2017034640 | ISBN 9781683245704 (hardcover : alk. paper)
Subjects: LCSH: Married people—Fiction. | Parent and child—Fiction. | Loss (Psychology)—Fiction. | Nigeria—Fiction. | Domestic fiction. | Psychological fiction. | Large type books.
Classification: LCC PR9387.9.A319 S73 2017c | DDC 823/.92—dc23
LC record available at https://lccn.loc.gov/2017034640

For my mother, Dr. Olusola Famurewa,
who continues to make our home
a wonderland where every room
brims with books,
with love and gratitude.

And in memory of my father,
Mr. Adebayo Famurewa,
who left behind a library and a legacy:
I miss you still.

PART ONE

1

I must leave this city today and come to you. My bags are packed and the empty rooms remind me that I should have left a week ago. Musa, my driver, has slept at the security guard's post every night since last Friday, waiting for me to wake him up at dawn so we can set out on time. But my bags still sit in the living room, gathering dust.

I have given most of what I acquired here—furniture, electronic devices, even house fittings—to the stylists who worked in my salon. So, every night for a week now, I've tossed about on this bed without a television to shorten my insomniac hours.

There's a house waiting for me in Ife, right outside the university where you and I first met. I imagine it now, a house not unlike this one, its many rooms designed to nurture a big family: man, wife and many children. I was supposed to leave a day after my hair dryers were taken down. The plan was to spend a week setting up my new salon and furnishing the house. I wanted my new life in place before seeing you again.

It's not that I've become attached to this place.

I will not miss the few friends I made, the people who do not know the woman I was before I came here, the men who over the years have thought they were in love with me. Once I leave, I probably won't even remember the one who asked me to be his wife. Nobody here knows I'm still married to you. I only tell them a slice of the story: I was barren and my husband took another wife. No one has ever probed further, so I've never told them about my children.

I have wanted to leave since the three corpers in the National Youth Service programme were killed. I decided to shut down my salon and the jewellery shop before I even knew what I would do next, before the invitation to your father's funeral arrived like a map to show me the way. I have memorised the three young men's names and I know what each one studied at the university. My Olamide would have been about their age; she too would just have been leaving university about now. When I read about them, I think of her.

Akin, I often wonder if you think about her too.

Although sleep stays away, every night I shut my eyes and pieces of the life I left behind come back to me. I see the batik pillowcases in our bedroom, our neighbours and your family which, for a misguided period, I thought was also mine. I see you. Tonight I see the bedside lamp you gave me a few weeks after we got married. I could not sleep in the dark and you had nightmares if we left the fluorescent lights on. That lamp was your solution. You bought it without telling me you'd come up with a compromise, without asking me if I wanted a lamp. And as I stroked its bronze base and admired the tinted glass panels that formed its shade, you asked me what I would take out of the building if our house was burning. I didn't think about it before saying, *Our baby,* even though we did not have children yet. *Something,* you said, *not someone.* But you seemed a little hurt that, when I thought it was someone, I did not consider rescuing you.

I drag myself out of bed and change out of my nightgown. I will not waste another minute. The questions you must answer, the ones I've choked on for over a decade, quicken my steps as I grab my handbag and go into the living room.

There are seventeen bags here, ready to be carried into my car. I stare at the bags, recalling the contents of each one. If this house was on fire, what would I take? I have to think about this because the first thing that occurs to me is *nothing.* I choose the overnight bag I'd planned to bring with me for the funeral and a leather pouch filled with gold jewellery. Musa can bring the rest of the bags to me another time.

This is it then—fifteen years here and, though my house is not on fire, all I'm taking is a bag of gold and a change of clothes. The things that matter are inside me, locked up below my breast as though in a grave, a place of permanence, my coffin-like treasure chest.

I step outside. The air is freezing and the black sky is turning purple in the horizon as the sun ascends. Musa is leaning against the car, cleaning his teeth with a stick. He spits into a cup as I approach and puts the chewing stick in his breast pocket. He opens the car door, we exchange greetings and I climb into the back seat.

Musa switches on the car radio and searches for stations. He settles for one that is starting the day's broadcast with a recording of the national anthem. The security guard waves goodbye as we drive out of the compound. The road stretches before us, shrouded in a darkness transitioning into dawn as it leads me back to you.

2

Even then, I could sense that they had come prepared for war. I could see them through the glass panes on the door. I could hear their chatter. They did not seem to notice that I had been standing on the other side of the door for almost a full minute. I wanted to leave them standing outside and go back upstairs to sleep. Maybe they would melt into pools of brown mud if they stayed long enough in the sun. Iya Martha's buttocks were so big that, if melted, they would have taken up all the space on the concrete steps that led up to our doorway.

Iya Martha was one of my four mothers; she had been my father's oldest wife. The man who came with her was Baba Lola, Akin's uncle. They both hunched their backs against the sun and wore determined frowns that made their faces repulsive. Yet, as soon as I opened the door, their conversation stopped and they broke into smiles. I could guess the first words that would come out of the woman's mouth. I knew it would be some lavish show of a bond that had never existed between us.

"Yejide, my precious daughter!" Iya Martha

grinned, cupping my cheeks with moist and fleshy hands.

I grinned back and knelt to greet them. "Welcome, welcome. God must have woken up thinking of me today-o. That is why you are all here," I said, bending in a semi-kneel again after they had come in and were seated in the sitting room.

They laughed.

"Where is your husband? Do we meet him at home?" Baba Lola asked, looking around the room as though I had stashed Akin under a chair.

"Yes, sir, he is upstairs. I'll go and call him after I serve your drinks. What should I prepare for food? Pounded yam?"

The man glanced at my stepmother as though, while rehearsing for the drama that was about to unfold, he had not read this part of their script.

Iya Martha shook her head from side to side. "We cannot eat. Get your husband. We have important things to discuss with the two of you."

I smiled, left the sitting-room area and headed for the staircase. I thought I knew what "important things" they had come to discuss. A number of my in-laws had been in our home previously to discuss the same issue. A discussion consisted of them talking and me listening while on my knees. At those times, Akin pretended to listen and jot notes while writing his to-do list for the next day. No one in the series of delegations could read or write and they were all in awe of those who could. They were impressed that Akin wrote down their words. And sometimes, if he stopped writing, the person speaking at the time would complain that Akin was disrespecting him or her by not noting anything down. My husband often planned his entire week during such visits, while I got terrible cramps in my legs.

The visits irritated Akin and he wanted to tell his relatives to mind their own business, but I would not allow it. The long discussions did give me leg cramps, but at least they made me feel I was part of his family. Until that afternoon, no one in my family had paid me that kind of visit since I'd got married.

As I went up the stairs, I knew that Iya Martha's presence meant some new point was about to be made. I did not need their advice. My home was fine without the important things they had to say. I did not want to hear Baba Lola's hoarse voice being forced out in between coughs or see another flash of Iya Martha's teeth.

I believed I had heard it all already anyway and I was sure my husband would feel the same way. I was surprised to find Akin awake. He worked six days a week and slept through most Sundays. But he was pacing the floor when I entered our room.

"You knew they would come today?" I searched his face for the familiar mix of horror and irritation that it wore any time a special delegation came visiting.

"They are here?" He stood still and clasped his hands behind his head. No horror, no irritation. The room began to feel stuffy.

"You knew they were coming? You didn't tell me?"

"Let's just go downstairs." He walked out of the room.

"Akin, what is going on? What is happening?" I called after him.

I sat down on the bed, held my head in my hands and tried to breathe. I stayed that way until I heard Akin's voice calling me. I went to join him in the sitting room downstairs. I wore a smile, not a big one that showed teeth, just a small lift at the corners of my mouth. The kind that said, *Even though you old people know nothing about my marriage, I am delighted, no, ecstatic, to hear all the important things you have to say about it. After all, I am a good wife.*

I did not notice her at first, even though she was perched on the edge of Iya Martha's chair. She was fair, pale yellow like the inside of an unripe mango. Her thin lips were covered with blood-red lipstick.

I leaned towards my husband. His body felt stiff and he did not put his arms around me and pull me close. I tried to figure out where the yellow woman had come from, wondering for a

16

wild minute if Iya Martha had kept her hidden under her wrapper when she came in.

"Our wife, our people say that when a man has a possession and it becomes two he does not become angry, right?" Baba Lola said.

I nodded and smiled.

"Well, our wife, this is your new wife. It is one child that calls another one into this world. Who knows, the king in heaven may answer your prayers because of this wife. Once she gets pregnant and has a child, we are sure you will have one too," Baba Lola said.

Iya Martha nodded her agreement. "Yejide, my daughter, we have thought about and slept on this issue many times, your husband's people and me. And your other mothers."

I shut my eyes. I was about to wake up from the trance. When I opened my eyes, the mango-yellow woman was still there, a little blurry but still there. I was dazed.

I had expected them to talk about my childless-ness. I was armed with millions of smiles. Apologetic smiles, pity-me smiles, I-look-unto-God smiles—name all the fake smiles needed to get through an afternoon with a group of people who claim to want the best for you while poking at your open sore with a stick—and I had them ready. I was ready to listen to them tell me I must do something about my situation. I expected to hear about a new pastor I could visit; a new

17

mountain where I could go to pray; or an old herbalist in a remote village or town whom I could consult. I was armed with smiles for my lips, an appropriate sheen of tears for my eyes and sniffles for my nose. I was prepared to lock up my hairdressing salon throughout the coming week and go in search of a miracle with my mother-in-law in tow. What I was not expecting was another smiling woman in the room, a yellow woman with a blood-red mouth who grinned like a new bride.

I wished my mother-in-law were there. She was the only woman I had ever called *Moomi*. I visited her more often than her son did. She had watched while my fresh perm was washed off into a flowing river by a priest whose theory was that I had been cursed by my mother before she died, minutes after giving birth to me. Moomi was there with me when I sat on a prayer mat for three days, chanting words that I didn't understand over and over until I fainted on the third day, cutting short what should have been a seven-day fast and vigil.

While I recovered in a ward at Wesley Guild Hospital, she held my hand and asked me to pray for strength. A good mother's life is hard, she said, a woman can be a bad wife but she must not be a bad mother. Moomi told me that before asking God to give me a child, I must ask for the grace to be able to suffer for that child. She said I wasn't ready to be a mother yet if I was fainting after three days of fasting.

I realised then that she had not fainted on the third day because she had probably gone on that kind of fast several times to appease God on behalf of her children. In that moment, the lines etched around Moomi's eyes and mouth became sinister, they began to mean more to me than signs of old age. I was torn. I wanted to be this thing that I never had. I wanted to be a mother, to have my eyes shine with secret joys and wisdom like Moomi's. Yet all her talk about suffering was terrifying.

"Her age is not even close to yours," Iya Martha leaned forward in her seat. "Because they appreciate you, Yejide, your husband's people know your value. They told me that they recognise that you are a good wife in your husband's house."

Baba Lola cleared his throat. "Yejide, I as a person, I want to praise you. I want to appreciate your efforts to make sure that our son leaves a child behind when he dies. This is why we know that you will not take this new wife like a rival. Her name is Funmilayo and we know, we trust, that you will take her as your younger sister."

"Your friend," Iya Martha said.

"Your daughter," Baba Lola said.

Iya Martha tapped Funmi on the back. "*Oya*, you go and greet your *iyale*."

19

I shuddered when Iya Martha referred to me as Funmi's *iyale*. The word crackled in my ears, *iyale—first* wife. It was a verdict that marked me as not woman enough for my husband.

Funmi came to sit beside me on the couch.

Baba Lola shook his head. "Funmi, kneel down. Twenty years after the train has started its journey, it will always meet the land ahead of it. Yejide is ahead of you in every way in this house."

Funmi knelt down, placed her hands on my knees and smiled. My hands itched to slap the smile off her face.

I turned to look Akin in the eyes, hoping that somehow he was not part of the ambush. His gaze held mine in a silent plea. My already-stiff smile slipped. Rage closed its flaming hands around my heart. There was a pounding in my head, right between my eyes.

"Akin, you knew this?" I spoke in English, shutting out the two elders who spoke only Yoruba.

Akin said nothing; he scratched the bridge of his nose with a forefinger.

I looked around the room for something to focus on. The white lace curtains with blue trimmings, the grey couch, the matching rug that had a coffee stain that I had been trying to remove for over a year. The stain was too far off-centre to be covered by the table, too far from the edge to be concealed by the armchairs. Funmi wore a beige dress, the same shade as the coffee stain, the same shade as the blouse that I wore. Her hands were just below my knees, wrapped around my bare legs. I could not look past her hands, past the long billowy sleeves of her dress. I could not look at her face.

"Yejide, pull her close."

I was not sure who had just spoken. My head was hot, heating up, close to boiling point. Anyone could have said those words—Iya Martha, Baba Lola, God. I did not care.

I turned to my husband again. "Akin, you knew about this? You knew and could not tell me. You knew? You bloody bastard. After everything! You wretched bastard!"

Akin caught my hand before it landed on his cheek.

It was not the outrage in Iya Martha's scream that stopped my words. It was the tender way Akin's thumb stroked my palm. I looked away from his eyes.

"What is she saying?" Baba Lola asked the new wife for an interpretation.

"Yejide, please," Akin squeezed my hand.

"She says he is a bastard," Funmi translated in a whisper, as though the words were too hot and heavy for her mouth.

Iya Martha screamed and covered her face with her hands. I was not fooled by her display.

21

I knew she was gloating inside. I was sure she would spend weeks repeating what she had seen to my father's other wives.

"You must not abuse your husband, this child. No matter how things appear, he is still your husband. What more do you want him to do for you? Is it not because of you that he has found a flat for Funmi to stay in when he has a big duplex right here?" Iya Martha looked around the sitting room, spreading her palms to point out the big duplex in case I had missed her reference to the house for which I paid half of the rent every month. "You, this Yejide. You must be grateful to your husband."

Iya Martha had stopped talking, but her mouth still hung open. If one moved close enough, that mouth oozed an unbearable stench, like stale urine. Baba Lola had chosen a seat that was a safe distance from her.

I knew I was supposed to kneel down, bow my head like a schoolgirl being punished and say I was sorry for insulting my husband and his mother in one breath. They would have accepted my excuses—I could have said it was the devil, the weather, or that my new braids were too tight, made my head ache and forced me to disrespect my husband in front of them. My whole body was clenched like an arthritic hand and I just could not force it to make shapes that it did not want to make. So for the first time, I ignored an in-law's displeasure and stood up when I was expected to kneel. I felt taller as I rose to my full height.

"I will prepare the food," I said, refusing to ask them again what they wanted to eat. Now that they had introduced Funmi, it was acceptable for Baba Lola and Iya Martha to have a meal. I was not ready to cook a separate meal for each person, so I served them what I wanted. I gave them bean pottage. I mixed the three-day-old beans I had been planning to throw in the bin with the freshly cooked pottage. Even though I was sure they would notice that the mixture tasted a little bad, I counted on the guilt Baba Lola was masking with outrage at my behaviour and the glee Iya Martha was hiding beneath her displays of dismay to keep them eating. In order to help the food down their throats, I knelt down to apologise to the two of them. Iya Martha smiled and said she would have refused to eat if I had gone on behaving like a street child. I apologised again and hugged the yellow woman for good measure; she smelled like coconut oil and vanilla. I drank from a bottle of malt as I watched them eat. I was disappointed that Akin refused to eat anything.

When they complained that they would have preferred pounded yam with vegetable stew and dry fish, I ignored Akin's look. On some other day I would have gone back to the kitchen to pound yam. That afternoon, I wanted to tell them to get up and pound the yam if they really wanted

23

pounded yam. I swallowed the words burning in my throat with gulps of malt and told them I could not pound because I had sprained my hand the day before.

"But you didn't say that when we first got here." Iya Martha scratched her chin. "You yourself offered to give us pounded yam."

"She must have forgotten about the sprain. She was really in pain yesterday. I even considered taking her to the hospital," Akin said, backing up my fairly obvious lie.

They shovelled the beans into their mouths like starving children, advising me to get the hand checked at the hospital. It was only Funmi who squeezed her mouth around the first mouthful of beans and looked at me with suspicion. Our eyes met and she smiled a wide red-rimmed smile.

After I cleared away the empty plates, Baba Lola explained that he had not been sure how long the visit would last, so he had not bothered to make any arrangements for the cab driver who had dropped them off to come back and pick them up. He assumed, the way relatives often do, that Akin would take responsibility for getting them back home.

Soon it was time for Akin to drop everyone off. As I saw them to his car, Akin jiggled his keys in his trouser pocket and asked if everyone was fine with the route he intended to take. He wanted to drop Baba Lola off on Ilaje Street and then drive

Iya Martha all the way to Ife. I noticed that he did not say anything about where Funmi lived. After Iya Martha said the route my husband picked was the best option, Akin unlocked the car doors and got into the driver's seat.

I stifled the urge to pull out Funmi's *jheri* curls because she slipped into the front seat beside my husband and pushed the small cushion I always kept there to the floor. I clenched my fists as Akin drove away, leaving me alone in the cloud of dust he had raised.

"What did you feed them?" Akin shouted.

"Bridegroom, welcome back," I said. I had just finished eating my dinner. I picked up the plates and headed for the kitchen.

"You know they all have diarrhoea now? I had to park by a bush for them to shit. A bush!" he said, following me into the kitchen.

"What is so unheard of about that? Do your relatives have toilets in their homes? Don't they shit in bushes and on dunghills?" I yelled, slamming the plates in the metal sink. The sound of cracking china was followed by silence. One of the plates had cracked in the middle. I ran my finger over the broken surface. I felt it pierce me. My blood stained the jagged space in trickles.

"Yejide, try and understand. You know I am not going to hurt you," he said.

"What language are you speaking? Hausa

or Chinese? Me, I don't understand you. Start speaking something I understand, Mr. Bridegroom."

"Stop calling me that."

"I will call you what I want. At least you are still my husband. Ah, but maybe you are not my husband again. Did I miss that news too? Should I switch on the radio or is it on television? In the newspaper?" I dumped the broken plate into the plastic dustbin that stood beside the sink. I turned to face him.

His forehead glistened with beads of sweat that ran down his cheeks and gathered at his chin. He was tapping a foot to some furious beat in his head. The muscles in his face moved to that same beat as he clenched and unclenched his jaw. "You called me a bastard in front of my uncle. You disrespected me."

The anger in his voice shook me, outraged me. I had thought his vibrating body meant he was nervous—it usually did. I had hoped it meant he felt sorry, guilty. "You brought a new wife into this house and you are angry? When did you marry her? Last year? Last month? When did you plan to tell me? Eh? You this—"

"Don't say it, woman, don't say that word. You need a padlock on your mouth."

"Well, since I don't have that, I will say it, you bloody—"

His hand covered my mouth. "OK, I'm sorry.

26

I was in a difficult situation. You know I won't cheat on you, Yejide. You know I can't, I can't do that. I promise." He laughed. It was a broken, pathetic sound.

I prised his hand away from my face. He held on to my hand, rubbing his palm against mine. I wanted to weep.

"You have another wife, you paid her bride price and prostrated in front of her family. I think you are already cheating."

He placed my palm over his heart; it was beating fast. "This is not cheating on you; I don't have a new wife. Trust me, it's for the best. My mother won't pressure you for children anymore," he whispered.

"Nonsense and rubbish." I snatched my hand away and walked out of the kitchen.

"If it makes you feel better, Funmi couldn't make it into the bush fast enough. She soiled her dress."

I did not feel better. I would not feel better for a very long time. Already, I was coming undone, like a hastily tied scarf coming loose, on the ground before the owner is aware of it.

3

Yejide was created on a Saturday. When God had ample time to paint her a perfect ebony. No doubt about it. The finished work is living proof.

The first time I saw her, I wanted to touch her jeans-clad knee, tell her there and then: "My name is Akin Ajayi. I am going to marry you."

She was effortlessly elegant. Only girl on the row who didn't slouch. Held her chin up, didn't bend sideways to lean on the orange armrests. Sat straight, shoulders squared, hands linked and held in front of her bare midriff. I couldn't believe I hadn't noticed her in the ticket queue downstairs.

She glanced to her left some minutes before the lights went out; our eyes met. She didn't look away like I expected and I straightened up under her gaze. She looked me up and down, sized me up. It was not enough that she smiled at me before turning to face the big cinema screen. I wanted more.

She seemed unaware of her effect. Appeared oblivious to the way I was gawking at her, enthralled, already thinking about the words that would convince her to go out with me.

Unfortunately, I couldn't talk to her at once.

The lights went out right after I came up with the words I had been trying to find. And the girl I was going out with at the time was seated between Yejide and me.

I broke up with the girl that night, right after the movie. I did it while we stood together in the foyer of Oduduwa Hall in Ife as the crowd that had come to watch the film show flowed past us. I said to her, "Please find your way to your hostel. I'll see you tomorrow." I clasped my hands together apologetically, though I didn't feel sorry. Would never feel sorry. I left her standing there with her mouth slightly open.

I pushed through the throng. Searched for a beauty in blue jeans, platform sandals and white T-shirt that showed off her belly button. I found her. Yejide and I were married before the end of that year.

I loved Yejide from the very first moment. No doubt about that. But there are things even love can't do. Before I got married, I believed love could do anything. I learned soon enough that it couldn't bear the weight of four years without children. If the burden is too much and stays too long, even love bends, cracks, comes close to breaking and sometimes does break. But even when it's in a thousand pieces around your feet, that doesn't mean it's no longer love.

After four years, nobody else cared about love. My mother didn't. She talked about my responsibility to her as a first son. Reminded me about the nine months when the only world I knew was inside her. She focused on the hardship of the last three months. How she couldn't get comfortable in bed and had to spend her nights in a cushioned armchair.

Soon, Moomi began talking about Juwon, my half-brother, the first son of my father's second wife. It'd been years since Moomi had used him as an example. When I was much younger, she was always talking about him. *Juwon never comes home with dirty uniforms; why is your shirt dirty? Juwon has never lost his school sandals; this is the third pair you've lost this term. Juwon is always home by three; where do you go after school? How come Juwon came home with prizes and you didn't? You are the first son in this family, do you know what that means? Do you know what that means at all? Do you want him to take your place?*

She stopped talking about Juwon when he decided to learn a trade after secondary school because his mother couldn't afford to pay his university fees. Guess Moomi felt there was no way a boy who was training to become a carpenter could ever measure up to her university-trained children. For years, she didn't talk about Juwon, and appeared to have lost interest in his life until she wanted me to marry another wife. Then she told me, as if I didn't already know, that Juwon already had four children, all boys. This time she didn't stop with Juwon but reminded me that all my half-brothers now had children.

After I'd been married to Yejide for two years, my mother began to show up in my office on the first Monday of every month. She didn't come alone. Each time, she brought a new woman with her, a potential second wife. She never missed a first Monday. Not even when she was ill. We had an agreement. As long as I continued to let her bring the women to my office, she would never embarrass my wife by showing up at our home with any of her candidates; she would never mention her efforts to Yejide.

When my mother threatened that she would start visiting my wife each week with a new woman if I didn't choose one within a month, I had to make a decision. I knew my mother was not a woman who made empty threats. I also knew that Yejide couldn't bear that kind of pressure. It would have broken her. Of the string of girls my mother paraded through my office every month, Funmi was the only one who didn't insist on moving in with Yejide and me. Funmi was the obvious choice because she didn't want much from me. Not in the beginning.

She was an easy compromise. She accepted a separate flat, miles away from Yejide and me. Didn't ask for more than a weekend every month and a reasonable allowance. She agreed that she would never be the one to go with me to parties and public engagements.

I didn't see Funmi for months after I agreed to marry her. I told her I had a lot going on at work and wouldn't be able to see her for a while. Someone must have sold the "a patient wife wins the husband's heart in the end" line to her. She didn't argue with me; she just waited until I came to terms with the fact that she was now a part of my life.

It had been more immediate with Yejide. I spent the first month after I met her driving two hours every day to be with her. I'd leave the office at five and spend about thirty minutes driving down to Ife. It took another fifteen minutes to get through the city to the university gates. Usually, I would enter F101 in Moremi Hall about an hour after leaving Ilesa.

I did this every day until one evening Yejide came out into the corridor and shut the door behind her instead of letting me in. She told me never to come back. Said she did not want to see me again. But I didn't stop. I was at F101 every day for eleven days, smiling at her roommates, trying to convince them to let me in.

On the twelfth day, she answered the door. Came out to stand with me in the corridor. We stood side by side as I begged her to tell me what I had done wrong. A mix of odours from the kitchenette and toilets wafted in our direction.

It turned out that the girl I'd been dating before I met her had been to Yejide's room to threaten her. The girl had claimed that we had had a traditional wedding.

"I don't do polygamy," Yejide said on the evening she finally told me what was going on.

Another girl would have found a roundabout way of saying she wanted to be an only wife. Not Yejide, she was direct, up-front.

"I don't either," I said.

"Look, Akin. Just let us forget it. This thing— us. This *thing*."

"I'm not married. Look at me. Come on—look at me. If you want to, we can go to that girl's room right now and I'll confront her, ask her to produce the wedding pictures."

"Her name is Bisade."

"I don't care."

Yejide didn't say anything for a while. She leaned against the door, watching people come and go in the corridor.

I touched her shoulder; she didn't pull away.

"So, I was being silly," she said.

"You owe me an apology," I said. I didn't mean it. Our relationship was still at the point where it didn't matter who was wrong or right. We hadn't arrived at the place where deciding who needed to apologise started another fight.

"Sorry, but you know people have all sorts of . . . sorry." She leaned into me.

33

"All right." I grinned as her thumb drew invisible circles along my arm.

"So, Akin. You can confess all your secrets to me now, dirty or clean. Maybe a woman who has children for you somewhere . . ."

There were things I could have told her. Should have said to her. I smiled. "I've got a few dirty socks and underwear. How about you? Any dirty panties?"

She shook her head.

Finally, I spoke the words that had been dancing on my tongue since the beginning—or a version of them. I said to her, "Yejide Makinde, I am going to marry you."

4

For a while, I did not accept the fact that I had become a *first* wife, an *iyale*. Iya Martha was my father's first wife. When I was a child, I believed she was the unhappiest wife in the family. My opinion did not change as I grew older. At my father's funeral, she stood beside the freshly dug grave with her narrow eyes narrowed even further and showered curses on every woman my father had made his wife after he had married her. She had begun as always with my long-dead mother, since she was the second woman he had married, the one who had made Iya Martha a first among not-so-equals.

I refused to think of myself as first wife.

It was easy to pretend that Funmi did not even exist. I continued to wake up with my husband lying on his back beside me in bed, his legs spread-eagled, a pillow over his face to shut out the light from my bedside lamp. I would pinch his neck until he got up and headed for the bathroom, responding to my greetings with a nod or a wave. He was incoherent in the mornings, incapable of putting words together before a cup of coffee or a cold shower.

A couple of weeks after Funmi came into our home for the first time, our phone rang shortly before midnight. By the time I sat up in bed, Akin was halfway across the room. I pulled my bedside lamp's cord twice, and all its four bulbs came on, flooding the room with light. Akin had picked up the phone and was frowning as he listened to the person on the other end of the line.

After he returned the phone to its cradle, he came to sit beside me in bed. "That was Aliyu, he's head of operations at the head office in Lagos. He called me to say we shouldn't open the bank to customers tomorrow." He sighed. "There has been a coup."

"Oh my God," I said.

We sat in silence for a while. I wondered if anyone had been killed, if there would be chaos and violence in the following months. Though I had been too young to remember the events, I knew that the coups of 1966 had ultimately thrust the country into a civil war. I comforted myself by thinking about how the tension after the last coup, which had made General Buhari head of state just twenty months before, had dissipated within a few days. The country had decided then that it was tired of the corrupt civilian government Buhari and his colleagues had ousted.

"But is it certain that the coup plotters succeeded?"

"Looks like it. Aliyu says they have already arrested Buhari."

"Let's hope these ones don't kill anybody." I

pulled the bedside lamp's cord once, switching off three of the bulbs.

"This country!" Akin sighed as he stood up. "I'm going to go downstairs and check the doors again."

"So who is in charge now?" I lay back in bed, though I would not be able to go back to sleep.

"He didn't say anything about that. We should know in the morning."

We did not know in the morning. There was a broadcast at 6 a.m. by an army officer who condemned the previous government and didn't tell us anything about the new one. Akin left for the office after the broadcast so that he could arrive at work before any protests broke out. I stayed at home, knowing already that my stylists in training would not come to the salon after listening to the news that morning. I left the radio on and tried to call everyone I knew in Lagos to make sure they were safe, but the phone lines had been severed by then and I could not get through. I must have dozed off after listening to the news at noon. Akin was home by the time I woke up. He was the one who informed me that Ibrahim Babangida was the new head of state.

The most unusual thing about the next few weeks was that Babangida referred to himself, and came to be referred to, not just as head of state but as president, as if the coup counted as an election. On the whole, things appeared to go on as usual and, like the rest of the country, my husband and I went back to our routine.

Most weekdays, Akin and I ate breakfast together. It was usually boiled eggs, toast and lots of coffee. We liked our coffee the same way, in red mugs that matched the little flowers on the place mats, without milk and with two cubes of sugar each. At breakfast, we discussed our plans for the day ahead. We talked about getting someone to fix the leaking roof in the bathroom, discussed the men Babangida had appointed to the National Council of Ministers, considered assassinating the neighbour's dog who would not quit yelping during the night, and debated whether the new margarine we were trying out was too oily. We did not discuss Funmi; we did not even mention her name by mistake. After the meal, we would carry the plates together to the kitchen and leave them in the sink to be cleaned later. Then we would wash our hands, share a kiss and go back into the sitting room. There, Akin would pick up his jacket, sling it over a shoulder and leave for work. I would go upstairs to shower and then head for my salon, and so we continued, days sliding into weeks, weeks into a month, as though it was still just the two of us in the marriage.

Then one day, after Akin had left for work, I went back upstairs to have my bath and discovered that a section of the roof had collapsed. It was raining that morning and the pressure of the gathering rainwater must have finally pushed through the already soggy asbestos and ripped the leaky square open in the middle so that water poured through it into the bathtub. I tried to find a way to bathe in that tub anyway because I had never used any of the other bathrooms in the house since we had got married. But the rain would not stop and the torn asbestos was located just so that I could not fit myself into any corner of my own bathtub without getting hit by the rainwater or bits of wood and scraps of metal that were making their way into the tub along with the water.

After I called Akin's office and left a message with his secretary about the roof, for the very first time I had to have my bath in the guest bathroom down the hallway. And there, in a space that was unfamiliar, I considered the possibility that I might end up having to take many showers in that tiny shower stall if Funmi decided to start coming over and insisted on spending her nights in the master bedroom. I rinsed off the soapsuds and went back to the master bedroom— my bedroom—to get dressed for work. When I checked on the state of the bathroom before going downstairs, the damage had not got any worse and the water was still flowing directly into the tub.

By the time I unfurled my umbrella and dashed for the car, the downpour had become torrential; the wind was strong and it tried its best to wrestle the umbrella from me. My shoes were wet by the time I got into the car. I took them off and put on the flat slippers that I used for driving. When I turned my key in the ignition, I got nothing, just a useless click. I tried again and again without any luck.

I had never had a problem with my faithful blue Beetle since Akin gave it to me after we got married. He took it in for servicing regularly and checked the oil and whatever else every week. The rain was still pouring outside and there was no use walking to my salon, even though it wasn't too far from the estate. The wind had already snapped several branches off the trees in our neighbour's front yard and it would have wrecked my umbrella within minutes. So I sat in the car, watching more branches struggle against the wind until they were broken and fell to the ground, still lush and green.

Funmi broke into my thoughts in moments like that, in the moments that did not submit themselves to my routine. And the idea that I too had become one of those women who would eventually be declared too old to accompany her husband to parties would flutter into my mind. But even then, I could trap those thoughts and keep them caged in a corner of my mind, in a place where they could not spread their wings and take over my life.

That morning, I brought out a notepad from my bag and began to write down the list of new items that I needed in the salon. I drew up a budget for my planned expansion for more salons. There was no point in thinking about Funmi; Akin had assured me that she would not be a problem and nothing had happened yet to prove him wrong. But I did not tell any of my friends about Funmi. When I spoke with Sophia or Chimdi on the phone, it was about my business, their babies and Akin's promotion at work. Chimdi was an unmarried mother and Sophia was a third wife. I did not think either of them could give me any useful advice about my situation.

A roof that had caved in and a car that would not start—if her day had begun like that, Iya Martha would have gone back to her room and spent the day behind locked doors and shut windows because the universe was trying to tell her something. The universe was always trying to tell that woman something. I was not Iya Martha, so when the rain slowed to a drizzle, I turned the key in the ignition one last time and got out of the car in my slippers. With my handbag slung over my shoulder, umbrella in one hand and wet shoes in the other, I walked to work.

• • •

My salon held the warmth of several women. Women who sat in the cushioned chairs and submitted themselves to the mercies and ministries of the wooden comb, the hooded hairdryer, to my hands and the hands of the stylists I was training. Women who quietly read a book, women who called me "my dear sister," women who made loud jokes that still had me laughing days later. I loved the place—the combs, the curlers and the mirrors on every wall.

I started making money from hairdressing during my first year at the University of Ife. Like most female freshers, I lived in Mozambique Hall. Every evening for the first week after I moved into the hostel, I went from room to room, telling the other girls that I could plait their hair for half the price they would pay to regular hairdressers. All I had was a small wooden comb, and while I lived at the university the only other thing I invested in was a plastic chair for my customers to sit in. That chair was the first thing I packed when I moved to Moremi Hall in my second year. I did not earn enough to buy a dryer, but by my third year I was making enough money for my upkeep. And whenever Iya Martha decided to withhold the monthly allowance my father routed through her, I did not go hungry.

I moved to Ilesa after my wedding and though I drove to Ife for classes on weekdays, it was impossible to continue the hairdressing business as before. For a while I wasn't making any money. Not that I needed to: apart from the housekeeping stipend, Akin gave me a generous personal allowance. But I missed hairdressing and did not like knowing that if for some reason Akin stopped giving me money, I would not even be able to afford a packet of chewing gum.

For the first few months of our marriage, Akin's sister Arinola was the only woman whose hair I wove. She often offered to pay me, but I refused her money. She didn't like elaborate styles and always asked me to weave her hair into the classic *suku*. Weaving her tresses into straight lines that stopped in the middle of her head bored me after a while. So I persuaded her to let me spend ten hours plaiting her hair into a thousand tiny braids. Within a week, Arinola's colleagues at the College of Education were begging her to introduce them to her hairdresser.

Initially, I attended to the growing stream of women beneath a cashew tree in our backyard. But Akin soon found a salon space that he told me would be perfect. I was reluctant about opening up a real salon because I knew I would only be able to work there over the weekends until I got my degree. Akin convinced me to take a look at the place he'd found, and once I stepped into that room, I could see that it would really be perfect. I tried to contain my excitement by telling him it was not sensible to spend money on a place that would be closed for five days a week. He saw through me and a few hours later we held hands in the landlord's living room as he negotiated the rent.

I was still using that salon space when he married Funmi. And that morning, although I arrived later than usual because of the rain and the trouble with my car, I was still the first in the salon. None of my apprentices was in sight when I unlocked the doors. They usually came in earlier to set up shop for the day, but even as I switched on the lights, the pitter-patter of rain picked up speed until it sounded like a hundred hooves were pounding on the roof. There was little chance that the girls would make it across town before the rain let up again.

I switched on the radio my father had given me when I went to university. It was now broken in several places but I'd put it back together with duct tape. I fiddled with the dial until I found a station that was playing music I did not recognise. Then I started setting out shampoos and pomades, styling gels and curling irons, bowls of relaxers and bottles of hair spray.

I did not bother to check if walking in the rain had ruined my braids in spite of the umbrella. If I looked in the mirror, I would have had to examine the shape of my face, my small eyes, my big nose; the things that could have been wrong with the dip of my chin or my lips, all the different ways in which any man, Akin specifically, might find Funmi more attractive. I did not have time to indulge in self-pity, so I kept on working because handling the equipment focused my thoughts on hair.

After the rain stopped, the girls trickled in one after the other. The last one came in just before our first customer showed up. I grabbed a wooden comb, parted the woman's hair in the middle, dipped two fingers into the sticky pomade and started my day. Her hair was thick and full, the tresses crackled softly as I wove them in tiny rows that gathered at the nape of her neck. There were four people waiting when I was through with her. I moved from head to head, sectioning hair, weaving strands into patterns, snipping off split ends and dispensing advice to the girls in training. It was bliss; time slipped by and soon it was well past noon. By the time I took a break for lunch, my wrists were hurting—almost everyone wanted weaving and braiding that morning and few easy wash-and-sets were coming our way.

That afternoon I went for rice cooked in eeran leaves and topped with palm-oil stew. There was a woman on that street who cooked it so well that after enjoying the bits of smoked fish and cowhide in the stew, I always had to fight the urge to lick the leaves clean. It was the kind of food that demanded a moment's pause after the plate was empty and induced a level of contentment that had me staring into space while the salon buzzed around me. Outside, the sky was still a threatening indigo although the rain had finally stopped. Cold air swept into the salon in draughts and battled the hairdryers to set the room temperature.

I thought she was a customer when she came in. She stood in the doorway for a moment, the overcast sky hanging behind her like a bad omen. She looked around the room with a frown on her face until she saw me. Then she smiled and came to kneel beside me. She was so beautiful. She had the kind of face that would complement any hairstyle, a face that would have other women looking longingly after her in the market, a face that would have some of them asking who her hairdresser was.

"Good morning, our mother," Funmi said.

Her words pierced me. I was not her mother. I was not anybody's mother. People still called me Yejide. I was not Iya This or Iya That. I was still merely Yejide. That thought tied my tongue and made me want to pull hers out of her mouth. Years before, nothing would have stopped me from punching her teeth down her throat. When I was a student at Ife Girls' High School, I was known as Yejide Terror. I got into fights every other day. In those days, we would wait until school was over before starting a fight. We would leave the vicinity of the school compound and find a path that none of the teachers passed through on their way home. And I always won—not once, not one single time did I lose. I lost a few buttons, broke a tooth, got a bloody nose many times, but I never lost. I never got one single grain of sand in my mouth.

Whenever I arrived home late and bloodied up from another fight, my stepmothers would scold me loudly and promise to punish me for my disgraceful behaviour. At night they whispered, with washed-out wrappers tied around their shrunken breasts, they whispered instructions to their children not to be like me. After all, their children had mothers, living women who cursed and cooked, had businesses and bushy armpits. Only motherless children, children like me, could misbehave like that. And it was not just that I did not have a mother, but the one I once had, the one who died seconds after she had pushed me out into the world, was a woman without lineage! And who impregnates a woman with no lineage? Only a stupid man who happened to be, well, her husband. But that was not the point; the point was that when there was no identifiable lineage for a child, that child could be descended from anything—even dogs, witches or strange tribes with bad blood. The third wife's children obviously had bad blood since insanity occurred frequently in her family. But at least that was known bad blood—my (possible) bad blood was of unknown origin and that was worse, as evidenced by the way I was disgracing my father by fighting like a street dog.

The whispered discussions in the rooms that each wife shared with her children were eventually reported to me in detail by my half-siblings. The words did not bother me; it was a game the wives played, trying to prove which woman had produced a superior stock of children. It was the threats that were never carried out, even when my fighting became a daily event, that bothered me. It was the whips that were not unleashed, the extra chores that were not assigned, the dinners that were not withheld that reminded me that none of them really cared.

"Our mother?" Funmi said. She was still on her knees.

I swallowed my memories like an oversized bitter pill. Funmi had placed her hands on my lap; her manicure was perfect. The nails were painted hibiscus red, like the matching mugs Akin and I had used to drink coffee that morning.

"Our mother?"

I never painted my fingernails anymore. I used to paint them when I was at university. Was it the nails that made her attractive to him? How did he feel when she raked those beautiful nails across his chest? Did his nipples tighten? Did he moan? I wanted . . . no . . . I needed to know immediately, in detail. What did she have of him that had always been just mine? What would she have that I had never had? His child?

"Our mother?"

"Who is your mother? You better get up now," I said.

There was an empty chair next to me, but she chose to sit on the arm of my chair.

"Why are you here? Who showed you this place?" I whispered because the background chatter between customers and stylists had stopped. Somebody had turned off the radio and the salon had gone quiet.

"I just thought I should come to greet you."

"At this time of the day? Are you jobless?" It was an insult, but she took it as a question.

"No-o. I don't have a job since our husband is taking good care of me." Her voice rose as she said "our husband," and it was obvious that everyone in the room had heard her. Chairs creaked as customers shifted in their seats and leaned back as much as possible in their attempts to listen in on the conversation.

"What?"

"Our husband is a very caring man. He has been taking good care of me. We thank God that he has enough money for all of us." She smiled at the top of my head.

I glared at her reflection in the mirror opposite us. "Enough money for what?"

49

"For us, our mother. That is why a man works, *abi*? For his wives and children."

"Some of us have jobs," I said, keeping my clenched fists firmly by my side. "You have to leave so that I can do mine."

She smiled into the mirror. "I will visit tomorrow afternoon, *Ma*. Maybe you will be less busy then."

Did she expect me to smile back? "Funmi, don't let me see your broomstick legs in this place ever again."

"Our mother, there is no need for all this-o; we have to be friends. At least for the sake of the children we will have." She went on her knees again. "I know people say you are barren, but there is nothing God cannot do. I know that once I conceive, your own womb too will be opened. If you say I should not come here, I will not come, but I want you to know that this bitterness can be one of the things causing the barrenness-o. Goodbye, *Ma*."

She was smiling as she rose to her feet and turned to leave.

I stood up and grabbed the back of her dress. "You! This wretched . . . this evil *egbere*. Who are you calling barren?"

I was not prepared for the confrontation. Even my insult was off the mark. Funmi did not look like the mythical *egbere*. She was not short; she was not carrying a mat or weeping incessantly.

50

In fact, when she turned to face me, she was smiling. I was surrounded by customers and stylists before I could land the first slap on her cheek.

"Leave her alone," the women said. "Let her go." They pulled my hands from Funmi's dress and pushed me until I was back in my seat. "My dear sister, please calm down. Just take it easy."

5

I bought new mugs.

"You know why I don't like white mugs?" Akin said at breakfast.

"Please enlighten me," I said.

"You can always see the coffee stains too clearly."

"Really?"

He pulled at his tie and frowned. "You sound angry. Is something wrong?"

I spread more margarine on my toast, stirred my coffee and clenched my jaw. I was prepared to keep my mouth shut about why I was upset until Akin asked me why at least five times. But he did not even give me a chance to sulk.

"I don't like these white mugs." He held a finger up and paused to drink some water. "Where are the old ones?"

"I broke them."

His mouth formed an *Oh* that it did not expel and he took another bite of toast. I could see that he assumed I had simply knocked the mugs over by mistake or dropped them as I was putting them away. There was no reason for him to think that I had slammed each hibiscus-red mug against the kitchen wall as the cuckoo clock in the sitting room chimed at midnight. He could never have imagined that I had swept the broken pieces into a dustpan, put them in a small mortar and pounded them until I was sweating from every pore and wondering if I had lost my mind.

"You know the internal auditors from the headquarters were in the office yesterday, we were so busy with them. I forgot to send someone to look at that roof. Today I'll—"

"Your wife came to my salon yesterday."

"Funmi?"

"Who else?" I leaned forward in my chair. "Or do you have another wife that I don't know about?" It was an idea I had not been able to shake since Funmi had left my salon the previous day, the possibility that there could have been other wives out there—in Ilesa, in any other city—other women that he could love, other women who made him less mine.

Akin covered one half of his face with a hand. "Yejide, I've explained my agreement with Funmi to you. You shouldn't let her bother you."

"She said you are taking good care of her." My words did not carry the power that I wanted them to, because I could not find any of the anger and disdain I had directed at Funmi the previous day. I wanted to be angry with him so I kept speaking; trying with my words to reach past what I really felt to the anger I was supposed to feel. "What does that mean? Explain to me what 'good care' means."

"Sweetie . . ."

"Hold it. Just hold it there. Please don't sweetie me again this morning." But I did want him to call me sweetie again, only me and no one else. I wanted him to reach across the table, hold my hand and tell me we would be all right. And I still believed then that he would know what to do and what to say just because he was Akin.

"Yejide—"

"Where were you yesterday night? I waited until well past midnight for you to come home. Where did you go?"

"The sports club."

"*Ehen*? Sports club? You must think I'm a fool. When do they close at the sports club? Tell me, when?"

He sighed and glanced at his watch. "You want to start policing me?"

"You said nothing would happen between you and that girl."

He grabbed his jacket and stood up. "I need to get to work."

"You are deceiving me, *abi*?" I followed him to the door, grappling for words to tell him I did not really want to fight with him, to explain that I was afraid that he would leave me and I would be all alone in the world again. "Akin, God will deceive you, I promise you. God will deceive you the way you are deceiving me."

He shut the door and I watched him through the

glass panes. He was all wrong. Instead of holding his briefcase in his hand, he gripped it to his side with his left arm so that his body tilted a little to the left, and he looked as though he was about to double over. His jacket was not slung over a shoulder but clutched in his right hand; the edge of a sleeve touched the ground and slid down the porch steps and through the grass as he walked towards his black Peugeot.

I turned away as he put the car into reverse. His coffee mug was still full, not one drop had left the cup. I sat in his chair, finished my toast and his and drank up his coffee. Then I tidied up the dining table and took the dirty dishes to the kitchen. I washed up and took care to make sure there was no coffee stain left in the mugs.

I did not feel like going to work because I was not ready for another confrontation with Funmi. It was clear to me that she would not stop showing up at the salon simply because I said so. I knew that women like Funmi, the kind of women who chose to be second, third or seventh wives, never backed down easily, ever. I had watched them arrive and evolve in my father's house, all those different mothers who were not mine, they always came in with a strategy hidden under their wrappers, they were never as stupid or as agreeable as they first seemed. And it was Iya Martha who was always caught unawares, stunned, without a strategy or a plan of her own.

It was becoming obvious that I had been a fool to believe for one second that Akin had Funmi under control. So I decided to take the day off to think things through. I stopped by the salon for a few minutes to give instructions to Debby, the most senior stylist in training. Then I took a taxi to Odo-Iro to get Silas, the mechanic who usually repaired my Beetle.

Silas was surprised to see that I had come to his shop alone and asked after Akin. Throughout the drive to my place he kept telling me in different ways that he would prefer to discuss the repairs with Akin before he did anything.

I cooked while he worked on the Beetle and offered him lunch when he was done. He washed his hands outside and ate the yam pottage quickly. I sat and watched him as he ate. I talked to him and he stared at me, grunting now and then, but mostly he just stared at me with a look of wonder as though he did not know what he could say in reply to my nonstop chatter. When he stood up to leave, I counted out the amount he had charged and gave the bills to him, then I followed him to his car, still talking as he drove off.

I sat on the porch calling out greetings to neighbours who passed by until Debby came to give me an account of the money that had been made at the salon. I invited her in and offered her some food, but she turned it down and said she was not hungry. So I insisted that she should have a bottle of Maltina. After she went home, there was nothing left to do. The car had been fixed, plates washed and dinner was ready, even though I knew by then that Akin would not be home until midnight. I could not delay thinking about Funmi any longer.

I went through several possibilities, from beating her to a pulp the next time she showed up in the salon to asking her to move in with us so I could keep her close enough to have my eye on her at all times. It did not take long to realise that the ultimate solution had little to do with her. I simply had to get pregnant, as soon as possible, and before Funmi did. It was the only way I could be sure I would stay in Akin's life.

I believed I was Moomi's favourite daughter-in-law. As a child, it was expected that I would call my stepmothers Moomi, even my father encouraged me to, but I refused. I stuck to calling them Mama. And whenever my father was not around, some of the women would slap me just because I refused to honour them by calling them "my mother." I did not refuse because I was being stubborn or trying to defy them as a number of them concluded. My mother had become an obsession for me, a religion, and the very thought of referring to another woman as Mother seemed sacrilegious, a betrayal of the woman who had given up her life for me to live.

One year, the Anglican church my family attended celebrated Mothering Sunday with a special service. After the vicar delivered his sermon, he summoned everyone who was below the age of eighteen to the front of the church because he wanted us to honour mothers with a song. I must have been twelve at the time, but I didn't get up until an usher poked me in the back. We sang a song that everyone already knew, an expansion of a popular saying. I managed the first line, *Iya ni wura, iya ni wura iyebiye ti a ko le f'owo ra*, before biting my tongue to choke back tears. The words, *Mother is gold, Mother is treasured gold that cannot be bought with money*, resonated with me more than any homily I'd ever heard. I knew by then that my mother could not be replaced with money, by a stepmother or anyone else, and I was sure I would never call any woman "Moomi."

Yet every time Akin's mother wrapped me in her fleshy embrace, my heart sang *Moomi* and when I called her the venerated title, it did not cling to my throat and refuse to climb out the way it used to when my stepmothers tried to slap it out of me. She lived up to the name, taking my side if any issue I had with Akin came to her attention, assuring me that it was a matter of time before I got pregnant for her son, insisting that my miracle would be waiting once I turned the right corner.

When Mrs. Adeolu, a pregnant customer, told me about the Mountain of Jaw-Dropping Victory, I went to Moomi that same day to discuss it with her. I needed her to authenticate the information; she was a treasure-house of knowledge about such things. Even if she did not know anything about a miracle house, she usually knew whom to ask and once she had checked out the stories, she was always prepared to accompany me to the ends of the earth to seek out a new solution.

There was a time when I would have ignored Mrs. Adeolu's words, a time when I did not believe in prophets who lived on mountains or priests who worshipped beside rivers. That was before I had so many tests done in the hospital and every one of them showed that there was nothing preventing me from getting pregnant. I hoped at one point that the doctors would find something wrong, anything to explain why my period still showed up every month, years after my marriage. I wished they would find something they could treat or cut out. They found nothing. Akin also went in to get tested and came back saying that the doctors had found nothing wrong with him. Then I stopped waving aside my mother-in-law's suggestions, stopped thinking that women like her were uncivilised and a little crazy. I became open to alternatives. If I was not getting what I wanted in one place, what was wrong with searching elsewhere?

My parents-in-law lived in Ayeso, an old section of town that still had a few mud houses. Their house was a brick building, with a front yard partially enclosed by a low cement fence. When I arrived at the house, Moomi was sitting on a low stool in the front yard shelling groundnuts into a rusty tray that sat on her lap. She looked up as I approached and looked down again. I swallowed and my steps slowed. There was something wrong.

Moomi always greeted me by shouting, *Yejide, my wife.* The words were as warm as the embrace that usually followed them.

"Good evening, Moomi." My knees trembled as they touched the concrete floor.

"Are you pregnant now?" She said without looking up from the tray of groundnuts.

I scratched my head.

"Are you barren and deaf too? I say, are you pregnant? The answer is either yes, I am pregnant or no, I still haven't been pregnant for a single day in my life."

"I don't know." I stood up and backed away until she was not within the reach of my clenched fist.

"Why won't you allow my son to have a child?" She slapped the tray of groundnuts on the floor and stood up.

"I don't manufacture children. God does."

She marched towards me and spoke when

her toes were touching the tips of my shoes.

"Have you ever seen God in a labour room giving birth to a child? Tell me, Yejide, have you ever seen God in the labour ward? Women manufacture children and if you can't you are just a man. Nobody should call you a woman." She gripped my wrists and lowered her voice to a whisper. "This life is not difficult, Yejide. If you cannot have children, allow my son to have some with Funmi. See, we are not asking you to stand up from your place in his life, we are just saying you should shift so that someone else can sit down."

"I am not stopping him, Moomi," I said. "I have accepted her. She even spends the weekends in our house now."

She held her thick waist and laughed. "I am a woman too. Do you think I was born last night? Tell me, why has Akin never touched Funmi? He has been married to her for over two months. Tell me why he has not removed her wrapper once. Tell me, Yejide."

I stifled a smile. "It is not my business what Akin does with his wife."

Moomi lifted my blouse and laid a wrinkled palm on my stomach.

"Flat as the side of a wall," she said. "You have had my son between your legs for two more months and still your stomach is flat. Close your thighs to him, I beg you. We all know how he

61

feels about you. If you don't chase him away, he won't touch Funmi. If you don't, he will die childless. I beg you, don't spoil my life. He is my first son, Yejide. I beg you in the name of God."

I closed my eyes, but tears still forced their way past my eyelids.

Moomi sighed. "I have been good to you, I beg you in the name of God. Yejide, have mercy on me. Have mercy on me."

She held me then, pulled me into her arms and muttered words of comfort. Her embrace held no warmth. Her words sat in my stomach, cold and hard, where a baby should have been.

6

Fear gripped my ankles as I climbed the Mountain of Jaw-Dropping Miracles. The heavily bearded man who trailed me did not ease my worries. He was my escort, sent from the mountaintop where the other faithful chanted words that the wind carried to us and carried away again. I could see about a hundred of them, clad in green robes and matching chef caps.

"No stopping," my escort said.

He must have noticed that my steps were slowing. The steep mountain was bare, with no trees to offer momentary shade from the sun. I was thirsty, my throat was dry and there was hardly any saliva in my mouth. There would be no reprieve for me. I had been asked to come fasting. No food, no water and, as the escort had informed me when he met me at the foot of the hill, if I stopped to rest as we climbed up the hill, I would be sent back home with no prayers and no meeting with the Highest Priest.

Mrs. Adeolu had assured me that the Prophet Josiah, the leader of this group, was indeed a miracle worker. Her protruding belly was convincing evidence. I needed a miracle fast. The only way I could save myself from polygamy was to get pregnant before Funmi; that way Akin might let the girl go. But as I pulled a small goat up the mountain, the only miracle I really wanted was that of water gushing from a rock so that I could quench my thirst. The way my escort stared at my chest was alarming. I was trembling not just from exhaustion but with foreboding. Each time my eyes met his blatantly roving ones, I wanted to run down the hill back to my car; yet I pressed on towards the crest. Funmi was still living in her flat in town, but I did not need a prophet to tell me that she would move into my home once she got pregnant.

"Can you help me with the goat?" I asked the escort, wishing the prophet had sent a woman to fetch me.

"No," he replied and moved a palm across my face. Just when I wanted to slap it away, he curved his palm and dragged rolls of sweat down my cheek.

He held my waist, presumably to steady me. I tried to quicken my trembling pace, but the goat had stopped. I pulled and pulled until the rope was chafing my hands. I would have dragged it on its side, but the instruction had been to bring a white goat without wound, blemish or a speck of another colour.

"It is the goat; I'm not stopping to rest." I was scared he might send me back.

"I can see that."

After a while, the goat started moving. We soon

arrived at the crest of the mountain. The faithful sat in a wide circle with their eyes closed.

"Enter the circle," my escort said. Then he sat down with the others and closed his eyes.

A man stood at the centre of the circle. His beard was even longer than the escort's and covered most of his face. His chef cap was bigger than that of the others and instead of dragging down his back, something had been stuffed in it to make it stand upright.

"Make way for our sister," he said.

The two faithful in front of me stood up and stepped farther into the circle without opening their eyes. I dragged the goat with me into the circle and went to stand by the man with the big cap. I looked around at all the faces and realised that they were all bearded, all men. I recalled the escort's lewd stares and felt faint. As if on cue, the men began to moan and tremble as though from some unseen stimulation. I thought of Akin and how beautiful our children would have been.

"You will have a child," the man beside me shouted and the moaning stopped. He opened his eyes. "Behold your child," he said, pointing at the goat. I glanced from the goat to the man's dancing eyes. I thought of running away from this crazy man, but I could see all of them chasing after me, deranged and drooling like rabid dogs, green robes flapping in the wind. I could imagine myself rolling down the steep hill to my death.

"You think I'm mad? The Prophet Josiah is mad?" He grabbed the back of my head and laughed in short cackles. "You cannot run from us until we are done. By then you will be with child."

I nodded until he let go of my head.

The moaning resumed. The man stooped beside the goat and removed the rope from its neck. Then he swaddled it in a piece of green cloth until only its face was showing. He thrust it towards me. "Your child."

I took the bundle.

"Hold it close and dance," he commanded.

The moaning stopped and the men began to sing. I shuffled along, holding the bundle to my chest, labouring under its weight. The singing switched to a quick chant and my pace quickened. I sang with them.

We danced until my throat was so parched that I could hardly swallow. And each time I blinked, I saw flashes of light and colour, like shards of a broken rainbow. We kept dancing until I felt I was on the edge of some divine experience. Then, beneath the brilliant sun, the goat appeared to be a newborn and I believed. We sang and danced until my ankles ached and I longed to fall on my knees. Hours must have passed before Prophet Josiah spoke.

"Feed the child," he said. His voice was like a remote control that switched the activity of the surrounding men. This time when he spoke, the singing stopped. I looked to his hand, expecting him to hand me some grass.

He tugged at the front of my blouse. "Breastfeed the child."

After he whispered those words, it was natural for me to reach behind my back and unhook the ivory lace bra I wore. To lift up my blouse and push up my bra cups. To sit on the ground with my legs stretched out, squeeze my breast and push the nipple to the open mouth in my arms.

I did not think of Akin and how he would have said I was going mad. I did not think of Moomi, who would have reminded me that my feet were shaky in her son's house without a child. I did not even think of Funmi, who might be pregnant already. I looked down at the bundle in my arms and saw the little face of my child, smelled the fresh scent of baby powder and believed.

When Prophet Josiah removed the bundle from my arms, they felt empty.

"Go," he said. "Even if no man comes near you this month, you will be pregnant."

I hugged his words close to me. They filled my arms and comforted me. I smiled as I walked down the mountain alone. I could still feel the wetness on my breast and my heart thudded with desperate faith.

7

Yejide told me she was pregnant on a Sunday. Woke me up around 7 in the morning to say a miracle had taken place the previous day. On a mountain of all places. A miracle on a mountain.

I asked her to please switch off her bedside lamp. Light hurt my eyes in the morning.

She still had a sense of humour back then. Wasn't above a practical joke once in a while. I thought she was building up to something hilarious. Maybe it was a stretch, me thinking she could joke about being pregnant.

I sat up when she switched off the lamp. Waited for her to deliver the punch line so I could slide back beneath the covers. But she just stood beside the bed, grinning. I wasn't amused. She was violating my Sunday policy. I practised strict observance of the day of rest, never voluntarily opening my eyes before noon. She knew that.

"I'll get you a cup of coffee." She pulled back the curtains a bit, let in a slice of sunlight.

I got up when she left the room. Went to the bathroom, turned on the cold water and put my head beneath the showerhead for a couple of minutes. I went back into the room without a towel. Let the water trickle down my chest and

68

back. Let it soak the waistband of my shorts a little.

She was back in the room when I got there. Sitting in bed with her legs crossed at the ankles. I noticed then that she was not in her nightgown. She was dressed in shorts and a blue T-shirt. Looked like she'd been awake for some time.

There was a tray beside her. Laden with plates of fried yam, a bowl of fish stew and two cups of coffee. The woman who could spend weeks complaining if I had a sandwich in bed had brought a bowl of stew into the room. I should have realised then that something was wrong.

I sat on the bed, took a sip of coffee. "When did you wake up?"

"Akin, I think it's going to be a girl."

Nothing had prepared me for a Yejide who thought she got pregnant on a mountain. Didn't know what to say to her. I ate my breakfast and watched her closely. Listened to her talk. By the time the last fried yam was gone, it was obvious she didn't think she'd got pregnant on that damned mountain. She was convinced she had.

I placed the tray on the bedside table, pulled Yejide close. "Look," I said. "You need to rest, sleep a bit more."

"You don't believe me."

"I didn't say that."

She wriggled out of my arms. "You haven't said you believe me either, you've just been eating all this time. You are not even excited or happy. You haven't said congratulations yet and you've had your coffee, so it's not that."

She wanted me to congratulate her. For getting pregnant on a mountain.

"Akin?" She gripped my hand, her nails dug into my palm. "Do you believe me? Tell me, do you believe me?"

"Things like that don't happen. You need to stop going to those places with Moomi. I've told you that before. All those people are liars, total con men."

She let go of my hand. "Your mother did not go with me."

"What? You are going to those crooks all by yourself now?"

"You need to believe." She frowned, shook her head. "Sometimes I feel sorry for you."

"What?"

"You don't believe anything."

"What is all this? Because I don't believe a man in a green robe waved a wand and made you pregnant?"

She sighed. "He didn't use a wand, I carried a—Never mind, you'll just think it's bizarre."

"I already think it's bizarre. What did you carry? God, I can't believe we are having this conversation."

"It doesn't matter." She smiled, laying a hand on her belly. "You know what? I'll go and get

70

tested at the hospital soon and then you'll believe too that something special happened on that mountain. I really think I might be pregnant."

"My God." I felt like I was talking to a stranger. "Yejide, let me make this clear. You did not get pregnant on that mountain. If you were not pregnant when you went up, you were not pregnant when you came down." I put a hand on her knee. "Do you understand me?"

"Akin. In nine months, you'll know they are not crooks." She held my chin, kissed my nose. "You'll see. Now, let's talk about something else."

The nose-kissing did it. Opened my eyes to the fact that I needed to do something before she lost her mind. At some point that Sunday morning, I decided it was time to get her pregnant. End all the crazy visits to priests and prophets once and for all. But first, I had to wait until she was ready.

"I may be going to Lagos next weekend," I said.

"What are you going to do in Lagos?"

"I need to see Dotun about some investments."

"Dotun and investments? Just be careful with your brother; sometimes I think he is nothing but trouble."

She was wrong about being pregnant, but she was right about Dotun.

8

My period was due the week after my visit to the mountain. It didn't show. By the end of the month my breasts were so tender that putting on a bra aroused me. I was vomiting every morning at 7 a.m. like clockwork.

I was sure that I was pregnant and I believed my body was telling me things a test would soon confirm. I knew the test had to come before any form of real celebration, but I was excited about how wonderful everything would be as soon as the doctors confirmed that I was pregnant. I did not talk to Akin about what was going on in my body because I did not want him to puncture my hopes. We were not exactly speaking to each other. He spent most evenings at the flat he rented for Funmi. I spent some of my evenings examining my stomach from different angles in the bathroom mirror.

"What are you doing?" Akin asked some weeks into my pregnancy. I had not seen him come into the bathroom.

"How is your wife?" I said, pulling down my blouse.

He moved closer and lifted the blouse. "What's wrong with you?"

I yanked the blouse down. "Why does there have to be something wrong with me?"

"I'm just concerned. Why were you—?"

"I told you. I am pregnant."

Akin stepped back as though I had hit him in the jaw. He stared at me as if I had grown a horn on the bridge of my nose. Then he laughed. It was a short sound that would haunt me in my sleep.

"Have you been having sex . . ." The laughter died with a gurgling sound in his throat. ". . . with another man?"

"I do not understand what you are saying."

His Adam's apple bobbed furiously, threatening to burst through his skin and splatter blood all over the white tiles on the bathroom floor.

"We both know you can't be pregnant. I have not even touched you in months. Except you . . . you . . ." His mouth hung open, but no words came out.

I walked out of the bathroom, dashed downstairs and out of the house before he could follow me. I needed the fresh night air to clear my head and the moon in the sky to renew my faith.

Akin did not respond when I greeted him the next morning. His hand trembled as he stirred sugar into his coffee.

"I am starting antenatal today," I said.

The cup of coffee was halfway from his lips. It fell on the table and soaked the white tablecloth with brown liquid.

"How could you cheat on me, Yejide?"

"I do not understand what you are talking about," I said and bit into a piece of toast.

He laughed. "So, this is an immaculate conception? And what shall we call this child? Baby Satan? When will a demon appear to inform me in my dream?"

I slapped the toast on a plate. "So now you can talk? You can blurt it all out? Who married another woman? In this house, who married another woman, tell me? Tell me now! Which bloody cheat did that?"

He traced the brown coffee stain with his thumb. "We've talked about that, we've settled it."

I was so angry I could hardly breathe. I stood up and leaned across the table to stick my face in front of his. "OK now. Something else is settled. I want a baby and since you are too busy at your new wife's place to try and get me pregnant, I can get a baby from any man I want."

He got up and grabbed my arms just above the elbows. The veins in his forehead popped. "You can't," he said.

I laughed. "I can do anything I want."

His nails bit into my arms through my shirtsleeves. "Yejide, you can't."

I wagged my head. "But I can. I can. I can."

He shook me until my head bobbed and my teeth rattled. Then he let go suddenly. I crashed into a chair, grasping the table for balance.

He picked up a saucer from the table and held it aloft. In one frightening moment I could see him breaking the delicate china on my head. He threw it across the room, then he pulled the tablecloth off the dining table. Plates, mugs, saucers and vacuum flasks crashed to the floor. My husband was not a violent man, and the man who lifted a dining chair and hit it against the dining table until the chair broke was someone I did not know.

Wesley Guild Hospital stank of antiseptic. The stench of chemically enforced cleanliness had me rushing out of the antenatal class twice to vomit. I would never have imagined that vomit could make me so happy. Yet I grinned at the mess I had deposited in the gutter and wanted to call passersby to come and take a look at it. The inability to keep food down, the extra sensitivity to touch and the general discomfort I felt were rites of passage into motherhood, initiation into a rank that I had always longed to attain. I was a woman at last.

A nurse explained what was going on in our bodies. She taught us a song about breastfeeding and discussed diet and exercise.

The nurse came to me after she dismissed the class. "Madam, congratulations! How is the body?"

"Thank you, *Ma*. You know how it is now,"

I chuckled. "I keep vomiting everything I eat and I can't eat much. Since last week, I've only been eating pineapples and beans, imagine the combination, my sister. Pineapple inside palm oil beans! I try and try to eat something else but no, nothing else is staying inside me."

"*Abi*, that is how it is. In fact with my last child I could eat only *eba*, no stew, no vegetables to go with it, nothing, just *eba* and water. Just imagine that. If I tried anything else, it came right out of my nose."

We laughed.

"Then the sleeping too, I can only sleep on one side," I said. "I wake up every time I have to turn."

The nurse stared at my stomach. "Your stomach is not that big yet." She frowned. "You shouldn't be having problems sleeping at this stage. I hope there is nothing—"

"There is nothing wrong with me—everything is going normally."

"Oh, how long has this been going on? The discomfort, how long?"

"Aunty Nurse, why are you bothering yourself? I said everything is fine; it is probably just me."

"Ah, ha. See you calling me Aunty Nurse. You don't know me? I get my hair done at your salon now, once every two weeks."

"Oh. Yes, yes," I said, trying and failing to remember her face.

"You remember now?" she asked.

I smiled and nodded. "Of course," I said, still unable to place her face.

"Congratulations, my sister. Those men, they don't understand, but thank God all your enemies have been put to shame. Every time they will be blaming the woman and sometimes it is their own body that has a problem." She hugged me tightly as if we were teammates in some unspoken game and I had just scored a winning goal against the opposing side.

Funmi was waiting outside my salon when I got back from the hospital. I had given my stylists firm instructions never to let her inside my salon after her last visit. But that afternoon, I was happy to see her. On that day, I would have been happy to see all my stepmothers lined up in front of the salon. The antenatal class had filled me with unconditional love for all living creatures.

"Come in, my dear," I said.

When I served her a bottle of Coke, she didn't drink it until I took a sip to assure her it had not been poisoned.

She said, "I have come to beg you."

But her clenched jaw told me she wanted to fight, not beg.

"Our husband fought with me this morning because of you. He said he would not visit me again because of you. Please let him come-o because I have tried for you. I have tried staying outside when my place is inside. Please-o." She said this in a tone low enough to give the impression that she wanted no one to hear her words, but loud enough for the stylists and customers who were unusually silent to hear. I knew then that she was a dangerous woman, that Funmi, the type of woman who would call you a witch just so you could beat her to death and end up in jail.

I was in a generous mood. I could have given away everything in my shop that afternoon. I was pregnant at last. I had attended an antenatal meeting and people in the antenatal unit had treated me with care: they had asked me to eat fruit, rest and exercise. Nothing else mattered. God had been generous to me and I had no reason to hoard my husband. Anyway, what was a husband compared to a child that would be all mine? A man can have many wives or concubines; a child can have only one mother.

"I will talk to him about it. You'll see him before this week ends," I said.

Funmi's mouth dropped open in what I assumed was surprise. She had come for a fight, for a story she could share over and over to prove that I was evil, and she was going away without that ammunition. She masked her disappointment, stood up and said goodbye. As she was about to step out of the shop, I said, "My dear, be among the first to know, I started my antenatal today. God has done it."

She whirled around and stared at me. I saw in her eyes the realisation that I was now a threat to her instead of the other way round. She gripped her forehead. Unable to fake joy, she walked away.

My stylists went crazy; they hugged me, laughed and sang praise songs. Even the customers joined in. I was a miracle, a vindication for good women like me everywhere. I stayed seated; sure that I had grown taller, sure that if I stood up my head would raise the roof.

The news of my pregnancy travelled fast, just as I intended. Funmi accompanied my mother-in-law to my home that evening. It was obvious that she was eager to play the good younger wife now that my stakes in Akin's life had been strengthened. They were waiting on the front porch when I arrived home.

I smiled, went into Moomi's embrace and nodded as she asked over and over, "Is it true? Is it true?"

Funmi grinned so widely, my cheeks hurt just from looking at her.

"You must give us twins. Two fat boys, fat baby boys. That is what you will give us," Moomi said, settling into a cushioned chair once we got inside.

"As I am, I am ready to give you six boys at once," I said.

"Let's start with a soft hand—two boys at first, just give me those two first. After that, I will leave you to do any magic you want to do."

"What will you eat?" I asked.

Moomi shook her head. "Not today. This news is more than enough to keep me from going hungry for days. Besides, I don't want you going up and down unnecessarily at all. Make sure you relax very well, don't be bending over to sweep or carry anything heavy. Even food, please don't pound yam at all. Maybe you should even get one of those girls that help around the house to help you for this time."

"I don't really need a house help," I said. "I think I can manage—"

"I can come and help," Funmi broke in.

"What?" I said.

"You don't have to pay for a house help. What if I come to live here so I can help around the house?" She smiled. "You should be very relaxed during this period."

"And that is true," Moomi said. "In fact, I think that is what you should do."

"Only if it's OK with you, *Ma*." Funmi leaned towards me. "Do you mind?"

I had been fooled again. For some reason, I was still stupid enough to imagine that the two of them had entered into my sitting room without a ready agenda. Yes, the pregnancy had made me generous enough to entertain Funmi in my salon, but I was not ready to allow her to move into my home. I was smart enough to know that if she moved in under the guise of assisting me, she would never leave.

I could not think of a way to say no to Funmi. At least there was no way to say it without Moomi thinking I was being disrespectful to her. In spite of everything, I wanted Akin's family to love me. I did not want my child to live under the banner of resentment against its mother as I did. In case I died, I wanted love for who I had been to compel the people left behind to care for my child. I was about to become a mother. The stakes were higher, I had to be calm and agreeable or at least appear so. The fate of my unborn child depended on it.

So I smiled while I boiled inside and said I would ask Akin. Moomi smiled in satisfaction, Funmi in anticipation of victory. My smile felt tight and I could hardly wait for them to leave so I could take it off. We would have made such a pretty picture, all three of us with our perfect smiles.

9

It began with the ultrasound scans. The machines claimed that there was no baby in my womb.

Dr. Uche was the first doctor to run the scan. She had small eyes that swam in a pool of stagnant tears that refused to fall. The sheen in her eyes glittered as she broke the news.

"Mrs. Ajayi, there is no baby."

"I heard you the first time and the second time too," I said.

She kept peering at me with her shimmering eyes as though she expected me to do something. Cry? Scream? Leap onto her table and start dancing?

She leaned forward in her seat. "How long have you been pregnant?"

"I thought you said there is no baby."

Dr. Uche smiled a cautious smile. I had seen that smile before, on my father's face. It was a small smile that looked like his mouth was prepared to burst into a loud cry for help at any moment. It was a special smile reserved for his third wife, the one who once went into the marketplace naked. The one who was always talking to people no one else could see.

"Can I have the results?" I said.

"I want to discuss this pregnancy with you," she said.

She obviously thought I was losing my mind.

"Have you heard of Perfect Finish?" I asked.

She nodded.

"You know Capital Bank?"

"Yes, I have an account there."

"I own Perfect Finish and my husband is the manager of Capital Bank. I got my first degree from Ife. I am not some mad woman off the street. Why are you discussing pregnancy with me when you just said there is no baby?"

Dr. Uche placed a palm against her forehead. "Madam, I'm sorry if I sounded patronising. I'm just worried about your health, your mental health."

She said "mental health" in such hushed tones, as if she was afraid to hear her own words. I wondered about the state of her own mind.

"Doctor, I am fine. Just let me have the results. You have a lot of patients waiting."

She handed the results over. "It happens, this kind of . . . pregnancy. To people who can't have . . . haven't had children. It happens—pregnancy symptoms are there but no baby. We are agreed that you aren't pregnant, right? Perhaps you could see a gynaecologist again about this issue? I can see on your file that you have had a number of tests done before, but maybe we could run some more tests?"

"I'll think about it."

I walked into the hallway with a hand on my slightly swollen stomach, undaunted by doubting Akin and the doctor. I felt like a balloon, filled with hope and a miracle baby. I was ready to float over the wards of Wesley Guild Hospital.

Akin laughed when I told him Funmi wanted to come and stay with us during my pregnancy. We were getting ready for bed; I was already in my white nightgown. He was still taking off his office clothes.

"That girl? What pregnancy anyway? Have they confirmed it at the hospital?" He yanked his belt off forcefully; it snapped against the bed like a whip.

"The doctor I met does not know what she is doing. She needs glasses, I'm telling you, saying she can't see my baby, *ehn*? The baby that has started kicking."

"Kicking?"

"Yes, now. You are shaking your head at me? Shake it well, shake it until it falls off your neck, you will see." I climbed into bed. "When I hold my baby in my arms, you will be put to shame, all of you who think I can't have a child. Even that stupid doctor will be put to shame."

"You know you sound crazy, right?"

"What are you saying?" I cradled my belly and waited for him to reply.

He stripped down to his boxers and lay beside me. "Yejide, please dim your lamp."

"What did you mean by what you said just now?"

He rolled onto his stomach and turned his face away from me.

"Akinyele? Me, I sound crazy?"

"You are not pregnant and Funmi is not coming to stay here. Can I sleep now?" He pulled the covers over his head.

His words crept across the room and clung undetected to my body like soldier ants would. Then they stung without warning in the early hours of the morning when I woke up to urinate for perhaps the tenth time in the course of that night. As I sat in bed and sipped water from the nearly empty bottle that I now kept on my bedside table, his words played back in my head, triggering questions.

I was now about four months' pregnant, my stomach was growing bigger each day, yet my husband chose to believe some incompetent doctor. He kept telling me I sounded crazy. Was he blind? Could he not see my stomach? Could he not see my puffy face? Even strangers could see it. Everywhere I went, people greeted me: *L'ojo ikunle a gbohun Iya a gbohun omo o—May we hear the mother's voice and the baby's voice when you deliver.* Strangers wished me well, they prayed for my survival and that of my child.

People alighted from full taxis so I could enter; I did not have to queue in the bank anymore, I was asked to go to the top of the line by those in the queue. Did Akin think I was a crazy woman who stopped people on the road to tell them that I was pregnant? Since the day we got married, I had never told him I was pregnant before, why did he find it so hard to believe me now?

I lay back in bed and clasped my hands over my belly. I could feel tension in my head, the beginnings of a headache. Beside me, Akin was stirring; he stretched in his sleep. I stared at his hairless chin and clenched my fist to keep from stroking it. I was still staring at him when he opened his eyes.

He rubbed his eyes with the back of his hands. "Didn't you sleep?"

"Why do you hate me so much?"

He scratched his neck. "You've started again. Get some sleep, Yejide."

"If I do a test, and it shows I'm pregnant, will you believe?" I tried to read his face in the hazy light of dawn. I could not.

"Yejide, you need to sleep more. It's too early for this."

I converted the empty room beside the kitchen into a playroom. I created a special place where I could spend time with my baby, a space for just the two of us. The playroom was not something

I planned; I converted it because Akin stopped talking to me. He stopped visiting Funmi in the evenings. Instead, he planted himself in the sitting room, watching the evening news, reading newspapers, but mostly not speaking to me, even if I was seated beside him. He responded to questions with a grunt, to insults with silence.

I gave up on trying to provoke or persuade Akin to talk and stayed in the spare room instead of the sitting room. I arranged the toys I had bought for the baby on the floor of the room. I put in a cushioned chair and bought my own newspapers so that I had something to read while I waited for the kitchen timer to ring. In that room, surrounded by teddy bears and brightly coloured rattles, I read about the military officers who had been accused of planning a coup. I was drawn to the profile of two of the men. There was Lieutenant Colonel Christian Oche, who had been a PhD candidate at Georgetown University in the United States until he was summoned back to the Supreme Headquarters. I kept wondering what course his life would have taken if he hadn't been recalled and had been left to complete his thesis. Perhaps he would have read about the events in the lower right-hand corner of some American newspaper. I also wondered if, when he boarded the plane back to Lagos, he had felt an enervating sadness that he ignored until it was replaced with the excitement of being back home.

And then there was the man whose fate fascinated the country, Major General Mamman Vatsa, sitting minister, award-winning poet and close friend to the head of state. Vatsa and Babangida were childhood friends who had been classmates in middle school; they were commissioned into the army on the same day and had commanded neighbouring battalions in the civil war. Babangida had even been the best man at Vatsa's wedding.

I was spending more time in the playroom than anywhere else in the house at this time, but the day I read that Vatsa, Oche and eleven others had been sentenced to death, I sat with Akin in the sitting room and tried to discuss the events with him. But he kept redirecting the conversation to my bulging stomach, so I retreated to the play-room and didn't bother to ask if he thought it would help when Wole Soyinka, Chinua Achebe and J. P. Clark met with Babangida. The writers' appeal for clemency made sense to me; after all it had not even been a proper coup attempt: the men had been tried for their *intentions*. The next day, I wept when I learned that ten of the officers, including Vatsa and Oche, had been executed. Vatsa maintained that he was innocent until the end, but it would be years before other military officers would question the evidence used to convict him. At the time, Nigeria was still in the honeymoon phase of her relationship with

Babangida, and like most new brides she wasn't asking probing questions, yet.

I did not go into the sitting room while the defence secretary announced the executions, but I could hear him from the playroom because Akin had turned up the volume. I wanted to go to him, not even to talk, just to be next to him and feel him squeeze my arm. But I was afraid he would stare at my stomach mutely with the expression of a man looking at vomit.

Eventually, Akin's icy silence melted into warm words spoken softly. He even came into the playroom a few times. His words took up too much space in the room and it was hard for me to breathe. Since I had told him I was pregnant, he had sealed his mouth about the baby, but when he visited me in the playroom, it was the only thing he wanted to talk to me about. He wanted to talk sense into me, only he couched his sermons in questions that I soon stopped answering. He asked me several times if I thought my baby would save the world. He asked if I saw visions of the child. He asked me to describe the angels I had seen, even after I told him I had never seen an angel in my life. One night, he asked me if I thought my baby would have superpowers and I decided I had had enough. I went to my salon the next morning and informed my shop girls that I would not return until the next day. Then I drove to the teaching hospital in Ife.

There was no electricity in the hospital when I arrived. After he booked my appointment, the nurse informed me that the generator would not be switched on until 2 p.m. and since there were people in line ahead of me, I might not get to see a doctor until 3 p.m. It was just 11 a.m. now. I decided to go into the market to buy a few items for my salon. I got the usual setting lotions and shampoos that I used in the shop, and then I stopped by a gift shop to buy a wooden flower vase that would look nice in the playroom.

I was on my way out of the market when I felt a hand grab my wrist. I turned and found myself face-to-face with Iya Tunde, my father's fourth wife. I had not seen her since my father's burial.

"Yejide, so it is you? I saw the person and I told myself, no, it can't be Yejide, Yejide would not come into this market without visiting my stall. Is that the way this world is? A child can now visit the market without branching off to her mother's stall?" Iya Tunde said.

"Good afternoon, Iya Tunde." I could not resist reminding her she was Iya Tunde, not my mother. "How is the market?"

"We are begging God for a good market day. Still, we thank God because we are not going hungry."

For the first few months after she had married my father, Iya Tunde sold fruit in a small shed behind our house. When she got pregnant, my father moved her into the stall he'd built for Iya Martha in the market and he asked them to share it because a pregnant woman should have sufficient shade and space to do her business. He promised Iya Martha that he would build a new stall for her elsewhere in the market. I don't know how she did it, but by the end of the year Iya Tunde had taken over the stall and Iya Martha was selling her wares in the wooden shed behind our house. My father never built another stall for Iya Martha.

"Greet everyone at home for me," I said. "I have to get going."

"Wait, wait, let me rejoice with you, I can see you are now two in one? You are pregnant!"

"I thank God."

"Your mother is not sleeping in heaven-o, she is praying for you. Even though she had no lineage, or at least we did not know her lineage, it is obvious now she is a good mother." She could not let me go without throwing her own jab at me. According to my father, my mother had been part of a nomadic Fulani group when she got pregnant by him and refused to travel on with her own people. But my stepmothers would go to their graves calling her a woman of "unknown lineage."

"I really must go."

"Remember to visit us once in a while, try and

91

show us your face now and then. After all, it is still your father's house."

Every time he married a new wife, my father would tell his children that family was about having people who would look for you if you got kidnapped. He'd then add that he was doing his best to build an army just in case one of us did get kidnapped. It was a bad joke and I was the only one who ever laughed. I laughed at all his jokes. I think he believed in this myth of his large harmonious family. He probably thought that I would still visit my stepmothers after his death.

"Goodbye, Iya Tunde."

"Goodbye-o. Greet your husband for me."

The polythene bags I was carrying suddenly felt heavier. I was grateful when the bus conductor took them from me as I climbed into the bus. I had left my car at the hospital to avoid putting unnecessary strain on its old engine. I fought off thoughts of my lonely childhood, rubbed my stomach through my clothes and was comforted. I did not need to be afraid. Even if Funmi ended up taking Akin from me, I would soon have someone all my own, my own family.

I was just in time for the appointment.

After the scan, Dr. Junaid cleared his throat. "How long have you been pregnant?"

"About six months now."

"When did you have the last scan?" He wrote something in the open file before him.

"At three months, and that was three months ago. I met one young doctor like that, maybe that is why she made a mistake—lack of experience."

He stopped writing and looked at me. "Hmm, you think she made a mistake?"

"That is why I'm here to confirm. She said there was no baby there." I patted my protruding belly. "You can see for yourself and I'm sure it is not kwashiorkor."

I laughed. Dr. Junaid didn't.

"Have you seen any fertility specialists? Did you see any, before you got, um, before you came to think you were pregnant? Did you have any tests done?"

"Yes, of course. I saw someone in Ilesa, I did all the tests. They said I was OK."

"And your husband, did he see a specialist?"

"Yes, he did."

We went to the hospital together once. Akin answered most of the doctor's questions. When the doctor asked about our sex life, Akin held my hand before he answered and stroked my thumb as he said, *Our sex life is normal, absolutely normal.*

Dr. Junaid shut the file he'd been writing in and leaned forward. "So your husband, was he tested? Did they run any tests and—?"

"Yes, he was tested," I said. "Look, doctor, what about my baby?"

"Madam"—he drummed his fingers on his desk—"there is no baby."

I clapped my hands three times and laughed. "Doctor, are you blind? I don't want to insult you, but can't you see?"

"Please, let me explain. These things happen sometimes. Women think they are pregnant, but they are not."

"Listen to yourself. I don't think I am pregnant. I *know* I am pregnant. I have not seen my period in six months. See my stomach. I have even felt the baby kick! I don't *think* I am pregnant, doctor. I *am* pregnant. Can't you see? I am pregnant."

"Madam, please calm down."

"I am leaving. I don't even know if it is the machines you work with that are faulty or your brains."

I slammed the door as I left the room.

As the pregnancy approached eleven months, I decided to visit the Mountain of Jaw-Dropping Miracles again. On the day I went there, Akin was in Lagos for a meeting and had travelled with his colleagues in the bank's official car. I drove his car to the flat expanse of land at the base of the mountain. When I arrived, there was only one car in the space, a Volvo parked in the shade of an almond tree. I recognised Mrs. Adeolu's plate number.

As I climbed up the mountain, everywhere was

still and quiet. It took me over two hours to get to the crest because I stopped from time to time to sit on rocks and drink from the bottle of water I carried with me. The sun was relentless. Sweat streamed down my back into the crack of my buttocks. I pulled my dress back and forth at the neckline to get some air on my skin.

When I arrived at the crest, there was no living creature in sight. I wandered around until I found a wooden slate on which someone had scrawled: *Prophet Josiah on travel. Plis come back in next month four your miracul.* Too bad for Prophet Josiah, I thought to myself, patting the wad of naira notes in my pocket—I wanted to give him some money. He had not asked for any money the first time I came, and I figured giving him a gift would not hurt. The bottle of water was now empty and I was parched and felt faint. Afraid that I would collapse on my way down the mountain, I went around the crest, hoping to find a forgotten bottle of water, praying I would not get cholera from whatever I found. That was when I found the shed—it was made from four wooden posts arranged to form a rough rectangle, and palm fronds covered it at the top.

In the shed, Prophet Josiah and Mrs. Adeolu were having sex. I could see her face; her eyes were closed in what could have been ecstasy. The Prophet's distinguishing chef cap was about to fall off; his robes were bunched up around

95

his waist, exposing his thrusting buttocks. His bare legs were so skinny.

I left before either of them could see me and spent the next two months at home, waiting for the baby to come. I stopped going to the salon and left Akin to attend to the head stylist when she came to give account in the evenings. I did not cook or do housework. Akin bought meals from *bukas* in town and sat with me in the playroom to make sure I ate something. He also brought newspapers that I did not read. One morning I told him that I was conserving my energy so that when the baby was ready, I would be strong enough to push. He did not tell me there was no baby, or ask me why I had not done this when the pregnancy had lasted for nine months. He just kissed me on the chin and left for work, but when he came back that evening, he explained that if I wanted to be strong for the baby, I needed to be active. There was no mention of psychiatrists and he did not sound as if he was joking or humouring a crazy person. He spoke to me the way I'd wanted him to all the while, like an expectant father. I took his advice and went back to work the next day.

One Saturday afternoon, I opened the door of my home and found Funmi on the other side, surrounded by several boxes and bags. The taxicab that dropped her off raised a cloud of dust as it drove away.

"Move and let me pass," she said.

I stood by the door like a guard as she swept in. I watched as she dragged her bags into the house one after the other, and littered the sitting room with them. She wore a navy-blue *boubou*, complete with a matching scarf that she had tied around her braided hair like a band. Her bright skin shone in the sunlight that streamed in through the open doorway.

"Where is my room?" she said when she was done lugging her bags.

"In this house? Are you dreaming?"

"You, this woman—I have tried enough for you-o. Don't try any more nonsense with me. This is my husband's house too. Why must you keep me outside this house?" She removed her scarf and tied it around her waist. "Why? You wicked woman, I asked you to shift so that we could both sit down. If you are not careful, I will push you off the seat totally."

"You see, I am not the one who married you. Your so-called husband is not in. When he's back, you can ask him stupid questions." I pointed to the door. "Now, get out of my house."

"You know what? I can only see your mouth moving, I can't hear a single word. Let me tell you, there is only one thing that can get me out of this house, one thing!"

97

"I said, get out!" I slapped my thigh in time with each word.

"The one thing that will cause me to leave you in peace is for you to lift up your blouse and let me see your stomach. This pregnancy of yours is over a year old now. Let me see what is there, because we have heard the news all over town that it is a calabash you are carrying about under your cloth—yes, you have been exposed." She laughed. "But you can prove them wrong, prove the evil people wrong. Let me see your stomach for myself and I will leave you in peace. I swear to God."

I cradled my chin in one hand and wrapped the other across my distended stomach.

"Won't you speak?"

What could I have said? That my pregnancy was real? I still had not seen my period and if I had lifted my blouse and opened my wrapper, no calabash would have clattered to the ground; no pillow would have fallen at my feet. She would have seen my taut, distended stomach and the stretch marks crisscrossing the skin. I could have said my pregnancy was not real, that scan upon scan said there was nothing there, even as the baby's kicking woke me each night. That some of my stylists thought I was crazy and the last doctor I saw had referred me to a psychiatrist.

I could not say any of those things; there was only one thing left to be said. The thing she was not expecting me to say. I shut the door and turned to her. "Follow me. Let me show you your room."

I led her to the playroom.

I was not stupid. I understood that it was a matter of time before Moomi showed up to make sure that Funmi started living in the house. If I fought with Funmi, it would only make things worse. Moomi could ask me to leave and though Akin kept telling me how much he loved me, I no longer believed him. But I wanted to believe him. I had no father, no mother, and no sibling. Akin was the only person in the world who would really notice if I went missing.

These days I tell myself that is why I stretched to accommodate every new level of indignity, so that I could have someone who would look for me if I went missing.

PART TWO

10

I'm digging my father's grave. Doing more than I should because my sister's husband overestimated his abilities when he promised to do it. As my father's first son, I'm supposed to shovel the first and last clumps of sand out of the grave for safekeeping. My father's son-in-law is supposed to do the rest, or pay someone else to. I thought Henry would pay labourers to do this since that's what most people do these days.

Yejide, you must remember how I told you years ago that this tradition would die out soon. It was after your father died. While your family made arrangements for the funeral, you told them that I should join in the grave digging even though we were not yet married. Of course, your stepmothers wouldn't allow it. And you wept until the whites of your eyes turned pink. I tried to comfort you, told you that it didn't really matter because everyone would be hiring labourers to dig graves in a few years anyway. I'm not sure you heard me or cared. You cried yourself to sleep that night.

I couldn't tell you at the time, but I was relieved I didn't have to dig your father's grave. I believed in ghosts then, was terrified of graveyards. Yet, if your stepmothers had agreed to let me dig, I would have done it to please you. You must know that, no matter what you think of me now, there are few things I wouldn't do to make you happy. I'm certain now that there are no ghosts, because if there were, I would be haunted already. So here I am, about two feet deep, helping Henry out so that the work will be done by the time we leave for the wake.

Henry's doing this to prove a point to my parents. For three years my parents insisted they were not giving their only daughter in marriage to Henry because he was not Yoruba. They stood by their word until my sister ended the arguments by getting pregnant by Henry. Then the people who had sworn that they would be dead before he married their daughter invited Henry to pick any date for the wedding so that it could be done before the pregnancy started showing. Henry now speaks Yoruba fluently, knows more about our traditions than I do. And here we are, slaving silently beneath a blazing sun, because Henry is still trying to prove to my parents that he is good enough for their daughter. It's obvious now from his heavy breathing that he'd stretched the truth to the breaking point when he claimed he could do this "the way it should be done."

The sun is so hot, feels like there's a furnace

on my back. My arms ache each time I lift the shovel, but I keep going. I think about Dotun as I shovel, miss him for the first time in all these years. If he were here, he would have broken this silence, found a way to make Henry and me laugh. He called me this morning, around 7. He didn't introduce himself, he didn't have to. Once he said, "Brother Akin, good morning," I recognised his voice. He said he was calling from the airport hotel, had received the letter I had sent to him about the funeral arrangements and would be leaving Lagos by noon to get to Ilesa in time for the wake. Our first conversation in over a decade lasted less than one minute. When I got off the phone, I felt none of the anger I'd expected to feel, instead I had a sudden desire to stay in bed and spend the day sleeping. Dotun's phone call made me ask myself if you'll honour my invitation. I wonder if you'll show up at the wake, if you'll agree to sit beside me and sing hymns.

This ground is getting harder as we dig deeper. It doesn't look like a grave, just a long hole in the ground. I clear my throat. "I think we should call someone to finish this thing."

Henry smiles and collapses against the grave's wall. It's as if he's been waiting all day for me to say this. He frowns. "Arinola—"

I wait for him to finish his sentence, but he says nothing. I watch his furrowed brow; try to understand what his silence means. "You don't want me to tell her we abandoned this?"

"She was very touched that I'd be digging the grave."

"OK, we'll tell her you dug the grave." It's the truth—stretched, but still true. Besides, what would be left of love without truth stretched beyond its limits, without those better versions of ourselves that we present as the only ones that exist?

Timi tells me Moomi has refused to come downstairs for the wake. As I wonder why, it occurs to me that my mother might be grief-stricken over my father's death. I almost laugh. I know as I climb the stairs, two steps at a time, that it has to be something else. I don't think they were ever in love. But they did tolerate each other until my siblings and I left home. Then Moomi stopped bothering with tolerance, and unleashed her long-held anger and resentment. My father didn't fight back, poor man had little energy left after dealing with his four younger wives. Now that he's dead, I expect Moomi to feel some sadness, but mixed with a measure of triumph— she has outlasted him. I turn left at the landing and step into Moomi's sitting room. Her bedroom door is wide open. She sits on her bed, dressed in white like the other widows, arms folded across her chest.

"Moomi, Timi says you don't want to come downstairs. Why?"

She sighs. "Akinyele."

It's never a good sign when she calls my name in full. I walk across the room, sit in a cushioned chair, wait for her to continue.

"If a lie travels for twenty years, even a hundred years, it will take one day—" She raises her right hand, points the index finger at the ceiling. "It will take one day for the truth to catch up with a lie. The truth has caught up with you today, Akin. Today is the day I know you have been lying to me about Dotun—didn't you tell me he called you this morning? You said he would be here by now. Where is he? Akinyele, where is my son?"

I reach into my trouser pocket, bring out my phone, dial the number Dotun called with in the morning, put the phone to my ear.

The number you are calling cannot be reached at the moment. Please try again later.

"See, I just tried to call him, *Ma*. The number cannot be reached."

"You can't deceive me anymore. Do you think I will break down if you tell me the truth? Even if the truth will kill me, am I too young to die?"

"You need to believe me." I'm tired of trying to convince her that I've not been lying to her, just want Dotun to show up today and put an end to her anxieties.

"Although what could kill me is knowing

that you and your brother never settled that quarrel and that Dotun went to his grave without forgiving you." Moomi sighed. "And I could have talked sense into your heads, but no, you two didn't tell me why you were fighting."

"Again, we resolved things long before he went away."

Dotun needs my forgiveness, not the other way around. But I'm sure he still thinks I need to apologise. Yejide, I've realised that it's your forgiveness that I need. Questions of forgiving Dotun or begging his forgiveness become secondary as Moomi sheds the first tears I've seen since her husband died. These tears have nothing to do with my father—they are all for Dotun, her favourite son.

"How can you tell me my son is alive when he has not come home to see his own father, his own father buried? Akin, you are deceiving me, I'm now sure that you have been deceiving me all this time." Moomi's voice shakes but she doesn't sob, the tears just come.

"Please wipe your tears, Moomi. See, let's go downstairs so the wake can start. Everyone is seated, it's almost four. I'm sure he will arrive during the service."

"If you don't bring Dotun into this room, I am not attending that wake." She removes her scarf, folds it into a square and places it on her bedside table.

"Moomi, you are just getting upset over nothing. He will soon be here."

She lies down on the bed, turns to face the wall.

This delay makes me think Dotun is still the same man he was when he left the country without informing anyone in the family; the type who will arrive when the wake is over, offer no apologies, make a joke and expect everyone to laugh.

"Moomi, please stop crying, Dotun is not dead." I glance at my watch. It's about five minutes to four. "Moomi, I hope you can hear me. When it's five, if Dotun is not here, we will start the wake."

"Without me?"

"I will ask the priest to delay for an hour. I can't ask for more than that, *Ma*."

"The priest will not start without me."

"I'll ask Timi to come and call you when it's a few minutes to five." I stand up. "Please put your mind at rest, Moomi."

I go downstairs, back into the front yard where the canopies have been set up. I bend over to greet people as I pass through the noisy crowd to the front row; all the while I am looking out for your face.

In the front row, I talk to the priest, then whisper to my stepmothers that the wake will now start at five. I head to the back of the canopy without answering their question about why Moomi has not come downstairs. I need to get away from the noise, call the grave digger, confirm that my father's resting place is ready.

I step out from under the canopy as a yellow-and-black Lagos cab pulls up behind it. I can see Dotun in the back seat; he is alone. He gets out of the car, looks up and our eyes meet. He is balding too, his face a sagging version of the one I remember.

I stand with my hands in my trouser pockets, watching him. He stays beside the taxi for a moment, then walks forward, towards me. And for the first time in over a decade, my brother and I are face-to-face.

I try to think of something to do, something to say. He beats me to it, prostrates himself on the red sand. When he gets up, he says two words, "Brother *mi*."

I don't know who reaches out first, but it doesn't matter; we are hugging, laughing. I think one of us has tears in his eyes.

Yejide, I hope it will be this way between us when you come. If you come.

11

O ne day, I came back from a trip to Lagos and found Funmi at the dining table, eating fried rice with a fork. She stopped eating when I came in, walked towards me smiling, wrapped her arms around my neck, kissed my chin. Her breath smelled like garlic.

"Welcome, my husband." She took my briefcase. "How was your journey?"

"Great," I said. Didn't think I had any cause for alarm. Thought she was just visiting for the day.

"Is Yejide upstairs?" I asked as Funmi poured me a glass of cold water.

Funmi pursed her lips, sighed, pulled me into the sitting room. "The traffic in Lagos must be terrible as usual, *abi*?"

"It was OK."

We sat in silence as I drank the water.

Funmi often tried to chat with me, but we had a problem. We had nothing in common, apart from the fact that we were married. I usually said little when we were together.

"Should I bring something for you to eat?" Funmi asked.

"No, thank you."

111

"I made fried rice, but if you want something else I can cook it. Do you want pounded yam?"

Someone must have convinced her that feeding me at every chance she got would change my feelings about her. She was constantly offering me food or drink.

"I ate lunch at Dotun's place before leaving Lagos. I'm not yet hungry."

"Oh, OK. Later, *abi*?"

I nodded, dropped the empty cup on a stool and began to get up. Funmi put a hand on my knee.

"I want to ask you for something," she said.

"What is that?"

"Sweetheart, I want you to spend the night with me."

The word "sweetheart" always sounded strange on her lips. It was a word she did not mean and I did not believe. But she kept saying it as if she thought repeating it would make it true. I considered telling her not to call me that a number of times, but it would have been a cruel thing to do.

"Funmi, you know that I can only come to your flat at the weekend."

"No, my sweetheart. I live here now."

"What did you just say?"

"I moved in two days ago. Aunty Yejide showed me to my room. She doesn't mind at all-o; in fact, she welcomed me with open arms."

My first instinct was to tell Funmi to pack her

things immediately and leave. Knew I couldn't balance things with Yejide and Funmi under the same roof, the pressure would be too much— something was bound to go wrong. But I fought that instinct because I knew Funmi already had her suspicions—if I told her to leave, she could have screamed them at the top of her lungs. I had to wait for the right moment to get her out of the house.

"My sweetheart," Funmi said, holding my chin in her hand. "Are you angry with me for not asking for permission before moving in?" She went down on her knees. "Don't be angry with me."

"Of course not. It's OK; please get up. No need for all that."

She smiled, putting her head on my knees. I decided then to watch out for the right moment to get her out. Not just out of the house, but out of my life. Marrying her was a terrible miscalculation. I knew as she took off my shoes that I had to fix the equation as soon as I could.

I was sure that a perfect moment would present itself for me to divorce Funmi, just as one had presented itself for me to marry Yejide in '81. That year, Bukola Arogundade, a student at the University of Ife, was murdered. This was years before some of the protest marches in universities would become compulsory, mandated by so-called union boys who chased freshers out of their rooms. The protest in '81 to demand justice for Bukola Arogundade was pure, propelled by a collective anger that shivered in bloodstreams, an unspoken assurance that if we just got to the palace and screamed loud enough, someone would pay attention.

I was courting Yejide then, driving to Ife every day after work just to breathe in her scent. I caught the feverish anger from her enchanting words. I'd never seen her act the way she did that day, was enthralled by the veins that stood out in her neck as she spoke. I agreed with everything that came out of her mouth; it was as if she was reading my mind. It was new, strange, exciting: the way she mirrored me in those moments, mirrored my passion and dreams for a better country. I was convinced more than before that I had found my soul mate. I took a day off work and joined the protest to demand a thorough and transparent investigation into the murder.

Yejide and I marched side by side, singing and chanting. The clouds gathering ahead did not dampen our ardour. We marched with the crowd to the school gate, we were not even tired, or even breathless. The chants became louder as we marched out of the gates into town. When the rain started, I saw it as a blessing from above, a mark of approval. Believed as I got drenched that the protest would produce results that would propel the rest of the nation forward. I could see the uprising as I blinked against the shower—at first in the universities, students and lecturers trooping into the streets demanding change, an end to corruption, consistent power supply, better roads. I could see it all so clearly. Though the protest was heading in the opposite direction, I imagined it sweeping into Ibadan, carrying the people of that city like a flood, dragging them along with us into Lagos, all the way to the government house. The possibility was as real to me as raindrops on my lips and in my mouth as we sang:

SOOOO-lida-RITY For-EEEE-VER
SOOOO-lida-RITY For-EEEE-VER
SOOOO-lida-RITY For-EEEE-VER
WE SHALL ALWAYS FIGHT FOR
  OUR RIGHTS
SOLI SOLI SOLI
SOOOO-lida-RITY For-EEEE-VER!

The policemen were waiting in Mayfair. Gunshots rang out. People started running all around me, screaming as they dashed into the bush, beating paths to unknown destinations. I was confused at first. Ran aimlessly forward like a chicken in its last throes of life after its head has been chopped off. Then I too ran into the bush. It was like diving into hell. Around me people screamed, prayed, cursed, slipped, collapsed. Some pulled themselves up again and continued running. A girl in tight jeans with an afro fell in front of me and lay still. I leapt over her, kept running as though she was a gutter in my way. I ran for what felt like years, the bush stretched on forever, teeming with tree branches that poked my eyes and mouth.

Then I was on the road again. The moment my feet touched tarmac, I wanted to run back into the bush. The road felt so exposed, with no place to hide. But there were too many people pouring out of the bush into the road. If I didn't move, I would have been knocked over. I kept running. Took a while before I realised I was back on campus. I ran to Moremi car park, where I'd left my car under an almond tree.

I was in the car before I remembered Yejide. Panic seized me by the throat. Where was she? She had been standing right beside me, holding a wet cardboard placard over her head. I tried to remember if she had been wearing jeans. I wondered if she was the one I leapt over in the bush. In that instant, I could not remember if she had an afro or not. The car park was in chaos, students were running around, into Moremi, farther down. I didn't know where to start looking for her.

Then she was there beside me, rapping on the car window. I'd never been so happy to see another human being, wanted to strap her in the seat next to me, live with her in the car forever, never let her out of my sight again. I settled for hugging her until I could feel the rapid beat of her heart as though it was mine. Neither of us said anything. I couldn't speak, though my throat was clogged with words, clogged with emotions that paralysed my vocal chords. Even now I think I should have said something, told her how I couldn't stand to lose her, how the thought of it had almost made me lose my mind moments before, how I wanted to bind myself to her, so that she could be safe, so I could go with her everywhere she went.

I said nothing until the next day, when we learned that three students had died in the protest.

"Marry me now," I said. "Life is short, why should we wait until you finish your degree? I'll give you my car, you can drive from Ilesa; you can even stay in the hostel if you want. But let's tell your father that we are ready."

I knew she would say yes, because it was the right moment. At any other time, she would have insisted that she didn't want to be a married student. But that day in June, she held my hand and nodded.

I dreamed about the dead students a lot in the first year of our marriage. I used to see them lying in an endless row on the tarmac, all dressed in tight blue jeans. Yejide was always standing at the other end of the bodies. I would try to get to her, but there were too many bodies in my way.

12

Two weeks before the armed robbers wrote us a letter, a new salon was set up right beside mine. The owner was Iya Bolu, a fat illiterate who belched in between her words. If she said good morning to you, you got an accurate idea of what she had eaten for breakfast, along with a spray of spit that followed every word she spoke. Children spilled out of her salon like water from a fountain and littered the passageway that we shared. They were all over the place—crawling, sitting or lying about. They were all little girls with dirty hair. The oldest was about ten and the youngest about four—six daughters in six years. I disliked the woman so much in the first week after she arrived that, in a wild moment, I considered moving my salon to another location.

Iya Bolu was always shouting at her daughters. And the few customers she had went home with more spittle in their hair than setting lotion. She had about two customers each day and sometimes none at all. As much as she tried to lure my customers by greeting them with too many words and very wide smiles, the spittle fountain that was her mouth must have put them off. She was soon spending a lot of time in my salon. She would come in shortly before noon so that she could listen to the midday news on my radio. The radio was not just old, it had become temperamental. Sometimes, to get clear reception, Iya Bolu would need to stand beside it and hold the antenna. Once the news was over, she'd settle in a chair that squeaked under her weight and dispense unsolicited styling advice.

It was Iya Bolu who brought me the letter her family had received from the armed robbers. Her family lived on our estate and every family in the estate had received a letter from the thieves. She asked me to read her letter to her after the customers and stylists had left.

The letter was in the same format as the one addressed to us; only the address and salutation were different.

> Dear Mr. and Mrs. Adio,
>   We greet you in the name of the Gun.
>   We write to inform you that we will visit your family before the end of this year.
>   Prepare a package for us. We accept a minimum amount of a thousand naira. We will give you time to gather this money. We will write you again to tell you the specific date of our visit.

"Is that all?" Iya Bolu asked.

"Yes."

She frowned. "I must think about this matter.

119

Where do they want us to find that kind of money? It's enough to buy a car."

"I am sure it is a joke. It is just a stupid prank, *jare*," I said.

This was long before that kind of thing became a regular occurrence. I could not imagine then that one day in Nigeria thieves would be bold enough to write letters so that victims could prepare for their attacks, that one day they would sit in living rooms after raping women and children and ask people to prepare pounded yam and egusi stew while they watched movies on VCRs that they would soon disconnect and cart away.

Only a few people like Iya Bolu believed the letter was real. I attributed this to her lack of formal education. I didn't think much about the first letter. I didn't even show it to Akin. There were other things on my mind. After Funmi moved in, I began seeing a psychiatrist on Wednesdays. I'd never heard of pseudocyesis until then and though it sounded to me like a made-up word, I went for my appointment every week and my body began to revert gradually to its normal size.

I took to walking to and from work because my psychiatrist recommended exercise. I actually found it calming to walk the short distance, away from Funmi and back to her. I tried to focus on my salon, but it was hard not to notice the changes she was making in the sitting room.

She moved the chairs around and placed a vase of plastic flowers on the centre table. I did my best to avoid running into her and spent most of my time upstairs. Akin was busy at work and usually came in after I was fast asleep, but during the weekends he wanted to talk about how my treatment was going. To make him happy, I assured him that I no longer had days or even moments when I believed I was pregnant.

Iya Bolu became a permanent fixture in my salon. She slept through the working hours, snoring through her open mouth while her daughters roamed around, getting up only to stand by the radio when the news came on.

When we got the follow-up letters from the armed robbers, the days began to speed along like a videocassette on fast-forward. These letters were different from the initial ones. They were not identical notes that a bored teenager could have cooked up. They were personalised, addressed to each family by people who had to have been watching us, studying us, and perhaps living among us.

The robbers congratulated the Agunbiades on the birth of their twin daughters. They congratulated the Ojos on the brand-new Peugeot 504 station wagon they had just bought, consoled the Fatolas on the loss of their chieftaincy title and advised the Adios (Iya Bolu's family) to consider family planning. They promised to show up within three weeks, advised everyone not to move out of the estate and promised to hunt us down if we dared move. They knew so much about us that we believed they would find us if we tried to run away from the estate. Our hearts stopped beating and began to thump loud rhythms. We jumped when rats scurried by and stopped taking evening strolls. Even children were less noisy.

The estate committee employed a group of hunters to guard the estate. There had been no estate committee before the threats. We were all so educated and modern in our individual duplexes, honking hello when we drove by each other in town. We visited when it was necessary, for naming ceremonies, birthdays and the occasional funeral. But we did not send pounded yam and egusi stew in enamel bowls to each other at Christmas or distribute fried ram at Ileya. Instead, we wished each other "Merry Christmas" and "Ramadan Kareem" without leaving our porches and waved as we got into our cars or went into our houses.

Yet, once the second set of letters from the thieves arrived, an estate committee was formed. Everyone in the estate joined. The first official meeting was rowdy but we managed to agree to employ five policemen and a group of hunters to join the security guards. We also decided to pay three naira per household as security due. Akin and Mr. Adio were dispatched to Ayeso police station immediately to request that policemen be sent down to us.

The committee got a letter the next day from the robbers. They wrote that the police were on their payroll. We laughed at this and nodded in agreement at the committee meeting when Mr. Fatola (ex-chief Fatola) said we had outwitted the robbers and their last letter was evidence to that effect. The policemen resumed duty within the next week. The sight of policemen with automatic pistols and hunters with Dane guns patrolling the estate reassured us and we soon forgot about the letters.

Then Iya Bolu called a "women of the estate" meeting.

It was the first time I had entered Iya Bolu's home. I was surprised to discover that it was so clean and tidy. From what I saw of Iya Bolu at the salon, I had expected her sitting room to stink of caked urine and be littered with used nappies. Instead it smelled tangy and fresh, like lime. I could tell from the way the other women looked around that they had expected something similar. None of her children surfaced throughout the meeting. I kept wondering if she had hidden them in a room or in a shoe cupboard.

Iya Bolu started the meeting once the last woman was seated. "We must be ready for the thieves. These people rape, they rape children.

123

We must be armed with sanitary pads." Her eyes opened wider with each word until they looked like they might pop out and roll under a chair.

"With sanitary pads? Do they put bullets in them now?" Mrs. Fatola said, shaking her head.

One person laughed, then another, and soon we were all laughing except Iya Bolu, who looked as if she might begin to cry.

"Shut your mouths!" Iya Bolu screamed. "I have six daughters, do you know what that means? The oldest one is already growing breasts. Some of you have daughters too, daughters already seeing their monthly things. Anything can happen with those thieves, and what about you yourselves, how many of your husbands will take a bullet rather than have a group of robbers rape you? I am sure they are finding a way to hide in the ceiling."

"There are no thieves coming, we have policemen," Mrs. Ojo said. She had studied in England for a year and she always spoke in a fake British accent, even when she was speaking in Yoruba.

"Yes, there is no need to scare ourselves over nothing," I said.

Mrs. Fatola applauded. Nobody else joined in the applause.

Iya Bolu hissed. "Let me say my own. Soak the sanitary pads in red wine or liquid from boiled Zobo leaves. Wear it every night in case these people come, so that if they come they will think you are seeing your monthly thing."

"Is this woman crazy? Even if she is right, all the women in a whole estate menstruating at the same time? Who would believe that?" Mrs. Ojo said in English with her strangled British accent.

Mrs. Fatola shook her head and got up.

"It's her illiteracy—an impoverished mind, I must say," Mrs. Ojo said.

"I don't have time for this. I need to get to work," Mrs. Fatola said.

"What are they saying?" Iya Bolu asked me.

"That there is nothing to worry about, just relax," I said to her in Yoruba. "We have the police."

"Tell me, did the police help Dele Giwa?" Iya Bolu asked.

Mrs. Fatola fell into her chair as though pushed back by the weight of Iya Bolu's words. The room was quiet and Mrs. Ojo glanced about as though afraid there was a secret service agent listening in on our conversation.

In the months after Dele Giwa had been assassinated, rooms would fall silent with fear whenever his name was mentioned. It did not matter that none of the women in Iya Bolu's sitting room was editor-in-chief of a news magazine, Giwa's fate still felt like something that could befall any of us because the bomb that killed him was delivered to his home in a parcel. Receiving a parcel was such an innocuous everyday thing, and we could all imagine sitting at a desk in our home to cut one open. And though I could not imagine my parcel with a sticker that bore the Nigerian coat of arms and the inscription *From the office of the C-in-C,* I knew that if, like Giwa's son, I had received similar packages in the past for my father from the head of state, I would not hesitate to take it to him in his study. When Giwa, who was with a colleague, received the parcel, he said, *This must be from the president,* and opened it after his son left the study. He died in a hospital later that day, though his injured colleague survived.

"To be honest," Mrs. Fatola said, "I ask the housemaid to open our letters now, even the ones from these so-called robbers."

I had taken no precautions with the letters my family received. When Dele Giwa was killed, I was busy spending my time indoors, conserving my energy so I would be strong enough to push when the baby came. I was paying no attention to the news. By the time I returned to work, Giwa's death had taught Nigeria to be afraid of her leaders. But probably because I learned about the events in retrospect, I was not terrified enough to stop opening my own letters.

At the salon, Iya Bolu pestered me for the wording of my family's letter. She went around asking all the women for the details of their letters, then sat in my salon trying to figure out what the robbers might want from each family. She seemed to care about protecting us all from what she saw as impending doom. She really cared.

I told her the details of the letter addressed to Akin and me. The robbers told us not to leave the estate for Funmi's flat in an attempt to avoid them.

"How come they know your rival's house? I tell you, they are real, they are going to come," Iya Bolu said.

The woman was so scared, sometimes I was touched by her concern; at other times her fears irritated me. Didn't she see policemen standing guard in the estate?

13

My husband's brother was one of those men who won an argument because he could yell louder and longer than everyone else, even if his view was stupid. He also had a way of twisting his neck around as far as it could go in the heat of an argument. It gave the impression that he might strangle himself to death if his audience did not agree with him. Most people eventually did. I always thought they let him have his say and his way because they did not want to be responsible for his death.

I did not like my brother-in-law, but then I was married to Akin and Dotun came as part of the package. Whenever Dotun came to visit, I was glad that he lived in Lagos and his visits were spaced out enough to give me breathing room. He was always telling all sorts of strange jokes that were not funny at all. He laughed so loudly, too loudly, at his own mirthless jokes. It was tiring to be around him; I always had to laugh at things that were not funny. I also had to figure out when I was supposed to laugh, as his jokes had no detectable punch line. He was not a man to be taken seriously; amid all that laughter, he made many promises—promises he would never keep.

Dotun had promised us a child once; he'd said he would send one of his sons to live with us until I conceived. When he said it, I went on my knees and thanked him. Moomi had suggested months before that I look for a child, a toddler who could live with me until I conceived. She'd said that children have a way of calling other children into the world. Having a foster child's voice around me constantly would call up my own children; hurry them along into the world. The only problem was that I had no full siblings and I hadn't spoken to my half-siblings in years. I had no relative who would entrust me with their child. I forgot about the idea until Dotun somehow got to hear about it and promised to send his youngest son.

The boy's name was Layi: he was two years old at the time. I furnished a room for him upstairs. I bought toys, picture books, drawing books and colouring pencils. I waited. The items in the room became dusty. I waited, dusted each toy and each book with a soft cloth. I asked Akin to call his brother and follow up. The items gathered more dust. Akin told me that Dotun had changed his mind. I packed up all the toys and gave them away.

Yet I was glad when Dotun showed up on our doorstep one Saturday morning just as the sun was coming out of hiding after a downpour. Funmi had travelled to visit relatives and Akin kept following me around the house, asking for details about my treatment in the hospital. It was as though he knew that there was still a part of me that did not totally believe that the doctors were right. That morning, he had managed to question me until I screamed at him that it was possible that everyone was wrong and I was right.

"You need to tell your doctor what you are really thinking," he'd said. "Stop saying what you think he wants to hear."

I was happy to see Dotun because I felt he would distract Akin. They enjoyed each other's company and spent hours on the phone arguing about sports, politics and the weather. Sometimes, when Akin thought I was not listening, I overheard them discussing which was better, a busty woman or one with a really round ass. I assumed that with Dotun around, Akin would ease off the pressure he was putting on me.

"I'm here-o," Dotun yelled when I opened the door. He pushed me aside to lunge at his brother. They embraced, and then Dotun stepped back and bowed. "Brother *mi.*"

Akin was so tall that he always had to bend before passing through a doorway. His skin was bronze-brown and in the sun it took on a glossy sheen. Dotun was the same height as my husband, but he was fair-complexioned and lean, with cheeks that looked as if they had been hollowed out. I knelt down to greet him. We were the same age, but because he was my in-law I was expected to treat him as though he was older than me. I believed he was a typical *oniranu*, a totally irresponsible man, but I gave him due respect every time he came around.

"Welcome, sir. I hope you have had a good journey," I said.

Dotun settled into an armchair, stretching his legs out on the mahogany centre table. "My wife sends her greetings—she's on a night shift this weekend. I can't handle the boys on my own; their fighting would have convinced me to drive into a tree on the way here, so they are in Lagos. How did our mother survive with us? This is payback time for me. The boys are with their aunt, my wife's sister. Yejide, I hear you have become two in one; you have swallowed a human being! Come, let me see you clearly."

I stood in front of my brother-in-law, and then turned around for inspection. The smile that had been sitting on my husband's face since Dotun showed up fell off his lips.

"She is not pregnant," Akin said. "She has a condition, she's seeing a doctor."

"But Moomi said—" Dotun began.

"I am pregnant," I said, clutching my tummy, willing the baby to kick at that time, willing it to prove itself to me, to everyone in the room, and put a permanent end to Akin's unbelief.

"Brother *mi*, it is the woman that will say if she's pregnant," Dotun said.

"Ask her how long she has been pregnant," Akin said.

Dotun focused his gaze on my belly, squinting as though I had somehow shrunk and he had to try really hard to see me.

"Akin, you can't tell me what I am feeling in my body."

Akin stood up and grabbed my shoulders. "You have been sent away from antenatal classes, Yejide. You had five scans, five different doctors, in Ilesa, Ife and Ibadan. You are not pregnant, you are delusional!" Saliva foamed from the sides of his mouth. "Yejide, this has to stop. Please, I beg you. Dotun, please talk to her. I have talked and talked, my mouth is starting to peel off because of all the talking." His hands were hurting my shoulders.

Dotun's mouth was open; he closed it and opened it again. I had never seen him speechless.

"What do doctors know anyway?" Dotun said when his voice returned to him from its wandering. "It is a woman that knows if she is pregnant or not."

He believed me. There was no mockery, no doubt in his eyes. They met mine evenly. His eyes held something I hadn't seen in Akin's eyes for so long, for far too long. Faith in me, in my words, in my sanity. I wanted to hug

132

Dotun close to me until his faith in me restored my dwindling hope and drove away the familiar despair that was eating me up.

"Your brain is melting, Yejide. It is melting," Akin said. "Dotun, I'm tired of reasoning with this crazy woman. I'm going to the club, are you coming?"

He had never spoken to me like that before. His words would replay themselves to me for weeks and cause me to cringe each time. *Your brain is melting, Yejide. It is melting, melting.* Dotun started to say something in my defence, but I didn't wait to listen. I pressed my palms against my stomach and stumbled up the stairs, blinded by tears. As I entered our bedroom, I could hear Akin's car pulling out of the front yard.

Sometimes I think my husband's words made it easier for me to let Dotun comfort me. I think they made me weak enough to lean against him as he held me while I wept, as he kissed my earlobes and took off my clothes. It was over before I could blink, leaving me with semen and a dry ache between my thighs. I felt a strong sense of pity for my poor sister-in-law. Was this it? All she got out of Dotun week in, week out? I had at least expected to feel more, a tingle at the very least in spite of myself, even if it was against all I thought I believed in—until that weekend.

"It will be better next time; I'll be better.

You are too beautiful . . . you . . . I've always thought . . ." Dotun said as he pulled on his trousers hastily. And even as I tried to deny the knowledge, I knew there would be a next time. There was something different about being with him, something fuller. I wanted to try it again. My first instinct was to tell Akin, but how does one tell one's husband: *I want you to fuck me the way your brother did?*

I hid in the room for the rest of the weekend. I left the door open so I could hear Akin and Dotun laughing or hear their voices rising in disagreement. I heard nothing; all was quiet downstairs. The silence was a presence that reached up to punch me hard in the stomach until I lost my miracle baby in a flood of guilty tears.

When he came to bed on Sunday night, Akin found me curled up. I was moaning, *My baby, my baby.*

He stood by the door. I was sure he would not come near me—that he would walk out. I was sure his brother's hands had left prints on my skin. Prints that shone for my husband to see under the fluorescent tube that lit our room, prints that the hot showers I had taken would not wash away.

Akin closed the door, removed his shirt and singlet, carefully folded them at the foot of the bed and lay down beside me. He stretched out my limbs, trailing the tips of his fingers over my skin.

"I'm sorry," he said. "I'm so sorry."

He whispered my name, *Yejide, Yejide.* It was so soft on his lips, an exotic sound that was a caress in itself. I wanted him to know what I could not say, that my baby, the pregnancy I had nursed, was gone. Gone. I was empty again.

He kissed my face until I started moaning his name instead.

I wanted to run downstairs to Dotun, to tell him, *See! See what Akin can make me feel on just my face. SEE!*

He whispered my name, his breath hot against my skin. I shivered and covered his lips with mine. He moved to my neck and I shut my eyes. This time, I could not drown in the tingly sensations his tongue and fingers gave. Pleasure was suspended by my fierce hope that everything would be perfect, positioned just right for me to conceive.

Dotun left on Monday morning. His hand lingered too long on my shoulder when he said goodbye. And I wondered if I saw Akin grind his jaw as we both waved at Dotun's departing car.

14

When they finally came, the armed robbers sounded like a group of men who were lost and had come into our sitting room to ask for directions. They spoke impeccable English, sat in chairs like visitors and requested something to drink (no alcohol on duty, please). Then they pointed a gun at each of our heads and asked us to pack up all our electronics.

Initially, it was more of a visit than an attack. One of the men even said thank you when he was done with his bottle of Limca. Then a few minutes after Akin, Funmi and I went back into the house, after we had loaded our electronics into their van, we heard a gunshot, then a scream that punched holes into the silent night. Several gunshots followed, leaving echoes that would keep residents of the estate awake with sweaty faces and dry mouths for months to come.

Akin pushed me down after the first gunshot and threw his body over mine. We stayed that way, trying our best not to breathe loudly. I was aware that Funmi was somewhere in the sitting room too; she whimpered until Akin told her to shut up. We stayed on the ground until dawn; Akin did not shift once, not even when Funmi asked him if he did not care about protecting her too.

When we stood up in the morning, Funmi began to sob.

"You don't love me," she said to Akin. "You don't care at all."

Akin didn't reply. He asked me if I was OK and went outside to check on our neighbours. I went upstairs, leaving Funmi alone in the sitting room.

It turned out that the shots had all been fired into furniture, walls and car windows. No one had been hurt; although Mr. Fatola fainted the minute robbers entered his home. He came to after the robbers had left and his wife poured a cup of ice-cold water on his face. The estate committee wrote a petition to the police station at Ayeso when the hired hunters informed us after the robbery that none of the policemen had shown up for work the day the robbery took place. After they said this, Mrs. Ojo announced in her British accent that one of the policemen had been among the thieves. No one paid her any attention. It was obvious the police were involved in some way, but that they would take up arms against us themselves? We did not think things had become that bad yet.

While Iya Bolu worried about the robbers, I had better things on my mind. My stomach was bulging with child—even the ultrasound machines agreed this time. I tucked the glossy scan result under the wooden frame of my mirror, at the top corner, where I could see it when I combed my hair every morning. I ate fruits and Akin cooked vegetable stew for me every night. There were stones in it most times, but I did not complain. I refused to change my wardrobe, so that the pregnancy would strain against my too-tight clothes. I kept this up until a dress ripped from armpit to knee as I rose up to join the congregation in sharing the grace at a Sunday service.

I became known as "the pregnant woman with the ripped dress," even after the baby was born. But I did not care that people pointed and smiled behind their hands during a hymn or the Nicene Creed at the church. I had become immortal, part of a never-ending chain of life. New life kicked within me and soon I would have someone that I could call my own. Not a stepmother or half-brother. Not a father shared with two dozen other children or a husband shared with Funmi, but a child, my child.

These thoughts filled me with so much happiness that I was gripped with fear. It seemed too much that any human being should be so happy and fortunate. More than once, in the early months of pregnancy, I would take my hands off the steering wheel while driving and place them over my belly, splaying my palms to cover as much of the belly as they could. I tried to hold the baby in, lest, in a wave of misfortune that my infinite joy of those months had me overdue for, the baby burst to the floor of my Volkswagen and left my stomach hanging open.

The hoots of horns and curses from other motorists reminded me that an accident would be a surer way to lose the baby. To my amazement, I was never involved in an accident during my tummy-clutching moments. This reaffirmed my belief that bad luck would soon come knocking. That my happy life was too good to be true and would soon come crashing down on my head. I set about blocking off all possible avenues for bad luck. I became nice to Funmi, shared tips about Akin, from his favourite shade of lipstick—a bright red that would look garish on her—to how he liked his beans—watery and with lots of pepper. I was ready to share. A man is not something you can hoard to yourself; he can have many wives, but a child can have only one real mother. One.

Against my worst imaginings, the pregnancy was smooth. The doctors were happy every time I went in for an examination. And by the third trimester my anxiety disappeared and I settled in to enjoy the pregnancy. I loved the aching back. I bragged about the enormity of my feet and complained incessantly about how difficult it was to find a sleeping position. It was the best time of my life.

15

We called the baby Olamide and twenty other names. She was soft yellow and turned pink in the face when she cried, which was almost all the time, except when a nipple was stuck in her mouth. Her ears were a shade of brown that matched the back of Akin's hands. Moomi assured us that Akin had been that way too and soon our pretty girl would ripen from soft yellow to the brown shade of her ears.

The naming ceremony was a carnival. Olamide had been born on a Saturday, the most convenient day of the week. Her naming ceremony seven days later was attended by hundreds of people, as it didn't have to compete with working hours or a Sunday service. My stepmothers arrived on Friday; they came wearing smiles to mask the disappointment that lurked in the corners of their eyes. They peered into the cot where Olamide lay as though expecting to discover a pillow wrapped in a shawl instead of a baby. They gushed appropriately about how happy they were and mentioned names of pastors and priests they had visited to pray for me to conceive. I acknowledged their lies with an appreciative smile, then herded them out of my bedroom before they could actually touch my child.

Dotun came down from Lagos with his wife and children. They arrived before the ceremony, about the time the DJ was whispering *Testing, testing, one, two, one, two* into the microphone. I was in the bedroom, sitting on a bucket that contained a mixture of hot water, alum and antiseptic, wondering why all the masters of ceremony had to say those words and never something else. Moomi was standing guard to make sure that I did not stand up until enough steam had entered my vagina to tighten the walls.

Moomi cackled. "Not long now, Akin's fingers will start probing under your wrapper in the dark again."

I wished for more than her son's fingers to probe at that later date, but I did not share this with my mother-in-law, whose thinly veiled references to sex were already making me uncomfortable.

It should have been a relief when Dotun's wife came in, liberating me from Moomi's hypotheses about her son's sexual prowess and offering me a reason to escape the steam that was making my sore vagina burn as though red pepper had been shoved into it. Instead, the heat in me increased as I rose to hug my weeping sister-in-law. Ajoke sobbed into my bare shoulder and I gripped her hand, afraid that she would break loose and pour the alum water mixture on my head. Surely she knew and I was doomed to disgrace on the happiest day of my life.

She pulled back and laughed her peculiar laugh that always seemed to come from every part of her being, right from her toes up until it erupted from her mouth. "The Lord is good. Our God is so good." She smiled, her eyes full of pure joy and relief that mirrored what I felt in the first moment I held my daughter in my arms. Ajoke had never said anything to me at family gatherings about a baby; she was a woman who hardly ever said anything to me or anyone at all. I was surprised and shamed by her unusual display of emotion. I hugged her again so she could not see my eyes. Moomi joined in the loose hug. I was surrounded by their laughter and mine. Ajoke made delighted sounds that pricked me like a fork.

Olamide yelled throughout the naming cere-mony and if there hadn't been a microphone, nobody would have heard the vicar call out her names. I went back upstairs to feed her until she slept. Downstairs the party continued until the early hours of the morning. Long after the live band had stopped performing, food and beer flowed until most of the guests dropped off to sleep on the blue metal chairs. I did not join in the festivities, even when a drunken Akin sang love songs and tried to drag me downstairs with him. I was not ready to leave my child with someone else, not even my mother-in-law. I thought of my mother. If she had been alive, I could have given Olamide to her and gone downstairs to dance.

The next morning, Olamide was the first to wake up in the house. Her cries startled me out of my sleep. I bathed her and breastfed her. She soon fell asleep, still suckling at my breast. I waited for her mouth to loosen its grip on my nipple before tying her to my back with a wrapper. Then I went downstairs to find something to eat.

I screamed as my feet hit the first step. I staggered downstairs still screaming, holding onto the banister for support. At the bottom of our flight of stairs, Funmi lay lifeless. She was dressed in a pink nightgown unlike anything I had ever seen before. It had only one strap on her left shoulder, the right side of the gown stopped at her navel, leaving her yellow breast bare. So this is all it takes to snatch a man from his wife's bed, I thought, even as I screamed for help and lifted Funmi's head from a small pool of blood; a bare yellow breast and a pink nightgown.

Funmi's body was already cold. I shook my head and screamed her name. My mother-in-law raced downstairs with a wrapper tied haphazardly over her breasts; Akin and Ajoke were a few steps behind her.

"What happened?" Moomi yelled, even though she was already standing beside me.

"Funmi?" Akin was squinting at his wife as if

he didn't know who it was. His breath stank, like a mix of garlic and alcohol.

Moomi knelt beside me, lifted Funmi's hand and watched it fall heavily to the ground. She tried to force a finger through Funmi's clenched teeth while calling the girl's name over and over.

"Ahhh, I'm stuck, I am now firmly stuck in a tight place," Moomi said as she stood up. Then she threw her hands in the air and began to dance. She hit herself and shuffled left and right, bending her knees and screaming at intervals. "I have accrued a debt I cannot pay back; I'm in trouble. Funmi, what do you want me to tell your mother? Ahhh, I'm stuck."

It was Ajoke who thought to check Funmi's pulse and heartbeat.

I clung to Akin as Ajoke bent over Funmi, digging my nails into his arm. Moomi continued to slap her head, but was quiet when Ajoke looked up at us.

"She is gone," Ajoke said softly.

"Ahhh! I'm in hot oil! Funmi! Ahhh! I'm in debt-o. Eternal debt," Moomi screamed and began to dance again.

"What is going on?"

We all turned to the staircase. Dotun stood at the top, wearing only boxer shorts.

I shut my eyes and wished Funmi had picked a better day to die. A day unattached to my Olamide's birth and naming ceremony. I wasn't supposed to think like that; I should have been sad. Instead, I felt inconvenienced, upstaged even, but not sad, not at all.

We changed the tiles in the sitting room because Funmi's blood wouldn't come out. Sometimes I stood at the base of the stairs where I had found her body and stared upstairs. I half expected her to sashay downstairs one more time in the heels she wore around the house, with her footfalls sounding like nails being driven into concrete. I kept expecting her to turn up on our doorstep, her hand held just so I could see her new manicure. Sometimes, as I grated okra into a bowl of water, I could feel her eyes on the back of my neck, but she was never behind me when I turned around, it was just the kitchen door swinging on its hinge. She wasn't in the room she had shared with my husband. Even her clothes were gone from the wardrobe. There were rows of naked hangers that her sister hadn't packed when she came for Funmi's things.

The sister was a startling copy of Funmi, just a few inches taller. I needed a third look at her flat slippers to convince myself she was not Funmi in heels. She did not speak to anyone as she lugged her late sister's possessions out of our house. I was relieved when she left. I had been expecting drama, a slap or two on my cheek for out-living my rival—surely that made me a suspect in Funmi's sudden death? I had been afraid someone would suggest I had pushed the poor girl down the stairs, but no one did. It was agreed that, groggy and probably drunk after Olamide's naming ceremony, Funmi had slipped on her way up the stairs at some point in the night.

I didn't attend her funeral; Moomi believed it would enrage her family to see me. Akin attended and apart from a moody evening he spent downing bottles of beer when he returned from the funeral, he did not seem to mourn Funmi's death at all. There was no staring into space, no angry outbursts at the newscasters on TV or a stool that stood in his way, no long nights away from the house which ended with him staggering home and vomiting in the hallway.

He spent his evenings singing made-up songs to Olamide and reading newspaper articles aloud to her. My daughter knew all about the proceedings of the constitution review committee and the constituent assembly before she was three months old. It was the most beautiful thing, watching my husband tell my daughter things she could not understand. It was so perfect, so surreal that I wanted to press the pause button on life in those moments.

Funmi faded from my mind, slowly, like a bad dream.

Soon Akin's hands were groping me in the early hours of the morning. He reached across

Olamide's sleeping form to squeeze my breast and whispered about us making another baby. And though, by this time, Moomi had poked three fingers into my vagina and assured me that it was tight enough before terminating the alum-water treatment, I was not ready for sex. I told Akin this, but he ignored my words, seducing me with words of his own about how beautiful our lives would be with another child.

I caved in like I always did under the weight of his husky voice.

Olamide would darken beyond Akin's brownness to my shade, my mother's shade, a midnight black that would glow ethereally in the fierce sun. She would get all the prizes and I would stand up throughout the prize-giving ceremonies at her school, clapping loudly so that everyone would recognise her as my child. She would go on to university, of course, become a doctor or an engineer, an inventor, a Nobel Prize winner in medicine, chemistry or physics.

I could see all of this in her eyes when she suckled my breast, and I was already proud.

16

About a month after Olamide was born, I went to church for the first time since I had married Yejide. Stopped bothering with the Sunday services when I was at university, but I still showed up for Easter and Christmas celebrations before I got married. Hadn't been back in church on a Sunday morning since then, because I didn't think I had an extra hour in my week to spend sitting in a pew. But two weeks after my daughter was born, I started having nightmares again, dreaming up the same images from the protest march I joined in Ife in '81. Kept seeing the jeans-clad girl lying in the rain—only difference was that this time I knew that each girl on the floor was Funmi. So I went back to church.

I didn't sit in the back pew where many men, dragged to the Sunday service by nagging wives, dozed with their mouths open or read newspapers. I went as close to the front row as I could get. Sat in a pew where I had a clear view of the stained-glass windows behind the altar. The glassy scene showed Christ and the twelve at the Last Supper: eleven disciples at the table; the twelfth, presumably Judas already on his way out, his back to Christ.

When the vicar mounted the pulpit, the old woman to my right hung her head as though about to pray. Soon, she started to snore softly. The vicar began his sermon by reading out the Lord's Prayer from the massive Bible that resided permanently on the marble pulpit. He stopped at *Deliver us from evil* and breathed heavily into the microphone. He whispered the words, repeating the line over and over, pausing after each word, his voice rising with each repetition until he was shouting into the microphone: BUT. DELIVER. US. FROM. EVIL.

Beside me, the old woman was startled out of her sleep. She looked around the church, then rested her chin on her chest again.

"We often ask the Lord to deliver us from evil," the vicar said. "And we should. However we must also consider the unspeakable evils that we seek out by ourselves. What are we doing about the terrible evils that we can deliver ourselves from? Why must we always wait for the Lord when we are perpetrating so much evil with our own hands? Have we stopped to think about the evil we deliver into the world? The list is endless, but let me try to remind you: adultery, sloth, envy, jealousy, bitterness, anger, drunkenness . . ."

The vicar's eyes roamed the rows as he spoke. Our eyes met when he mentioned drunkenness, as if he knew something about me, something hidden, secret. His gaze lingered on me; maybe he wanted my heart to quiver. I shook my head from side to side, slowly, as I imagined saints did when they heard all about the sins of the worldly.

Fact is, I'm not a drunkard. I don't drink a lot. There are months when I don't take any alcohol, not even a glass of wine. If I had to count the number of times I have been drunk during my whole life, you could count them all on one hand. First time I got drunk, I was a teenager. At the time, my father would send me to buy him a gourd of fresh palm wine every evening. Dotun often went with me. On our way back home, we'd drink a bit of the wine and chew raw ewedu leaves to get rid of the smell before we got into the house. One day, we decided to drink everything in the gourd. The plan was to tell Baba that we'd been attacked by rogues who had snatched the gourd from us. That was the last time Baba sent us to get palm wine.

According to Moomi, Dotun and I arrived on our street drunk, beating the gourd, singing church hymns. We went past our home, marched into our neighbour's compound, calling for lost souls to repent. Moomi blamed Baba for sending her young children to buy alcohol. He blamed her for raising boys who couldn't keep their drink down. The argument lasted the whole year, dying down to rise again at unexpected moments in Moomi's shrill voice and Baba's studied silence.

Moomi ripped our buttocks with a stick every day for a week, extracting a promise not to touch alcohol until we died with each stroke. She gave me double the number of strokes Dotun got, reminded me that she expected more from me because I was her firstborn son, *the beginning of her strength.* I discovered beer during the next week. Best thing about it was that Moomi couldn't recognise the smell on our breath because Baba didn't drink it at the time. Dotun and I would pour beer into plastic cups, then drink under Moomi's nose and tell her that we were sharing a bottle of malt.

As the vicar continued his sermon that Sunday, I made a note in my jotter to get a crate of beer ready for Dotun's next visit; he planned to stop over in Ilesa for a few days on his way to Abuja at some point in the next couple of weeks. When I glanced up, I didn't look at the vicar, stared instead at the stained-glass windows. Struck for the first time by Judas's downturned lips, I wondered if he already regretted what he was about to do. I had regrets that Sunday morning, about getting drunk during Olamide's naming ceremony. I had had my first beer after Dotun arrived from Lagos with his family around ten in the morning, just before the ceremony began. I'd stood in the storeroom beside the kitchen, the place where nobody would have looked for me. Swallowed gulp after gulp of warm beer until

I'd emptied three brown bottles back-to-back. It was easier to smile when I rejoined the crowd that had gathered in our home to celebrate with Yejide and me. Even then, my words were not slurred when I read out the twenty-one names that Olamide would bear.

Each name was a contribution from a key member of the family. Even Yejide's stepmothers contributed names. Olamide was Yejide's choice, but everyone thought it was my choice since it was the first name I called out. But I did not give that child any name, not one. The beer made the names roll off my tongue as if they were names whose layers of meaning I, father of the child, had pondered upon before agreeing to include them on the handwritten list that I read from. It was so much easier to be a father after three bottles of beer.

Everyone was congratulating me. They called me Baba Aburo, Baba Ikoko, Baba Baby, then after the names had been given, Baba Olamide. Colleagues slapped me on the back, told me that the next baby had to be a boy. Friends said I had allowed Yejide to start with an easy hand by having a girl; next it was time for a boy—better still, boys. Two, three, four boys, as many as I could knock into her at once. Then somebody remembered Funmi, remembered that I was now pulling double duty.

My colleagues and friends decided that I

needed reinforcement. The kind any man would need if faced with the task of getting two beautiful women pregnant with boys. It was time to start getting ready, one of my friends said. We were all seated around a metal table beneath the large tarpaulin tent that was used for the naming ceremony. We were drinking beer and eating fried meat as the conversation took place. I was not as drunk as most people at the table when Dotun suggested that I should drink several bottles of *odeku* in preparation for the task ahead.

It was Dotun who then brought the crate of stout to our table. He handed me the first brown bottle, while the other men at the table chanted: *odeku odeku odeku.* The men stood up to hand me the subsequent bottles, as though each one was a gift—their own contribution to solidifying my virility and populating my family with enough children to make up for the years when quite a number of them had asked me to do something about the barren woman in my house. They gave me bottle after bottle, cheered me on each time I slammed an empty brown bottle on the table like a warlord returning from battle holding an opponent's head.

I don't remember how Funmi came to join us at that table, how she too became involved in the drunken preparation for the task of filling our house with a dozen children. But soon enough, Funmi and I were swapping beer bottles, laughing like fools. That day was the first time I saw Funmi drink stout. No, drunkenness has never been a problem for me or the women in my life. And as the vicar began to wrap up his sermon that Sunday about a month after Funmi died, I decided that drunkenness was not something I needed to be delivered from.

"Perhaps when we ask the Lord to deliver us from evil, we are really asking him to deliver us from ourselves." The vicar wiped his forehead with a white handkerchief. "I admonish you today, to deliver yourself from every evil that you have brought into your life with your own hands. Let us now bow our heads for prayers."

I tried to shut my eyes and pray, but I couldn't stop thinking about Funmi. I could see her clearly as I studied the stained glass. I could hear her final yelp, see the way her hands tried to grab the banister after I pushed her down the stairs.

17

When I was a child, my stepmothers would usher their children into bed to tell them stories. But always behind closed and bolted doors. I was never invited in to listen, so I lurked around in the corridor, moving from doors to windows as I tried to determine which woman's voice was loudest each night.

I consoled myself by saying that being motherless meant that I got to pick and choose my stories. If I did not like the story one wife was telling her children, I could simply move to the next doorway. I was not trapped behind the bolted doors like my half-siblings. I told myself that I was free. Sometimes, I did not check the floor very well before sitting down and I would sit in chicken or goat shit. Some of the women were just dirty; they did not bother to clean up their part of the corridor before settling in for the night.

I loved the riddles best because I knew them so well. The thin rod that touches both heaven and earth? Rain. The one who eats with the king, but does not pick up the plate? The housefly. I mouthed the answers from my spot in the corridor, usually before a half-sibling screamed it inside the room. And when the other children were asked to clap for the one who had got the answer right, I would smile and my face would feel warm, as if they were actually clapping for me.

I would sing along to the choruses that came in the middle of the tale, but always under my breath. If my voice was heard on the other side, if one of the mothers came out to check, I would have been in hot soup. My ear would have been twisted and pulled until it was hot enough to boil water on. In our polygamous home, eavesdropping was not just rude, it was criminal. Everyone had secrets, secrets that they were ready to guard with their lives. I learned to be light-footed, to listen for the footfalls of anyone coming to the door during the tale. I learned to listen and run to my room without making noise.

My favourite story was the one about Oluronbi and the Iroko tree. Initially, it was difficult for me to believe the version my stepmothers told. Their Oluronbi was a market woman who promised to give her daughter to the Iroko tree if it could help her to sell more goods than other traders in the market. At the end of the story, she lost her child to the Iroko. I hated this version because I did not believe that anyone would trade a child for anything else. The story as my stepmothers told it did not make sense to me, so I decided to create my own version. I added new bits and pieces each time one of my stepmothers told the tale. After a while, I would tune out whenever they told Oluronbi's story and concentrate on building my own version of it.

That was the version I told my Olamide. I started telling her stories after Moomi left. She would have thought it was strange that I was telling stories to an infant who could not comprehend what I was saying. But I had been waiting all my life for a child, my own child, a child I could tell stories to. I was not ready to wait one more minute. I told the stories in the afternoon, when Olamide and I were alone in the house. I made up new stories in addition to those I remembered from my childhood. But I told my version of Oluronbi's story most often. And I think Olamide liked it as much as I did.

In my version, Oluronbi was born a very long time ago, at a time when human beings still understood the language of trees and animals. Oluronbi's family loved her and she was everyone's favourite. She was like water; she had no enemies in her family. Oluronbi's mother loved her so much that she took Oluronbi along to the market every day. This was how Oluronbi learned to trade very well, so that even as a young girl she knew how to manage a stall. Oluronbi was an obedient child, very beautiful. She never told a lie, never stole; she never snuck out at night to talk to boys behind a wall.

Oluronbi was living happily until one fateful day. On that day, Oluronbi's father was harvesting a lot of yams on his farm. This farm was next to a forest. He asked Oluronbi's mother and all the children to follow him to the farm to help out. But Oluronbi was asked to stay behind to manage the stall. When she got back from the market in the evening, she prepared a big meal for the people who had gone to the farm. Then she waited and waited for them to get back. The sun disappeared from the sky and they didn't return from the farm. When the sun came up the next morning, Oluronbi went to the market. She assumed that her family had decided to sleep at the farm the previous night. But when she got back from the market, there was still no one in the house. There was some light in the sky, so she hurried into the forest and went to her father's farm. There was nobody there. She walked the length and breadth of the farm, calling out the names of each member of her family. There was no response.

By the time Oluronbi got back to the village, it was dark. She went home, and when she discovered there was no one there, she began going from house to house, asking if anyone had seen her family. While the sun slept that night, Oluronbi went to every house in the village to ask if anyone had seen her family members. No one knew where they were.

The moment the sun woke up and started its work in the skies, Oluronbi went to the king's palace to report the strange occurrence. The king sent out a search party into the forest to look for the missing people. Oluronbi didn't leave the king's palace until the search party returned two days later. The search had been fruitless.

"Maybe your family decided to leave this our village," the king said to Oluronbi.

Oluronbi pleaded with the king to send the bravest hunters in the village into the depths of the forest. The king agreed, but after five days, the hunters returned empty-handed. They too had been unable to find Oluronbi's family. The king advised Oluronbi to get on with her life because there was nothing left to be done. "Maybe your family decided to leave the village," he said again.

Oluronbi did not believe the king; she knew that her family would never abandon her. So she decided to search for them again in the forest. Every day of the week she went deep into the forest, asking all the trees if they had seen her family. But the trees refused to tell her anything.

Then one day she asked the king of trees, the Iroko tree.

"I know where your family is," the Iroko said.

"Are they alive? Tell me—are they still alive?" Oluronbi asked.

"Yes, they are still alive," the Iroko said. "But I don't know how long they will last."

Oluronbi screamed. "Iroko, tell me where they are so I can rescue them quickly!"

"No," the Iroko said.

"Please, Iroko, tell me where they are. I will do anything—anything you ask me to do, I will do."

"No way," said the Iroko.

"Please, Iroko, I will give you anything you want, anything you ask, just tell me where they are."

"Anything I want?" the Iroko asked.

"Anything." Oluronbi was on her knees before the Iroko tree.

"I want your first child," the Iroko said.

"Iroko, but I don't have a child," Oluronbi said. "Ask me for anything else, and I will give it to you. Do you want a cow?"

"No," the Iroko said. "I want your first child."

"Do you want a goat? I can get a very big goat."

"No," the Iroko said. "I want your first child."

"But I don't have a child to give you," Oluronbi said. "I am not even married."

"You can fulfil your vow when you have a child," the Iroko said.

Oluronbi did not say anything for a long time. She was on her knees before the Iroko, thinking about her family, her father, her mother, her brothers, her sisters—all gone.

"All right," Oluronbi said. "I will give you my first child."

"You must swear," the Iroko said.

"I swear that I will give you my first child."

"You must go and swear before the king of your village," the Iroko said. "When you come back, I will tell you where they are."

Oluronbi ran into the village and swore before the king that she would give the Iroko her first child if the Iroko revealed where her missing family was.

When Oluronbi got back to the forest, her family members were all standing beside the Iroko tree.

She was so happy, she hugged all of them. "Where have you all been?" Oluronbi asked. "What happened?"

"We can't remember," they said.

"How did you find them?" Oluronbi asked the Iroko.

"That is a secret of the forest," the Iroko said. "I can never tell you."

"Thank you," Oluronbi said.

"Don't forget your vow," Iroko said.

"I will never forget it," Oluronbi promised.

Oluronbi went back into the village with her family. Whenever she remembered her promise to the Iroko, she became very afraid. She stopped going into the forest to gather firewood for her cooking; she stopped going to the forest to gather herbs to sell.

Many years passed and Oluronbi never saw the Iroko.

However, any time someone from Oluronbi's village went into the forest, the Iroko would ask about Oluronbi.

"How is Oluronbi doing?" the Iroko would ask.

"She is going to her husband's house tomorrow. In fact, these twigs that I am gathering will be used to cook at the wedding."

"How is Oluronbi?" the Iroko would ask. "Is she enjoying her husband's house?"

"Oluronbi is too lucky, she married the best man in the world. She is even pregnant already. She is very happy. I only wish I were as lucky as Oluronbi. Why did I have to marry a foolish man like my husband?"

"How is Oluronbi?" the Iroko would ask.

"Have you not heard? She just had a baby girl. They named the child Aponbiepo."

"How is Aponbiepo?" the Iroko would ask.

"She is the most beautiful child in the village. Her skin is so fair, so spotless. I have never seen anything like it. You don't need to ask if she is Oluronbi's daughter, she is exactly like her mother from head to toe. If only my own daughter were that beautiful, what kind of luck do I have?"

As Aponbiepo grew older, she was warned never to go into the forest. Every morning, Oluronbi warned her child never to go near the forest.

But one day, while Aponbiepo was playing with her friends, they decided to go into the forest.

"Come with us," they told Aponbiepo.

"My mother says I must never go into that forest," Aponbiepo said.

"But there are beautiful trees there with sweet fruit."

"My mother says I mustn't go there."

"Why?" they asked.

"I don't know."

The other children laughed. "So you have never been in the forest?"

"No."

"Never in your life?"

"No," Aponbiepo said.

The other children laughed and laughed and laughed. "So you have never seen the forest?"

"No."

"You have never seen the deer?"

"No."

"You have never seen the very tall Iroko that is the king of all trees?"

"No."

"Then you have not seen anything; you don't know anything. You have not seen anything in your life," they said.

"Goodbye," the other children said, "we are leaving for the forest. We are going to find some twigs and eat sweet fruits. We are going to say hello to the Iroko, the king of trees."

"I'll go, I'll go," Aponbiepo said. "Let me go with you. I want to see the king of trees."

The children went to the forest and that was the last time anyone ever saw Aponbiepo. The other children came back to the village with the twigs. They did not even notice Aponbiepo was not with them until Oluronbi came out and asked, "Where is my daughter?" They searched every inch of the village for Aponbiepo but nobody could find her. The only place left to search was the forest.

When Oluronbi got to the forest, the Iroko refused to say a word to her. Oluronbi pleaded and pleaded, but the Iroko would not speak. Oluronbi never saw her child again and the trees stopped talking to human beings after that.

The reasons why we do the things we do will not always be the ones that others will remember. Sometimes I think we have children because we want to leave behind someone who can explain who we were to the world when we are gone. If there really was once an Oluronbi, I do not think she had any children after she lost Aponbiepo. I think the version of her story that survived her would have been kinder to her if she'd left behind someone who could shape the way she would be remembered. I told Olamide several stories, expecting that one day she too would tell the world my story.

18

A mother must be vigilant. She must be able and willing to wake up ten times during the night to feed her baby. After her intermittent vigil, she must see everything clearly the next morning so that she can notice any changes in her baby. A mother is not permitted to have blurry vision. She must notice if her baby's wail is too loud or too low. She must know if the child's temperature has risen or fallen. A mother must not miss any signs.

I'm still sure that I missed important signs.

I had decided as soon as she was born that I would breastfeed Olamide for at least one year. I still had a long way to go on the morning that I missed the important signs; she was just five months old. I was feeling sleepy that morning because I'd had to wake up several times during the night to feed her. At dawn, I showered, gave Olamide her bath, rocked her to sleep and laid her in the cot. Then I climbed into bed to get a few hours of sleep, fully expecting her to wake me up with her wails within a few hours.

I woke up around half past noon and was relieved that Olamide was still napping in her cot. I went downstairs to get some food and must have spent about thirty minutes in the kitchen.

After I finished eating, I went back upstairs, expecting to find my daughter awake. She did not always cry when she woke up; sometimes she would stay in the cot, gurgling and amusing herself.

When I leaned over her cot, Olamide seemed unusually still. It took me about a minute to realise that she was not breathing. I picked her up and screamed her name. I shook her and tried to check her heartbeat. I ran downstairs with my baby in my arms, still screaming. I rushed about the sitting room trying to find my car keys. I probably spent a few minutes searching for the keys, but it felt like a year. When I'd checked every surface and kicked the cushions out of the chair, I stood in the middle of the room for a brief moment, holding my limp baby close to my breasts.

I remember picking up the phone and calling Akin's office. I know that I spoke with him, but I do not remember what I said. I remember dropping the phone and leaving the house, running out of the estate into the street where I flagged down the taxi that took me to the hospital.

19

Yejide was sitting in the corridor when I arrived. Not on one of the benches but right on the cemented floor. I could see her as soon as I left the hospital parking lot. Wasn't sure she was the one at first because there were no shoes on her feet. Should have known when I saw the bare feet that something had gone very wrong.

I crouched when I got to her side, put my arm around her shoulder, even waved a greeting at a nurse that I recognised.

"Get up," I said. "I'm sure she'll be OK. Has the doctor said anything?"

I assumed that Olamide had been admitted, figured they might have found out what had caused whatever was wrong and had given Yejide an update before I arrived.

"Do I need to pay for anything? Yejide, please get up. No need to sit on the floor. Relax, she'll be fine. You know they say children are resilient. *Oya*, stand up."

She stared up at me, eyes wide and mouth open.

"Yejide?"

She blinked and swallowed.

I shook her a bit because I could tell that she was not fully present with me. Her hair was in disarray, so I placed my hand on her head, pushed her tresses backwards.

"What did they say happened? Have you spoken to any of her doctors?"

"They have taken Olamide to the mortuary."

My hand fell off her shoulder and I fell to my knees beside her. "What do you mean by 'mortuary'?" I said.

"I'm sorry," Yejide said, holding her head in her hands as though its weight had all of a sudden become too heavy for her slim neck to bear. "Akin, I'm so sorry. I didn't take long. I was hungry. I just wanted to make something to eat. I didn't know. I'm so sorry."

"No," I said, sure that I wasn't processing what she'd said quite right. It didn't make any sense for her to mention Olamide and the mortuary in the same breath. "Wait, wait. Calm down, please. Olamide, where is Olamide?"

She ran her hands through her hair, slapped her head, then spread her arms. "They have taken her to the mortuary, Akin. They say she is dead. They say my daughter is dead. They say Olamide is dead. They say . . ."

I stood up, rubbed my eyes with the back of my hand because I felt as though everything I was seeing was tilted. I walked down the corridor, away from her, stopped when I could no longer hear her voice, then turned back to look at her. She kept slapping her head, but there were no tears. She did not scream, just kept hitting herself, her breasts, her thigh, her face.

Don't know how long I stood at the end of the corridor, just watching her, trying somehow to absorb the fact that after everything Yejide and I had done to have a child, we had, without warning, lost Olamide. Didn't think it was possible for the world to change so suddenly. I was aware of other people moving up and down the corridor: I heard heels clicking, people speaking, felt some bodies push past mine. But I felt so alone, as though within the space of time it had taken Yejide to say, "They have taken Olamide to the mortuary" I had been transported to a planet with no human life.

Eventually, I went back to Yejide, held her hands as she stood up, led her to the car, and helped her into the passenger's side.

Still don't know where I got the strength to walk into the emergency ward. Only know that I found myself in front of the matron on duty.

"I'm Mr. Ajayi," I said. "My daughter was brought in some hours ago—Olamide."

She led me away from the ward into a cubicle, offered me a chair as she opened some drawers. She placed some documents in front of me, asked if I wanted to see the body before signing. Took me a few minutes to realise that by "the body" she meant Olamide. I shook my head because I couldn't speak and started signing the documents.

169

Didn't read a word of the text, simply looked out for the signature boxes on each page and appended my signature.

The matron offered her condolences when I got up to leave, assuring me that the doctors had done their best, but the baby had been dead on arrival. I shook her hand, said thank you; told her that I appreciated their efforts.

Yejide was sitting still as a rock when I got back to the car; I could only tell for sure that she was alive when she blinked. I was supposed to offer words of comfort, tell her something to alleviate her pain. I'd done it before on condolence visits, spoken to colleagues who'd lost spouses or relatives, had found words to tell them everything would somehow still be all right.

I jammed the key in the ignition, gripped the steering wheel and stared through the windscreen at the people walking up and down in the sunny parking lot as though it was just any other day. I did my best to think of something to say to my wife, even found enough words to string together into a sentence or two. And because I wanted my words to have maximum impact, to give comfort for what I couldn't yet fully comprehend, I turned to look her in the eye.

Then I noticed the breast-milk stain on the front of her green blouse. I could tell she wasn't wearing a bra and the stain was right in front of her right nipple. It was a fresh stain, small,

170

about the size of a baby's hand, Olamide's hand. I simply forgot whatever it was I had wanted to say. As I watched the milk stain spread downwards, I realised that the ground under our feet had just been pulled away, we were standing on air, and my words could not keep us from falling into the pit that had opened up beneath us.

20

Moomi said Olamide was a bad child, an evil girl who had chosen to die. I almost slapped her when she said it.

It was her way of comforting me, convincing me that my Olamide wanted to die, that there was nothing any mother could have done. It was not working and she knew it. I could not stop thinking of my baby, how wicked it was that she was forever trapped in soft yellow and her skin would never match her ears.

I was untouched by the downcast faces of mourners who filled my sitting room. It was their silence that touched me, squeezed my heart, the almost total silence of the mourners broken only by soft words meant to comfort and encourage. If my Olamide had grown older, if she had married and had children before dying, if it was me or Akin who had died, the mourners would have been wailing openly, not biting their lips and shaking their heads and asking me to forget because there would soon be another child.

It squeezed me inside that no one wailed or screamed. Everyone was so organised. There was no chaos, no crashing chairs or utensils, nobody rolling on the floor or tearing their hair out. Even

Moomi did not dance. No one was lost for words. They all knew what to say. *Don't worry, you will soon have another child.*

There was no framed photograph on a table with a condolence register beneath it.

It was as if nobody would miss her. No one was sorry that Olamide had died. They were sorry that I had lost a child, not that she had died. It was as though, because she had spent so little time in the world, it did not really matter that she was gone—she did not really matter. One would think we had lost a dog that was dear to our hearts. It squeezed me deep inside to see people so calm, as if nothing much had been lost. And when voices from the too-calm stream of consolers told me to imagine how terrible it would have been for this to have happened at a later date, on the eve of her graduation or the eve of her wedding, I wished I could wail, scream, roll on the ground and give her the mourning she deserved. But I could not. The part of me that could do that had gone into the morgue's freezer with Olamide to keep her company and to beg her forgiveness for all the signs I had missed.

The funeral took place within five days. Akin and I were not allowed to attend and we would never know the burial spot. My mother-in-law kept reminding me that I should not pester anyone about the spot that had been chosen. She whispered into my ears that I must never see her grave because then my eyes would have seen evil, then I would have experienced the worst thing that could happen to a parent, which was to know a child's burial place. I did not respond to my mother-in-law's words. I lay on the sitting-room couch through the morning, holding myself perfectly still, waiting for the moment they would place her little coffin in the ground. I was sure that if I lay still enough, I would know. I lay motionless and watched the clock until it became blurry. Time passed in a haze. I vaguely remember Akin picking up his car keys and saying something to me at some point. I stayed on the couch until I realised the time was two o'clock. The interment would have been over by twelve noon. I had felt nothing all day. As still as I had been, I had not been vigilant enough. I screamed then, a short piercing sound that left me coughing. A sound I could not sustain as much as I wanted to. Even then there were no tears, not a single drop.

Moomi was by my side instantly, tracing her finger across my scalp. "Before you know it you'll be pregnant again. You will recover, you'll see," she said, as though I had a cold and only needed to rest a little so that I could get better. I wished she were dead instead of my child. I turned away from her and did not tell her that I was already pregnant. Walls of pain closed in on me from every side; I tried to push, but the walls were concrete and steel. I was mere flesh and miserable bones.

Akin hinted, advised, cajoled and finally insisted that I go back to putting in full hours at the salon. I had not told him yet that I was pregnant.

I actually never told him. When my stomach became too big to ignore, he leaned against the kitchen door's frame and asked me. "Are you pregnant?"

I picked up a knife from the plate rack.

"Again?" Akin added, as though he was just remembering that I had been pregnant before.

I cut through the water leaves, gripped the knife too tightly and exerted every muscle in my arm as if I was cutting a tuber of yam.

"Yejide?"

I stabbed the knife into the wooden chopping board and turned to face this man who was my husband. I clasped my hands over my protruding belly. "What do you think, Akin? Tell me what you think is in my stomach."

"Why don't you just answer my question?"

"You think I have strapped a calabash to my stomach? You, this man. Is that what you are thinking?"

He scratched his eyebrows and looked away, fixing his gaze on some point above my head. I turned my back to him.

He cleared his throat. "So you are pregnant?"

It was still a question. The man thought that my head had scattered, scattered to the point where I would strap a calabash to my stomach. That was why he was still asking a question: he could not believe. The weather was hot and the only thing I was wearing was a big T-shirt that stopped mid-thigh. Did he want to inspect my stomach? Maybe cut through the skin a little, just to be sure? I prised the knife from the chopping board and let my hands fall to my side. I nodded. "Yes."

He made a sound that I could not quite make out. It sounded like congratulations, it sounded like he was choking or holding back a sob. I stared out of the kitchen window, the knife's steel cold against my bare thigh.

"I'm sorry," he said after a while, "about the baby's death."

"Her name is Olamide," I screamed. I turned to face him, the other twenty names we had given my daughter ready to roll off my tongue. The doorway was empty; he was already gone.

On my first day back at work, I asked one of the girls to cut my hair. She refused, glaring at me as though I had asked her to chop my head off. All the girls refused to touch the scissors, even Iya Bolu refused.

"But you are pregnant again," she said.

I cut the tresses myself and left the rest of my hair in low uneven chunks. The customers looked horrified. If it had been Akin who had died, they would not have been so shocked to see my hair chopped off. Why then were they staring as though I had lost my mind?

My car had been taken for servicing that day, so I dragged myself home after I closed the salon. My feet felt like lead. I did not want to go home to the empty cot that was still beside the bed I shared with Akin.

Akin was home when I got there. He was working at the dining table. He had dozens of white sheets spread out and was punching numbers into a calculator.

"What happened to your hair?" he asked, pushing the calculator away.

"A bird chewed it off my head on my way home. What else could have happened?"

He went back to punching in his numbers.

I sat in an armchair with my back to the dining table.

"How low do you want it cut?" Akin asked.

"Skin cut," I said, trying to work out candle wax from the rug with my big toe. There were several stains on it. It had not been swept in weeks.

Suddenly, I felt Akin's hand on my head. He ran his hands through my shaggy hair, then I heard the sharp snips of a pair of scissors, tufts of hair fell across my face, sticking to my skin when they met with the tears falling silently down my cheeks. The tufts prickled my skin, but I did not pull them off my face. I would let them stay, all night, let my skin itch and itch until my face felt as if I had scrubbed it with a piece of raw yam.

"Go and shower," he said when he was through.

I couldn't stand up. Sobs tightened my chest, making it hard for me to breathe.

Akin knelt beside me and laid his head on my stomach, one hand clutching my dress, the other hanging limply over the edge of the armchair, still holding the scissors. He would never admit it, but I felt his tears that day, they plastered my dress to my belly and validated my grief. I threw my head back and I wept out loud. I cursed. I screamed. I cried. I apologised to my daughter, begged her to forgive my carelessness, pleaded with her to listen to me wherever she was. I cried throughout the night as hard as I could. I held my head and tried to cry out the pain. The next night I slept straight through. I did not dream of dead babies decomposing under the ground—I did not dream at all. For about six hours after I woke up, I thought my tears had washed my pain and guilt away. I did not know then that that was impossible.

21

Sesan was born on a Wednesday. I was at work when my water broke and it was Iya Bolu who drove me to the hospital. Her husband had just bought a new secondhand car and she had finally inherited his old Mazda and was learning to drive. Her driving experience had been limited to driving from the salon to her house and back, but she refused to put the red "L" sign in front of her number plates or anywhere on the car. I sat in the front seat and tried to give her driving tips in between contractions. I could have taken a taxi, but I let her drive me to the hospital. Perhaps because, on some level, I believed I deserved some punishment for what had happened to my daughter.

There were few people at Sesan's naming ceremony. It was a small gathering that took place in our sitting room. Guests sat on dining chairs we had borrowed from our neighbours, ate Jollof rice, and went home an hour after the ceremony. Moomi did not even come. Her daughter Arinola, who now lived in Enugu, had also had a baby around that time and Moomi left for Enugu about a week before I gave birth to Sesan. No one travelled down from Lagos or Ife. There was no live band, no tarpaulin tent outside, no microphone, no DJ. There was no dancing.

Sesan's middle name was Ige because he came feetfirst into this world. Those feet were good feet; there was no doubt in anyone's mind after a few weeks that my son's feet were as good as feet could get. Like all people with good feet, his arrival in our family was followed by all sorts of good things happening to us. For instance, Akin bought four plots of land for half the market value because the owner was swarming in debt and had to sell all his assets. That was not such a good thing for the poor man, but as with many things in life, sometimes one person's good fortune is a direct consequence of another person's ruin.

I was vigilant with Sesan. Akin thought I was becoming paranoid. He warned me that my son would grow up and never be able to marry because he would be overattached to me. And I wondered how on earth Sesan could be overattached to me when his life depended on him attaching his mouth to my breast. The way I saw it, the danger was in a child being underattached or not attached at all. I was fully prepared to padlock Sesan's wrist to my apron strings and drag him around for the rest of my life.

Sesan was a peaceful child. He cried only when he needed to eat and even then his cries were punctuated by polite pauses. Sometimes I would check on him in the middle of the night to find him wide awake in his cot, chortling with his hands and legs in the air, enjoying his own company, not demanding attention.

We bought a house on Imo Street, not far from the estate where we lived. It did not have a fence when we bought it, but we had one built before we moved in. It was higher than the roof and had rolls of barbed wire at the top. Armed robberies had become common across the country and fences were springing up all over town, some of them taller than the one that kept convicts in at the prison. Most neighbourhoods now employed at least one vigilante to walk the streets during the night, firing a shot from time to time to reassure residents. During the day burglars snuck into homes and took all they could before their victims returned. I began to leave the radio on whenever we were leaving home in order to give any would-be burglar the impression that there were people in the house. I observed that most people did the same and in many homes radios droned on nonstop until the stations shut down for the day.

Before our new house stopped smelling of paint, the salon graduated from a five-dryer salon to a ten-dryer salon. After a short while, Akin and I saved enough money and bought the two-storey building housing my salon. Even though Sesan brought us so much good fortune, it was Olamide that I thought about at night before I drifted off to sleep. When I woke up in the mornings, before I opened my eyes, I could see her—alive and looking into my eyes while she suckled, like someone who had known me before time.

22

Shortly after we moved into our new home, Dotun lost his job in Lagos and moved in with us. He never really moved in, in the sense that a married man with four children never moves in with another family except when he is leaving his wife; he just showed up one day and did not go back to Lagos. He claimed that he needed time to sort himself out so that he could get another job.

The truth was that he had lost his job a year before coming to us and spent his savings on setting up a bakery that failed within a few months. He tried to get another job after that, but the only openings he could find were for security guards or messengers—positions he did not take because with his MBA he felt overqualified. After walking the soles of his last pair of shoes off in Lagos, he sold his car, his wife's car, borrowed some money and tried to resuscitate the bakery business. This time he was duped by some fraudsters in circumstances he claimed were too embarrassing to share. He told me all this first, before telling Akin.

He came to Ilesa to hide from his creditors. And even when Akin gave him part of our savings to pay off his creditors, he did not leave. During the first few weeks of his stay with us, Dotun must have had at least three cartons of the locally brewed Trophy lager. He did very little other than eat meat out of my pot of stew and proclaim out of the blue how sexy I was as I tried to fix dinner before my husband returned from work.

He sang my praises every day, wearing at my patience, chipping away my defences until I realised what I thought was steel was actually plywood. If he had said I was beautiful, I would have resisted him. Akin said that all the time, with a tinge of awe that never went out of his voice as the years went by. Dotun, on the other hand, praised the perfect mound of my breast, the roundness of my buttocks and the seductiveness of my eyes.

"I love it when you burn the stew," he said one day, eyeing me over a bottle of beer.

I was coming out of the kitchen. I had just incinerated a pot of vegetable stew that I was making to go with Akin's rice that night.

Dotun placed the bottle by his feet. "Especially when you are upstairs when it happens. You run downstairs and when you run your breasts jiggle. And I keep thinking about you, that weekend I stopped over on my way to Abuja."

I did not like to think about that weekend. It was about two months after Olamide had been born and Akin had to go on an emergency business trip to Lagos after his brother arrived. Dotun and I were home alone with Olamide the entire weekend. The house was not big enough to keep us from running into each other. We were having breakfast on Saturday when he reached across to push hair out of my face, then he touched my ear and did not let go. It was not quick and furtive like the first time; he did not finish too soon. I felt guilty enough to stay away from him for the rest of the weekend and I promised myself that it would never happen again.

"I always think about that weekend," Dotun said.

My heart was beating faster as he spoke and I could feel my nipples harden. I was grateful for the good things in life, such as the padded bra I was wearing that day. "Look, it's not happening again."

"Don't fight it," he said. "It's normal for you to want it."

I inched away, though I knew Dotun would never try to touch me. I would have to go to him; he would never seek me out. "What are you talking about?"

"Let me know when you are ready. I'm always ready," he said and picked up his beer again.

I told myself that it was the drink that made him so bold. He was partially drunk, his words were slurred.

It was good for me that he said it this way— as though getting into bed with him was just a business transaction. It helped me put things in perspective and doused the fire that was smouldering in the pit of my belly, and stemmed the wetness gathering between my legs.

I should have told him to stop speaking to me that way. To stop pointing out that my breasts were still remarkably firm after nursing two children. He would have stopped; at least he would have if I had threatened to tell Akin. But I did not want him to stop. I loved the way his words coursed into my ear, spreading warmth everywhere in my body. Instead of reporting the lewd remarks to Akin and demanding that Dotun be evicted from our home, I pretended to ignore them. At night, I played the words over in my mind, complete with the husky tone with which he said them, while Akin lay on his stomach beside me, snoring with his mouth open. I began to have reasons to head back home after dropping Sesan off at school.

My head felt heavy. The weight doubled with each step I took towards Dotun's room, the room that once belonged to the child I did not give birth to, before it was passed on to Funmi. Dotun was sitting on the floor with his back to the door when I entered the room, writing an application letter. There were a dozen envelopes strewn across the floor, most were sealed and addressed. I did not know until then that he was making an effort to get work. I assumed that he drank beer and ate meat out of my pot all day. Akin had told me Dotun was staying just long enough to sort himself out.

I wondered why he talked to Akin about his grand schemes instead of the applications he seemed to write every day. I wanted to back out of the room. It felt as though I had stumbled on him doing something private and if I watched I would be drawn into some form of intimacy with him. He looked up. No backing out for me now. He swept the envelopes into a pile, but his gaze stayed on my face.

"What is the matter? *Se ko si*?" he asked.

"I . . . nothing . . . well . . . nothing."

He stood up. "There is nothing wrong? You're in my room."

"I came to . . . came here to . . . How are the applications going? Has anybody answered you yet?"

He sat on the bed and held his head in his hands, staring at the pile of envelopes. He was quiet. It was my cue to take off my blouse or do whatever one did to say *I'm ready to have sex with you again.* I felt stupid. Why had I come in? What did I know about seducing a man? Even a willing one. I had been a virgin when I married Akin.

"I was roped into a fraud at work, that's why I got sacked. Word gets around about these things—no one will employ me now. Nobody." He spoke in a rush, as though the words were burning his tongue.

187

I wished he had remained alone in his tortured world and said nothing. I did not want to know his secret pain or agony. I did not care and did not want to. I wanted just one thing from him.

"I didn't tell Brother *mi*. Don't tell him, please. Don't," he said.

I nodded.

"I was not involved in the fraud. I was just stupid enough to authorise some of the documents involved. It was a woman that actually did it; I was sleeping with her." He looked up, his eyes were bleak and beseeching.

I nodded. Of course he was sleeping with a girl in his office; according to his wife, he was sleeping with every woman on their street.

He sighed. "My wife, she doesn't believe me. Thinks I have money stashed somewhere. Some pretty girl waiting to spend it with me." He laughed. "I wish. Don't tell Bros Akin. Please . . . don't . . . don't. Maybe I should tell him every—" He lay back on the bed and covered his face with his hands. "I'm done for. I can't run a business. Nobody will employ me. I'm finished."

"It will be OK," I said, hoping he would shut up, hoping I could leave the room before he bared more of his soul to me.

I sat beside him on the bed. "You graduated with a first-class degree. You'll figure something out."

The laughter stopped. His heavy breathing punctuated the silence. "Thank you," he said.

My legs trembled as I left the room.

Sesan and I were about to leave the house for a communion service when I learned about the Orkar coup. Though he had only just started walking, Sesan was firm on his feet and insisted on descending the stairs without my assistance. It was while I trailed him down the stairs that I heard the coup broadcast on the radio we now left on at all hours. Once it registered that the voice on the radio was announcing the overthrow of Babangida's regime, I carried my son, shushed him when he protested, and rushed into the sitting room.

It wasn't 8 a.m. yet. Akin was sleeping in upstairs and Dotun was in his room, probably hungover. So I was alone with Sesan while I listened to what was a repeat broadcast of the takeover speech. I nodded as the speaker reeled out accusations against Babangida's government, but when he announced the expulsion of five northern states from the country, I was so shocked I decided to wait for the broadcast to be repeated again, just to be sure I'd heard him right.

I loosened my headscarf while the station played martial music; there was no point going to church now. There was a power cut before I'd finished folding the scarf. I sighed—it could be hours or days before electricity was restored; there was no predicting it anymore.

I took Sesan upstairs and tried to remove his bow tie. He was wailing his disagreement when Akin woke up.

"What's the matter with him?"

I released Sesan and he ran off to stand by Akin's side of the bed.

"Aren't you going to church?" Akin said, squinting at the wall clock. "It's already nearly nine."

"They've toppled Babangida," I said. "There has been a coup."

Akin shot up in bed. "Seriously?"

"I listened to the broadcast before the lights went out."

"I told Dotun someone would take this man down. That Dele Giwa matter was too fishy." He swung his feet to the floor. "Nobody can prove it was him, but still. And didn't he promise there would be elections this year and we would go back to a democracy? Where is the democracy now?"

"That's part of what these new ones are saying, that he would have made himself life president if they didn't take over."

"Not possible in this Nigeria." Akin stood up and Sesan hugged one of his legs. "This is not some banana republic."

"There was one strange thing they said,

though." I went over to Akin's side and grabbed Sesan's hand; he snivelled while I unbuttoned his shirt. "They said they are expelling some northern states from the federation—Sokoto, Borno, Kano—I can't remember the others but there were more."

"They are doing what?"

"I don't even understand that part. It's not possible, is it?"

The phone rang and we both jumped. We knew the pattern: once a coup took place, the lines would usually be down all day. Akin picked up the phone. I listened to his side of the conversation, and deciphered that his sister was on the other end of the line. They spoke for a while, and Akin assured her that he didn't think there was any trouble in town and we were all fine. Almost immediately after he returned the phone to its cradle, it rang again. This time it was Ajoke, Dotun's wife.

"She wants us to pray." Akin said after he got off the phone with Ajoke. "There's a face-off going on in Lagos; they can hear gunshots in their house."

"Oh my God, her children. Are they OK?"

"Yes, but she is afraid. The gunshots are loud." Akin pressed a palm against his forehead. "I think they'll be fine, though. There won't be civilian casualties."

I sat on the bed, imagining Ajoke and her

children huddled in the corner of a room. "God help them."

"If they are still fighting now, I don't think Babangida is going anywhere."

"You should tell Dotun that Ajoke called."

"Yes, yes." He lifted Sesan and piggybacked him out of the room.

"There's breakfast in the kitchen," I called after him. "I made *moin moin*."

I stayed in the room, worrying about what the next few days would be like. The more I thought about it, the more I hoped Babangida would manage to hold on to power, not because I liked the way he was running the country, but because the status quo was the devil we knew. If the new officers took over and really expelled the northern states, the situation would probably devolve into another civil war within a few weeks.

Akin yelled something and I went out to the landing.

"What did you say?"

"Dotun thinks he brought his transistor radio," he said. "He's looking for it in his room." Akin was standing in the middle of the sitting room. Sesan was now sitting on his shoulders, stretching to touch the ceiling.

I went downstairs. Since it was Dotun, it took forever for him to locate the radio and the right-sized batteries. When he finally switched it on, all the stations were playing instrumental pieces, signalling that things were still in a confused state and none of them was confident enough to return to regular programming. Dotun settled for a station that was playing what sounded like classical music. We sat unspeaking, surrounded by the sound of music, waiting for news. Suddenly the radio went silent and for a moment I thought the batteries were flat, but it soon crackled with static and a voice spoke to us.

I, Lieutenant Colonel Gandi Tola Zidon, hereby assure you that the dissidents have been routed. You are all advised to remain calm and await further announcements. Thank you.

Dotun got on the phone and spoke to Ajoke and the children. Then we all continued to listen to the radio until the batteries ran out. There were more announcements, speeches and broadcasts which told us that, yes, there had been bloodshed, but nothing had changed after all.

Iya Bolu was now my tenant. She held on to her salon after I bought the building and her husband paid the rent on the first day of every month. She had hardly any customers, so there was no way she could have afforded the rent without her husband's help. Yet she refused to close down the salon.

"I cannot just be sitting down at home," she would say any time I suggested that she should let the salon go. "Let me be waking up and coming here until I know of another job I can do."

She continued to spend most of her time in my salon and I began to stop customers from sitting in the chair I came to think of as Iya Bolu's chair. When her daughters returned from school in the afternoons, they ate lunch in her salon and did their homework there. If the girls wandered over into my shop, she shooed them away with the same words every time: *Go and read your books.*

"That Bolu is going to be a doctor by God's grace," Iya Bolu would say after the children had grumbled their way into the corridor.

Usually, my customers would say "Amen" as Bolu and her siblings disappeared down the corridor. But one day, one of my regulars, Aunty Sadia, was in the salon when Iya Bolu made her declaration. Instead of saying "Amen," Aunty Sadia laughed.

"Why are you laughing?" Iya Bolu said, standing up. "What is funny?"

I was removing Aunty Sadia's weave, using a blade to sever the thread that held the attachments to her hair. She looked into the mirror as she responded to Iya Bolu.

"That your yellow-skin daughter? Don't you see? She is already becoming beautiful. You think the boys will let her rest?"

194

She said the word "beautiful" as if beauty was a bad habit Bolu had developed, something bordering on criminal behaviour for which she would one day be justifiably punished.

Iya Bolu came to stand beside me, arms akimbo. "*Ehen*, so if Bolu is beautiful, she cannot read? She cannot go to the university?"

Aunty Sadia smiled into the mirror. "Just wait until her breasts are sweet oranges and all the men that see her start standing stiff like soldiers. Small time, pregnancy will come. Then you will understand what I'm saying."

"Not my daughter. God forbid." Iya Bolu leaned closer to Aunty Sadia and raised her voice. "My own daughter will go to school."

I stared at Aunty Sadia, waiting for her to apologise or say something to pacify Iya Bolu. She did not speak.

"There is nothing stopping a beautiful girl from facing her books, Aunty," I said finally, patting Iya Bolu on the shoulders. I was done removing Aunty Sadia's weave, so I motioned a stylist to loosen her cornrows.

I went to the corner of the salon where Sesan was asleep in his cot and held his wrist for a few moments, feeling the reassuring rhythm of his pulse.

"I'm just saying that the hard thing is sweet. *Abi*? Even you, her mother, if it was not sweet, would you have given birth to her?" Aunty Sadia had turned in her seat and was smiling at Iya Bolu. It was the closest thing to an apology that she would offer.

Iya Bolu shook her head. "My own daughter is going to be a doctor. After that, she can enjoy all the hard things she wants."

"OK, then she will be a doctor before the stiff soldiers get her. Not that the world will end if they get her first and then she becomes a doctor." Aunty Sadia laughed and slapped Iya Bolu's hand. "At least, we thank God it doesn't kill people."

Iya Bolu joined in the laughter. "Some of us would be dead if it killed. We thank God the pestle doesn't kill the mortar. If it did, how would we be able to enjoy wonderful pounded yam?"

"But this God is a great God-o. Iya Bolu, you know when that thing is asleep, just soft like that, you can disrespect it anyhow. But once it stands like this?" Aunty Sadia got up and stood at attention. "Hard like that? I just want to thank the God that made it that way."

Iya Bolu clapped. "It is that hardness that gives it value and honour, *o jare*."

"*Abi*?" Aunty Sadia sat down. "What do we want to do with a soft pestle? Can it pound yam?"

As they talked, I became uncomfortable. I thought about the last time Akin and I had made love and I wanted to ask Aunty Sadia questions— she seemed like the kind of person who would slap the back of my hand and give straightforward answers. But I bit my tongue because I was not the kind of woman who discussed her sex life with women in a salon.

The stylist was now done with Aunty Sadia. I went to her and stuck a comb in her hair. "So, which style do you want?" I asked.

"Madam, why is your face hard like this? *Abi,* you don't eat midnight-pounded yam?"

"Don't mind her—that is how she will be frowning as if she's a virgin." Iya Bolu pointed at Sesan's cot. "But we have evidence that she can do very well."

"Madam, which style do you want?"

Aunty Sadia stared at me for a while, a smile still playing at the corner of her lips. I felt nervous beneath her gaze and was worried that she would keep talking about sex.

"OK," she said. "Just weaving, all back. Weave all back."

I began to rub pomade into her hair, grateful that she had dropped the subject. I pushed the questions I wanted to ask away and let her soft tresses slide through my fingers.

She smiled into the mirror as I sectioned the hair. "I know your type. You will do your face as if you are Mary, but once the bedroom door is shut like this, you fire."

I bit my lower lip and said nothing.

23

About a month after Sesan started kindergarten, Akin took him to the hospital for some routine tests. It was the sort of thing Akin did, like buying hundreds of shares for Sesan on every birthday, or having a children's school-fees savings account that he deposited money in every month from the day we got married, or a yearly medical and dental checkup for himself. So I was not surprised when my son came home and proudly showed me the invisible spot that had been pricked on his finger for blood samples. He told me that he had not cried, though the doctor's needle hurt. I kissed the finger and told him he was the bravest boy in the world. He skipped away to Dotun's room to continue to show off.

By the time the test results were ready, Akin was in Lagos for a series of meetings that would last two weeks. I went to the hospital to get the results. Even then, I hated hospitals. The antiseptic smell that clung to one's nostrils for so long after one left the place. The horrid white dresses and coats most of the workers wore, white like funeral shrouds. The blood that assaulted your eyes even in places where you least expected it. The screams of pain and loss that spiralled through the corridors. I did not want to be there.

"Madam, where is your husband?" Dr. Bello asked before I could sit down.

"Away. He is in Lagos at the moment," I said.

The office was a cubicle that smelled of iodine.

"I would actually prefer to discuss this with him."

"What?"

"I said I would—"

"I heard. This is my son and you won't give me his test results? What do you mean?"

"OK, madam, please sit down," he said, inching back in his seat. "But you must tell your husband to come and see me."

"OK," I said. I knew then that he was not going to tell me everything that he knew.

"So, madam, about your son . . . you know about red blood cells?"

I swept through the recesses of my mind for some recollections from biology class. I remembered Mr. Olaiya, the biology teacher whose oversized trousers fell down to his knees on a few occasions and brightened up his boring class. I remembered nothing about blood cells, red, green or blue as they might be. I shook my head.

"Red blood cells carry oxygen to the—"

"*Oga*, doctor, is anything wrong? With my son?" I did not need a biology lesson. Besides, my heart was beating so fast, I was sure I would collapse before the doctor made his point if he did not get on with it.

"Do you know about sickle-cell disease?"

My heart stopped. My brain stopped. Every organ in my body stopped. The room felt airless. "Yes."

"Your son has sickle-cell disease."

"No," I said. "My God, no." For the next twenty-four hours I would mutter it, whisper it.

"I'm sorry. But it is not a hopeless condition. There are things you must know. First you need to bring him in for a full exam . . ."

The doctor's mouth kept moving, wrapping itself around words that trailed by my ears instead of sliding into them. When he shut his mouth, I stood up and left the office. I dropped the key many times before I could unlock my car. It was 2 p.m. I drove across the road to the Franciscan Nursery and Primary School to pick up my son.

He wanted to walk to the car as I led him out of his classroom. I carried him, squeezing him close to me until he yelped. I held on tighter. I kept glancing at him during the ride home, taking my eyes off the road for dangerous periods of time. He was telling me something about school in his still-warbled tongue. He was excited about this thing. He smiled, gestured with his hands and drew shapes in the air. He bounced in his seat as he babbled. I tried to hear what he was saying, to listen to this thing he was so excited about. I heard nothing. I could only see him. His dirty fingernails, dimpled brown cheeks, his yellow shorts and shirt that had grass stains on them again. He was the most beautiful child in the world. I wanted to tuck him back into my stomach and keep him safe from life, from hospitals, from stiff white caps and ward coats.

"Momma, what's wrong?" Sesan asked, holding up my bunch of keys. He looked irritated.

"Nothing," I said after we got inside.

I fed him lunch, and helped him with homework. I watched him watch television, gave him dinner, and bathed him. I sat on the rugged floor. I watched him watch more television until he fell asleep on the sitting-room couch. There were no curfews for him that night.

"Why are you crying?" Dotun asked. He had just come into the house.

I touched my cheeks. They were wet. When did I start crying?

"He is going to die too. Sesan is dying." Nervous laughter bubbled inside me. I clamped my lips together to keep it down. If I laughed, I knew I would laugh through eternity.

Dotun hurried to my side, put his ear to Sesan's chest and sat beside me frowning. "He's fine." His breath smelled like alcohol and cigarettes.

"He's a sickler. Sickler." The bubbling inside me broke free. Tears flowed, not laughter. It blurred my vision and clogged my nose. The only sounds I could hear were my sobs. They blocked out Sesan's soft snores. I needed to hear those snores. The sound was my life. I crawled to the couch to listen for them. But my sobs became louder and my eyes were blurred. I could barely see my son. My sobs swallowed Sesan's snores, swallowed me.

"It is OK. OK, he's OK." I felt Dotun's hand on my neck. Stroking. Calming.

I felt his arms around my waist. I was falling, drowning in my sobs.

He was there, holding me in his arms, his mouth whispering that it would be OK.

I kissed him to swallow that word "OK." To catch it from his lips and tuck it safely inside me, in the place where Olamide had been ripped from my navel. I wanted the word. I got it. Then I wanted more, needed more, craved more, feverishly. More. More. More.

His tongue, his hands, his hardness deep inside me again.

Later, when his hardness became limp inside me, it still was not enough. I craved more than ever.

He rolled off me. I crawled to the couch, placing my face beside my son's. His eyes were closed.

Did he see us? How could I have exposed him? Had he seen us? Oh God, *please* let him think it was a dream if he did. Oh God, *please. Please. Please.*

I sat there until dawn, naked, listening to my son snore, loathing the woman I had become.

24

I had been taught and I believed that education, the best that money could buy, was the greatest thing I could give my son. I was ready to indenture myself if necessary to give Sesan a good education. I revered degrees and the people who held them. The more, the better. The minute I felt he was old enough, I shipped my son off to the best primary school in town, a Catholic school that would teach him the fear of God too.

The day after his diagnosis, I wanted Sesan to stay at home, in bed where I could feed him, fan him and just watch him. I did not care if for the rest of his life my son was unable to add two and two to get four. It did not matter anymore if he never spoke English without the heavy Ijesa accent that refused to quit the tongues of some of his aunts and uncles. I did not care if he never became an engineer or a lawyer, or an accountant like his father. If, for the rest of his life, he did nothing but stay alive, that would have been enough for me.

At some point in the night, Dotun had thrown a wrapper over me. Then he left the house without telling me where he was going. I did not ask. As sunlight seeped in through an opening in the curtains, I tied the wrapper across my breasts and tapped my son awake; it was time to get him ready for school. I let him go that day, even though I did not want to let him out of my sight, because a mother does not do what she wants, she does what is best for her child.

My hands shook on the steering wheel as I drove Sesan to school. I stood in the parking lot and watched him run to his class. My son did not even look my way.

I drove to the roundabout, parked in front of the courthouse beside the Owa's Palace and went into the public library. I couldn't find a single volume on sickle cell. I read biology textbooks. I read about blood, red blood cells and haemoglobin. I read the textbooks again and again until it was almost 2 and I had to go and pick up Sesan. I moved him out of his room that night and reinstated him in the room I shared with Akin. He would sleep beside me, where I could watch him vigilantly.

Dotun came to me on a Saturday night, a night when he should have been out as usual drinking at Ijesa Sports Club on Akin's membership. He did not knock; he just walked in as though from the other side of the door he could see that I was sitting up in bed with my back against the wall. I had not seen him since the night he teased my body to orgasm after orgasm while my son slept on the couch. His brother was still away, due back in a few days.

Dotun's eyes were bloodshot, the irises stood out against the redness.

"Let's talk," he said, standing by the half-open door.

"Please go away." I did not want to talk to him.

He sat near my feet. He looked sorry, guilty and a little afraid. He could not even meet my eye. Instead he focused on my forehead as though it was a television screen. I never imagined that the loudmouthed Dotun knew the meaning of guilt. I expected some remorse; I was his brother's wife after all. But the way the sides of his mouth dipped towards his chin suggested shame. Shame was something I had never associated with him, he always appeared above it with his easy smile, his inappropriate remarks, and the way he picked his nose and scratched his balls in public.

"What we did—"

"Will not happen again," I said.

"I just . . . I don't know what came . . . the devil . . . Akin . . ."

It was the first time I would hear Dotun say his brother's name just like that, just the name, stripped of the honour due to his older brother, unprefixed with "bros" or "brother." Not Brother *mi*, not *egbon mi* or Bros Akin—just Akin, as if somehow my husband had become his equal in age at some point during the week, perhaps while Dotun lay with me on the sitting-room rug.

I leaned forward and grabbed his chin. "Your brother will never ever know about this."

The downturned lips were now trembling and it looked as though he would cry. I hissed, gripping his chin harder until my nails dug into his skin, "Stop shaking like waist beads *o jare*."

Perhaps it was guilt that loosened his tongue, a need to justify the desire that leapt into his eyes the moment my hand touched his chin, a way to excuse the naked need he struggled to swallow. Perhaps he assumed that I knew the things he was going to say, the secrets that Akin had hidden from me while carefully feeding my insecurities.

I did not want to believe Dotun, but I could not resist the truth, could not deny his words out loud and look like a fool. Dotun kept apologising. I smiled and told him it was OK. He finally shut his mouth and retreated from the room with his head hung like a condemned criminal.

His words were like a blow to my head—they made me dizzy and disoriented. I mumbled them to myself, trying to piece his sentences together again. I tried to fit it into the picture I had of my marriage, of my relationship with Akin from the moment I laid my eyes on him. The past flipped itself open like a spooky family album, revealing one familiar picture after the other, highlighting the things standing in plain view, which I had never seen. Things I had refused to see.

25

I met Akin when I was in my penultimate year at the University of Ife. That night, I had gone to Oduduwa Hall to watch a movie with some boy who paid for my ticket and bought *suya* for me to eat during the show. I was seeing this boy almost every day at that time.

I saw Akin in the ticket queue in front of us. He was smiling at something the girl with him had said; his lower lip was a deep pink that stood out against his brown skin. I felt like touching the lip to find out if he was wearing lipstick. The feeling came from someplace deep in my stomach, someplace that I had not known existed before that night.

Inside the hall I was a seat away from him. The girl he came with was seated in the chair between us but she did not exist that night, she was just thin air—even the chair she sat on did not exist. I could feel Akin's presence beside me as though he was right next to me. I ate the *suya*, chewing chunk after peppery chunk of beef without pausing to drink from the bottle of soft drink my thoughtful date had brought along.

"Wow, you are tough, eating all that pepper. My mouth would have been on fire by now," date boy had said.

I glanced at him just before the lights went out to signal the beginning of the movie, trying to remember who he was and why on earth he was talking to me. I tried to keep my eyes on the screen. It was impossible. My eyes were drawn to Akin like metal to a magnet; it was just not possible to resist the attraction. He was watching me too in the dim glow of the light from the screen. I tore my eyes away every time, afraid I would drown in his steady gaze. The movie finished too soon. I stood up and dragged myself after date boy, still struggling to remember his name, keeping my head down so I could steal a glance at Akin without turning my head.

Date boy was going to a lecture hall to spend the night studying. I reassured him that it would not be necessary for him to escort me to my room. He headed towards the Faculty of Arts and I went in the direction of Moremi Hall.

Akin had followed me. I felt his hand on my arm once my feet hit the pavement.

"Do you need a ride?" he asked.

"You want to carry me on your back?"

He laughed. "That would be great. My car is parked in front of the hall. I can bring it here or we can go and pick it up together. But if you prefer to ride on my back, it belongs to you."

"No, thank you." I had been drooling over him all night, but my brains hadn't fallen out of my mouth yet. It was past midnight and he could have been a kidnapper.

"I'm Akinyele and everyone calls me Akin," he said.

My feet for some reason became rooted to the ground. "Yejide."

He scratched his eyebrow. "Ye-ji-de. Lovely name."

I was suddenly incapable of producing more than one word at a time. "Thanks."

"So, you noticed I couldn't watch the movie because of you."

"You want me to give you a refund?" Ah! My tongue was back.

He smiled. "I wouldn't mind, not money *sha,* I'd like your room number. I want to see you again. Visit you."

"Will you be coming with your girlfriend?"

"My? Oh, Bisade. She was my girlfriend, but it's over now."

I bent my head to hide a smile. "Since when?"

"Since I saw you. Tonight."

"Does Bisade know this?"

He scratched the tip of his nose. "She'll know soon."

"F101 Moremi. My room number." The words came out of my mouth of their own accord.

He rubbed his palms together and smiled. "Come with me to my car," he said.

I followed him to his car, the Volkswagen

Beetle that would become mine after we got married. He held the door open while I got in.

"You know what they say about a Yoruba man opening the door for his wife?" he asked when he got in.

"What?"

"Well, when a Yoruba man opens the door for his wife, either the wife is new or the car is new."

"Oh," I said, like a moron.

"F101," he said, switching off the car's engine. We were in Moremi Hall's car park.

I nodded, trying to tear my eyes away from his lips. I failed. Instead I felt my own lips part. The car was silent. I could hear myself breathing through my mouth. I could have removed his hand when it touched my chin, tilting my face until our eyes met, his eyes questioning, silently seeking permission. I did not remove his hand. His force field pulled me closer. His lips touched mine.

It was my first kiss.

Of course, I had swallowed saliva from the mouths of a few boys before then, had had my lips uncomfortably crushed, and wondered why there were so many people under the trees at different points on campus, mangling each other's lips every night. I understood why when I felt Akin's lips on mine. His lips stopped time. His tongue teased mine until it danced with his.

When he drew back, I could not remember my name or anything else.

"I'll check on you tomorrow," he said.

I staggered out of the car and up the steps that led into Moremi Hall.

He showed up the next day, sat on my bed and leaned back until his head rested on the wooden panel that ran along the side of the wall. He looked at home, as comfortable as though he came every day and leaned back on my bed like that. I felt awkward. He said nothing, just looked at me with a smile dancing on his lips. I was overwhelmed with the urge to fill every silence with words. Silence to me was a void in the universe that could suck us all in. It was my assignment to block this deadly void with words and save the world. I told him about myself without him asking. He sat up, leaned forward and took in every word. I began to feel as though I was elucidating eternal truths.

Akin had the ability to listen to people, to focus his eyes and ears in a way that made you feel whatever you were saying was important, even crucial. It was 10 p.m.—too soon, but he had to leave the hostel along with other male visitors. As I walked him to his car, I realised that he had spent four hours in my room and I still did not know anything about him apart from his name. Yet somehow I felt as though I knew him.

I would learn later that Akin could keep himself

neatly folded in while he drew out other people. He was the kind of person that many claimed as a dear friend. Many of those people did not even know him, but they never knew they did not know him. It made me feel special, this awareness that Akin never really allowed anyone to know him.

As we grew closer and he became the one who talked to me nonstop for four hours, I felt as though I was being ushered into the most exclusive club—a club that only Dotun and I were allowed into. I would not realise until much later that Akin could talk for hours without saying anything and with that skill he had managed to make me feel like part of the inner circle.

I told Akin about my plan. I made the plan the day I started secondary school. Iya Abike, my father's youngest and favourite wife at the time, had looked me up and down in my new school uniform and told me that there was no need for me to go to school because I would end up a whore like my mother, pregnant by a man who would never marry her. None of the other wives said anything and I knew that Iya Abike, bolstered by her status as the favourite wife, had spoken for all of them, sure that she could get herself out of trouble with my father if I decided to report what she said. Until then I had wanted to train to become a hairdresser with the local stylist after secondary school. I decided that minute that I would go to university, that I would stay a virgin until I got married and have the blood-stained white cloth sent as proof to my father on my wedding night. Even back then, it was a tradition that only a few people followed, but I was determined to go with the practice and shove it in my stepmothers' faces when the time came. In my mind, the plan would be a declaration, a condition that I laid on the table for any man who wanted to be with me, a take-it-or-leave-it kind of thing. But with Akin, I pleaded. Although we had only kissed a couple of times before he asked me to be his girlfriend, I knew already that I was at the mercy of the pinkness of his mouth.

He agreed to wait.

The waiting was pointless. My father died shortly before our wedding. My stepmothers found an excuse not to attend the church ceremony, although they could not wriggle out of the traditional wedding since it was held in the family compound. When I went back home after the wedding reception to wait for a delegation from Akin's family to come for me, the house was empty. There was no female relative to accompany me to Ilesa, no younger sibling to keep me company on my first night as a wife. It was as though I was not just an orphan; it was as if I had no relatives at all.

The night Dotun walked into my room without knocking, told me the things in plain view that I had been blind to, before leaving with his head

213

hanging like that of a condemned criminal, I felt the loneliness of my wedding day again.

I woke Sesan up.

"Tell me about school," I asked him.

"Is it time for school, Momma?" He was still drowsy.

"No, I just need to talk to you." I needed to hear his voice, this person who was all mine, my son. I belonged to him in an unchangeable, irreplaceable way. I was his mother. I knew him, he could not betray me in the ways Akin had. He could not deceive me yet and, even if he did, I would always be his.

"I want sleep."

"Sit here." I pulled him into my lap and hugged him tight.

"Tell me, who is your friend in class?"

"Lemme alone," he protested, wrestling himself from me with surprising force. He rolled over to the other end of the bed and dropped off to sleep.

Loneliness wrapped itself around me like a shroud.

26

The day that Yejide told me that Sesan had sickle-cell disease I was in a hotel room in Lagos, somewhere in Ikeja. I would have left for Ilesa immediately if I could have, but I still had business meetings scheduled for the next few days. I assumed, when Yejide said that Dr. Bello wanted to see me once I returned to Ilesa, that he wanted to discuss treatment options. Didn't know enough about the disease to be as scared as she sounded on the phone. I trusted in medical science, believing it could fix Sesan if I spent enough money. And I was ready to spend all I had.

I went to the hospital to meet with Dr. Bello on the day I arrived in Ilesa. I didn't even go home first, drove straight to the hospital once I got into town. He was just getting back from the clinic when I arrived at his office.

"You don't remember me?" he asked as he unlocked the door to his office.

I tried to remember where we had met but I couldn't. "No," I said, following him into the office, sitting in the chair he pointed to.

He removed his ward coat and slung it on the back of a chair. "I came to your bank for a loan

215

last year; you were so helpful," he said. "You are sure you don't remember?"

"I'm sorry, but no," I said.

He rolled up his shirtsleeves. "It's OK, it's OK. Your madam told me that you were in Lagos. How was the trip?"

"It was great, really good. Thanks for asking."

He took a deep breath. "I'm guessing that your madam also told you that Sesan has sickle-cell disease?"

I nodded, waiting for him to tell me what could be done, to arm me with knowledge, give me a list of rules we would need to keep.

"I will get straight to the point, sir. I think you need to have a discussion with your madam." He took off his glasses and began to clean the lenses with a handkerchief. "There were some . . . er . . . discrepancies in the results of the genotype test we conducted for your son."

I moved forward in my seat, eager for him to go on, imagining for a brief beautiful moment that he'd discovered an error in the test results since Yejide had left his office, that he was about to tell me our son was healthy after all.

"So, let me start by explaining how sickle-cell disease works. It's an inherited disorder, and you need two parents who have at least one sickle-cell gene before a child can get it. So, for instance, your madam is AS, and that means she has the sickle-cell gene, but because she has just one of

216

the genes, she doesn't have the disease, but is a carrier. And that means she can pass on the gene to her children, but her children can only have the sickle-cell disease if the other parent, the man, is also a carrier. So you need two people with the AS genotype or one with the AS genotype and the other with the SS genotype before the possibility of even having a child who is SS arises. Does that make any sense?"

I nodded.

"Now here is the discrepancy I was talking about. I took a look at your files after Sesan's results came in from the lab and here is what I discovered: your madam is the only one with the AS genotype, sir. You are AA, which means that your child could never have sickle-cell disease. Sir, I am telling you this as a man to another man and because you were so helpful when I came in for that loan. You understand what I mean? So, I can tell you with all certainty that Sesan cannot be your son."

My limbs went limp. I covered my face with my hands and prepared an expression to meet the doctor's sympathetic gaze.

"Do you mean this?" I said. "Do you mean what you are saying? You mean that woman has been cheating on me? Are you serious? You mean this? Oh, my God! I'm going to kill her. I swear to God." I allowed my voice to rise to its highest pitch and pounded my fist on the doctor's table.

"Calm down, sir, you need to handle this like a man, OK? Please calm down. Be a man, sir. Be a man."

I made sure I seemed angry enough to Dr. Bello. Behaved the way I imagined a man would when discovering that a child wasn't his. I punched a wall, yelled and slammed the door as I left the office.

But I knew Sesan was my son. I loved him. I was planning for his future, had bought shares in his name. I often thought of the day I'd buy him his first bottle of beer. Could hardly wait to teach him how to play table tennis at the sports club. I knew I was the one who would do all those things. Nobody else was going to do them. There are things scientific tests cannot show, things like the fact that paternity is more than sperm donation. I knew Sesan was my son. There was no test result that could change that.

Besides, I already knew that Dotun was the sperm donor. That was how I thought about what he did for me—sperm donation. I knew Dotun would never claim he was Sesan's father, which is the reason I went to him when I eventually accepted the fact that I needed someone else to get my wife pregnant.

"Brother *mi*? What is this thing you are saying?" Dotun said after I laid out my plan.

"You need to spend just a weekend. Next weekend, she'll be ovulating."

"And Yejide? She agreed to this thing you are saying?" He looked as if he was about to vomit all over the green rug on his sitting-room floor.

"Yes." Truth is I hadn't discussed it with Yejide, but I just wanted him to agree to the plan so I could go to bed and forget the discussion.

He got up, went to stand by a window, stared into a black night unlit by stars or streetlights. I couldn't see his face clearly; the candle that stood on the centre table was burning out fast.

"Brother Akin . . . with all due respect-o, but this thing you are saying is nonsense. What if? No. No, I can't do it. I won't. It's wrong." He turned to face me when he said this, slashing the air with his hands the way he did when agitated.

I wanted to laugh. Dotun? *Wrong?* What the hell. He'd dated a mother and her daughter at the same time. He had a string of girlfriends on the side; one of them was even his poor wife's colleague at work. He was telling me about wrong?

"I'm not asking you to rape her, damn it. Just once, get her pregnant and that's it. I've told you my problem. Do you want me to beg?"

"It is an abomination. She is your wife. Shit. Your wife, you want me to sleep with my brother's wife? My elder brother's wife? No, I can't, there has to be another way."

"Dotun, you are the only person I can come to.

You are the only brother I have. Do you want me to call a stranger?"

He hit several surfaces—his thigh, the wall, the blank television screen. His burst of conscience surprised me. I hadn't expected him to jump at the idea, but somehow I'd never thought he'd be so torn, so afraid. But of what? Was he not Dotun?

"So she gets pregnant. Won't you want another child?"

"If we arrange things well, one weekend will do for each child. All things being equal, three kids are OK."

He looked me in the eye, searched my face and slumped into a chair. "You've thought about this. You've been thinking about this for a long time." His voice accused me of many things.

"I'm doing this for her."

"Even then, I can't. Maybe an outsider would be better."

Why did I tell him the story? Maybe a part of me knew that it was Yejide's pain that could move him, had intuited in the hugs and gazes that lingered too long that if my brother had met her first, the story could have been different. Perhaps because I knew even then that what Dotun was afraid of, what he wouldn't admit to himself, was that with Yejide it could never be just sex for him because a part of him had always wanted her.

I told him about the miracle baby: the call

from the hospital, the antenatal nurse begging me to come and get my wife, told him about the day I went to the antenatal class, described the wounded look in Yejide's eyes as I tried to escort her out of the class, the way she clung to a metal pole on the hospital corridor, not removing her hands to retie the wrapper that dropped as I tried to pull her away. I talked about it until he could see her in just her Ankara blouse and lace underskirt, the wrapper lying at her feet like a snake's discarded skin. I told him how she stayed that way until the antenatal class was over and the pregnant women left for their homes, some slinking by her in hurried steps, others turning off to take another route as they approached her.

"Is she going mad?" he asked.

"She has started seeing a psychiatrist. She is OK right now, but she could wake up tomorrow morning and say she has morning sickness."

"I can't!" He stood up, went back to the window.

"Dotun, I'm talking about you having sex with Yejide, my beautiful wife." I swallowed. It felt like forcing an iron fist down my throat.

My brother shifted from one foot to the other. I could see in the way his hips thrust towards the window reflexively that he was already in Ilesa, in our bedroom, fucking my wife.

"It's an abomination."

"So advise me, what do I do?"

221

"Brother *mi*, does Yejide know you are here right now?"

"She knows I'm in Lagos. Dotun, why are you prolonging this discussion? Why would it be different from all the girls you go around with? It will just be sex five times at the most and you are done."

"It would just be sex." He spoke slowly, as though testing the truth of the words by speaking them.

27

Akin was irritated by Sesan's presence in our bed, diagnosis or no diagnosis.

"I just want to be able to touch you anytime, anyhow I want. And this child is old enough, he will remember what we are doing," he said.

I wanted to laugh in his face. What were we doing?

"Sesan's health is our priority now, not touching," I said.

He sulked, but I did not care. I did not want his hands on my body again ever. His deception was cutting me open, but I did not have the time to deal with it or confront him. Sesan needed me, needed everything in me that could will him to live. Fighting Akin over Dotun's revelations would have been an unnecessary waste of energy.

After Sesan was diagnosed, I pulsed with adrenaline. I spent my days reading photocopied medical journals I borrowed from Sesan's doctor. My head was filled with images of haemoglobin and sickle-shaped cells. I learned how to use a thermometer to check Sesan's temperature and briefly considered training to be a nurse. The only thing that stopped me was that there would be little time out of the training schedule to actually care for my son. Many times I woke up in the dead of the night sweating, unable to remember what nightmares had propelled me upright in bed. After a few months I began to breathe again. Sesan was as healthy as ever, still dangling himself upside down from the banister and running around the house for no particular reason. He was also doing well at school and even placed second in his class.

The first crisis took my breath away. Sesan told me he had a headache when he returned from school. I administered paracetamol syrup and put him to sleep on the sitting-room couch. He did not respond when I tried to wake him up for dinner.

I pleaded with God in my heart as Akin drove us to the hospital. *Please, please, please,* I begged. I could not wrap my mind around anything more coherent. The car sped on and on. In the corner of my mind, some demon assured me that we were speeding away from the hospital and not towards it.

"Faster, faster. Drive! Do you know where we are going?" I yelled at Akin.

I threatened Sesan. "You, this child, I will kill you if you die."

I stumbled out of the car before Akin stopped it and ran towards the nearest building.

A nurse tried to take Sesan from me. I held on to him, still screaming.

"Let him go," Akin said.

I let the nurse take him. A ward attendant blocked our way when we tried to follow her. I screamed threats after the woman, the pain I would inflict on her if anything happened to my baby. I paced the corridor. I was alone. Akin was somewhere filling in forms to admit him. I pleaded with God again. Then I threatened: *If you . . . if my . . . I will . . . I promise you I will.* In that moment I hated God. I wished I could see God and rip His heart out. What had I done to Him anyway? Didn't I deserve some happiness? My mother, Olamide and now Sesan.

The days passed slowly, each minute pregnant with hope, each second tremulous with tragedy. Moomi came to the hospital and sat by me all night. Before she left the next morning, she reminded me that I had to be strong because I was a mother. I sat by his bed looking, waiting, searching for the faintest sign that he had decided to return to me. There was no sign. I was afraid to touch him, afraid that my touch might stress him and careen him into the unknown, away from me, forever. By the third day I was on my knees praying to him in muttered words only I could hear. *Saanu mi, malo, Omo mi, joo nitori Olorun. Saanu mi. Duro timi.* Have mercy on me, don't go, please. Stay with me. I ran to the bathroom and back. I did not eat or bathe.

He woke up on the sixth day. I screamed for the doctor even though she was at the next bed on ward round when Sesan woke up.

"Mummy smelling bad." Those were the first words my son spoke as he recovered. I remember them to this day.

My mother-in-law came visiting about a week after Sesan was discharged. She waved away Akin's greetings and shook her head when I offered her a drink.

"This is *Abiku*," Moomi said as soon as she settled into a chair. "I have been thinking about this child's sickness since I came to check on him in the hospital."

"It's just a sickness, Moomi, they have a name for it and treatment. It is not *Abiku*," Akin said.

Moomi snorted. "Do they have a cure? Can they cure him of this?"

"They can treat it," Akin said.

"Do they have a cure? No! See? You shake your head. That means this is *Abiku*. I have seen a lot of them in my day. This, this is just how it is. Look, these children, they have made a promise in the spirit world to die young. Let me tell you, their ties to the spirit world are stronger than steel. You think your hospitals can help you with that? We must do something."

Akin held his forehead as though a migraine was setting in. "It's just a disease, Moomi. And there is treatment, there's nothing spiritual about it."

"So you went to the white man's school and I didn't. But we have seen enough of you school types to know schooling is not wisdom, for many of you it is foolishness, like settling for treatment when there is a cure."

"Moomi, are you saying I'm a fool?" I could tell that Akin's irritation was turning to anger.

Moomi gave him a stare that said her response was a resounding yes and turned to me.

"Talk to me *jare*, my daughter. What do you think? We should just fold our hands against our bodies and watch the doctors treat what they cannot cure when we have another route we can take? Another route, my daughter! The whole world knows there are many routes into any marketplace. But the white man has deceived some of you, told you his way is the only way." She paused and glared at Akin, who was staring at the ceiling. "Some have been foolish enough to believe him without investigating for themselves. God save them all."

"Say what you like, Moomi," Akin said, "we are not taking my son to any of your crooks."

"Look at this Akin that doesn't know what pregnancy feels like, see the way he is talking. My daughter, don't mind him-o. You are the one that will decide because you know what it is like to kneel in labour. Do you think our people simply say that there is no god like a mother? Of course you do. No one bothers to complete the saying these days. Iya Sesan, pull your ears and listen to the full proverb, there is no god like a mother because nobody can support her child like she would when that child is in anguish. It is you who will decide for your son, not this Akin that wants to cure *Abiku* with a syringe."

Dotun came in then, reeking of alcohol. "Moomi! Here you are!"

Sesan had wriggled free from his grandmother's knees. He pulled at the hem of my dress. "What is *Abiku*?"

"It is a game," I said.

"Can we play *Abiku*?"

"No, it is a bad game," I said.

Dotun was weaving around Moomi, singing nursery rhymes. "Baa baa black sheep, Baa baa black sheep."

"Why is my son bleating like a goat?" Moomi asked.

"He is singing a song. An English song," Akin replied.

Moomi sighed and shook her head.

"I can jump like a frog. I can jump like a frog!" This time Dotun sang in Yoruba and Moomi needed no interpreter.

"Akin, don't watch me like this. Do something about your brother."

Although my husband had nothing new to say, he snapped to and steered the conversation away from Sesan's health to Dotun's joblessness and what he was doing and planning to do about it.

Dotun leapt around our sitting room like a child, singing various nursery rhymes. Sesan followed him, singing along.

"Who is in the garden? A little fine girl. Can I come and see her? No. No. No!"

Dotun stopped in front of me and in his drunken haze pulled me up from my chair towards himself with one hand and grabbed my breast with the other. I tried to pull away but he held on.

Akin pushed him and Dotun collapsed into a seat, laughing.

"Ah, abomination!" Moomi cried, placing a hand over her left breast as if to keep her heart from bursting through her skin.

"It is the alcohol," Akin said.

"My wife, please don't be angry," Moomi said.

"She is not angry. It is the alcohol, isn't it?" Akin asked me. A muscle kept flexing in his jaw as though he was chewing his teeth. His hands were balled into fists and the veins stood out. His gaze stayed on me, even though his mother was saying something to him. He was waiting for me to answer, to assure him that it had really been just the alcohol. I lowered myself into a chair, thinking he had no right to be angry, not if the things Dotun had told me were true. But I did not have enough energy in me to care too much about how Akin felt. Sesan was all that mattered. My son was all I had left.

28

I picked him up from the Franciscan school's sickbay. One of the nurses on duty was also a nun. She went to the hospital with me, holding my son and whispering prayers that I did not know. The only lines I recognised were from the Lord's Prayer:

Our Father who art in heaven, hallowed be Thy name . . .

Her words were soon drowned by his groaning. He writhed as though he was seeking a way to escape his own body. The groans were filled with too much pain for one so tiny. He was hoarse by the time we drove across the road into Wesley Guild. The nun held him and followed me as I raced ahead of her into the ward. The nurse on duty recognised me and led us to a bed immediately. The nun stayed with us, saying her prayers at the foot of the bed:

Thy kingdom come, Thy will be done, on earth as it is in heaven. Give us this day our daily bread . . .

I stood as close to the bed as I could. I wanted to take in the sound of his voice, absorb the unspeakable pain it bore. I had heard it too many times. It had seared my mind and played in my dreams. His eyes were shut and he was curled into a tight ball that the doctor and nurses tried to prise open. He whimpered my name: "Mom-ma. Mom-ma. Mom-ma." Each broken sound was a nail in my heart. I wanted desperately to stop his pain, in any way possible. But I couldn't.

And forgive us our trespasses . . .

"Mrs. Ajayi . . . Mrs. Ajayi, please hold his hand."

I inched closer to the bed. His hand gripped mine with pain-induced strength that crushed my knuckles together. I welcomed the pain in my hand, aware that it was only a tip of what he was feeling. I hoped that by holding me, he could transfuse his agony into my body and be free from it.

I remember this time because the nun went with us to the hospital. Sesan was being admitted to hospital so often now that one visit was hard to distinguish from another. The nun in her beige habit makes this memory stand out. Soon, the doctors asked me and the nun to wait outside and we joined the group of sitting and pacing relatives, companions in the valley of the shadow of death, waiting for someone in white to come and tell us our fate.

The nun held my hand, led me to a wooden bench and sat beside me. So we waited; the nun prayed and I thought about how much I was to blame. There was little room to escape the guilt I felt about Sesan's sickness and I did not even try. The way I saw it, 50 percent of his pain was my fault. I had made him sick. I had passed on my sickle-cell gene to him; my body had created the fault in his. I did not shirk from the despair, did not hide myself from his pain—it was only fair that I should share in what I had caused.

I refused to entertain the possibility that he would die. I did not give up on Sesan, I held on to him in my heart. I convinced myself that he would survive it all—the pain that made him scream until he was hoarse, the injections and painkillers being pumped into his body. I did not once wish that death would release him from his suffering. My only prayers were that he would survive it all and live. The doctors had told us that there were people who lived long and full lives in spite of SCD, and as far as I was concerned, there was no reason why my son would not be one of them.

I convinced myself that he would live because he deserved to, he wanted to, he was so brave, so hungry for life in spite of everything. But it was also because I knew already that I could not bear to lose another child—I could not even think about it. I knew I would not survive the loss.

The nun visited Sesan every day during the two weeks that he spent in the hospital. On the day he was finally discharged, Akin tried to carry him when we left the ward, but he scampered down and skipped ahead of us towards the car. He laughed and stretched his little arms forward as he tried to catch a red butterfly that was flying in front of him.

29

Mr. Ajayi. It's Mr. Ajayi, right? OK, good," the doctor said. "He is responding to treatment now, you should be able to see him in an hour or so. I'll let you know when you can. Please excuse me."

I went back to the corridor where I'd been sitting on a bench with Yejide. She was pacing the floor with her hands clasped around her large belly.

"*Oya*, come and sit down. There is no problem." I put an arm around her shoulder, led her to a bench. "I met one of Sesan's doctors on my way back from the toilet. He says Sesan is responding to treatment. We should be able to see him soon. So just relax, OK?"

"Thank God," she sighed and slumped against me. "The baby kicked again when you left."

I put my hands on her belly.

She chuckled. "Sorry, she has stopped already."

"Not fair." I moved closer to her so an old man could sit next to me on the bench. "Will you go home to have some breakfast? I'll wait here."

"*Lai lai*. Never, I'm not going anywhere without my son."

"He'll be fine, don't worry about it. You need to eat, Yejide." I got up. "Let me get you something

234

from those food vendors outside the gate. What do you want?"

"Maybe bread."

"Be back in a minute."

Yejide and I had woken up during the night to find Sesan writhing in pain. We'd ended up in the hospital before 3 a.m. The sun was just coming up as I went outside the hospital's pedestrian gate. Most of the wooden stalls that clustered close to the entrance were empty and I had to walk towards Ijofi Street before I found a woman who sold two fresh loaves of bread to me. Yejide was still eating when the doctor I'd seen earlier approached us; we stood up as he came closer.

"Please come with me. I'd like to talk to you," he said.

Yejide dropped her bread on the bench and we began walking up the corridor with the doctor.

The doctor stopped, glancing at Yejide's belly. "No, no. I meant just your husband, *Ma*. Please go and sit down, I need to talk just to him. Alone."

"Just him, *ke*? You don't need me?" Yejide said.

"No, madam. I just need to ask your husband a few questions. He'll be back with you soon."

Yejide shuffled back towards the bench as the doctor and I walked up the corridor. I could still hear the sound of her feet when the doctor and I stopped at the end of the corridor.

"Mr. Ajayi, how do I say this?" He stared at the floor for what must have been a full minute. When he looked up, his eyes were red. "This is my first call in paediatrics. I just became a doctor last year. I don't specialise in paediatrics. My Senior Registrar, the SR on call, was there too when we were fighting for Sesan's life. But she has gone to the toilet again. Dr. Bulus, that's her name, I think she may have diarrhoea. Maybe we should wait for her, I'm so sorry."

"What are you saying?"

He rubbed his eyes with the back of his hand and sighed. "We lost him. I'm so sorry, we lost him."

To this day I think about the way he said they'd lost him, as though there was still a chance of getting him back, of finding him hidden in a filing cabinet.

I went back to Yejide. "He is getting better," I said.

"When can we see him?"

"Not yet. They are . . . they want to observe him for two more hours before we see him."

She frowned. "Two hours? Why did he want to talk to you alone?"

"Do you have ewedu at home?"

"Ewedu?" She scratched her head. "Yes. Why?"

"He wants us to bring ewedu stew for him so that . . . because when . . . it's nutritious and he thinks it will help him. *Oya,* let's go home."

"For what?"

"Yejide, the ewedu now. We are not going to see him for two more hours anyway. Let's go quickly so that the stew will be ready when they let us in."

She pursed her lips. As we walked to the parking lot, she kept glancing back at the ward Sesan had been admitted to.

As we drove home, I thought about the best way to tell Yejide our son was dead. I knew before we drove out of the hospital it would be harder than anything I'd ever done.

Yejide put a hand on my knee when I parked in front of our house. "You haven't said anything since we left the hospital. What is wrong? What did that doctor say?"

It must have been something in my eyes, in the way I looked at her while I tried to come up with something plausible to say.

"It's Sesan, *abi*? That ewedu thing is a lie— you just wanted me out of the hospital. What happened?" She gripped my knee. "*Abi*, my son is dead?"

I couldn't lie, couldn't tell the truth, didn't have the energy to say a word. I just stared at her.

"Akin? Sesan is dead. *Abi*?"

I couldn't even nod. I was weak, exhausted. I didn't even try to hold her when she put her forehead against the dashboard and began to cry.

• • •

Moomi came to ask for permission the next day. She offered her condolences briskly and sat beside Yejide on our bed. "Just a few marks on his body," she lowered her voice, "and a little whipping."

"Moomi, I said no, there is no need." I couldn't believe what she was saying, was within an inch of telling her to leave my house.

"Next time we will be sure, we will know for sure when Yejide has another baby."

"I said no. Can't you hear me?" I knew the tradition. There was no need for her to explain it to me. You whip the *Abiku*'s body so that the next time he is reborn, the marks on the newborn would tell you that the dead child had returned to torment its mother. I didn't want my son ritually scarred, because I didn't believe he was some malicious spirit-child. I'd never believed in *Abiku*s at all.

"*Abiku. Abiku.* I said it and said it until my mouth was bleeding. But you said, what does an old woman know? You are a man, Akin. Just a man. What do you know? Tell me. Have you been pregnant? Have you held a child to your breasts and watched it die? All you know is stupid English. What do you know? Yejide, talk to me, *o jare*. It is your permission that I need. Can they do it? Just a few marks so we will know for sure?"

238

"Yes," Yejide said, covering herself with a blanket.

"Yejide? What rubbish, you can't let them do this."

"Please, I want to sleep," she said. "Go away, all of you. Please go away."

30

There were no incisions on my daughter's body, no lacerations, no scars, not one single lash mark from a previous life. Still they named her Rotimi, a name that implied that she was an *Abiku* child who had come into the world intending to die as soon as she could. Rotimi— stay with me. It was the name my mother-in-law had chosen, a name that until then I had thought was given to boys alone. I wondered if Moomi had picked Rotimi because it was mutable. If the right prefix was added later on, it would sound normal, stripped of the tortured history that *Abiku* names announced. Rotimi could easily become Olarotimi—Wealth stays with me. There was no getting around other alternatives like Maku—Don't die, or Kukoyi—Death, reject this one. I checked every inch of her body, even her palms and the soles of her feet. Nothing. I stared at her smooth unscarred cheeks and thought of Sesan, his body beaten, marked forever. I wished I could rub the marks off with my fingertips the way I had once rubbed his tears into his skin until they disappeared. First, I would have had to find out where they had buried him— if they had buried him—if his body had not simply been left in a bush far away from the city, far away from any place where human beings lived.

There was no way for me to ever know. Moomi did not answer my questions. She refused to say a word about Sesan at all. It was as though, to her, he was a bad dream that should quickly be forgotten and definitely not spoken about. Like me, Akin was not allowed around Sesan's dead body or funeral, and since my husband had not agreed to the marks in the first place, he did not go to Ayeso the day the marks were put on Sesan's body.

The day Rotimi was named, in a quiet ceremony that included only ten people, I took off my gold necklace just before the ceremony began and twisted it around her neck three times to form a multilayered necklace. The pendant, a crucifix, lay hidden beneath her white dress. This was the only thing I did for my daughter that day. My mother-in-law took care of bathing and dressing Rotimi, she even held her neck while I breastfed her. Moomi made an effort to be kind, but I could sense her irritated impatience with me, even though I was far away, nursing my Sesan, still trying to keep him alive, battling the blurry pictures that kept blocking my view of him. Moomi was another blurry picture, an awkward image that held my face in her hands and dragged her hands across my cheeks to catch tears—only I was not crying. I was just sleepy,

241

eager to curl up in bed and dream of Olamide and Sesan.

"You must be strong for this child," she said over and over until I covered my ears with my hands. She left our house the same day, even though there was no other grandchild for her to help look after. "She is your daughter. You take care of her, you are not dead," she said before walking out to meet Akin at the car. There was more she had to say; it was there in the anger and contempt in her eyes. The eyes that condemned me for grieving for too long, for being too weak to be a mother to my newborn child, for dwelling with the dead. I did not care what she thought or what her rheumy eyes were screaming at me; after all, she was just another blurry photo blocking my view. I was glad to see her go, until Rotimi began to scream and I had to get up from the bed to pick her up from the cot. Moomi would have done that if she had waited. She would have rocked the baby to silence while I dreamt.

I did not know what to do with the screaming girl whom we were already pleading with, every day, every moment we called her name: Rotimi— stay with me. I closed my eyes when she suckled at my breast, careful not to make eye contact with her. I had the washerwoman come in every other day to wash the baby things. I was not strong enough to love when I could lose again, so I held her loosely, with little hope, sure that somehow she too would manage to slip from my grasp. I let her have the gold necklace I'd put on her for her naming ceremony, and whenever we left the house I wrapped it around her neck, placing the crucifix beneath her cloth, next to her skin like a talisman.

It happened on a Monday morning while Rotimi was sleeping. She did that a lot, she hardly ever moved an inch in her sleep.

On that Monday morning, she was not too hot or too cold. Her breathing was faint but sure and sometimes she chortled in her sleep. Was it because of her that things happened the way they did? Because I wanted to stay in the room with her and could not be downstairs in Dotun's room? Sometimes I think that if I had been in Dotun's room downstairs, I would have heard the car pull up in front of the house. I might have dressed hurriedly and left his room. But I always wanted it to happen the way it did. Somewhere inside me, I wanted Akin to walk in on us. I wanted to look into his eyes when he did; I wanted to see him explode in some kind of passion and, that Monday, I got exactly what I wanted.

When Akin walked in on Dotun and me, I was at once fulfilled and disappointed. I was disappointed because, in spite of myself, I still cared about the pain in his eyes. I shut my eyes to gather strength and raised my knees to accommodate Dotun and the only thing in focus was my husband and what he was seeing—the arch of Dotun's back, the feverish thrust of the hips, the shudder and the collapse.

Akin stood by the door, silent and unmoving until Dotun rolled off me and yelped when he noticed his brother in the room. Then Akin turned round, locked the door and slipped the key into his pocket.

He removed his jacket, folded it and laid it on the bed.

Then the fires of hell overflowed their banks and spilled into our bedroom.

PART THREE

31

I arrive in Ilesa just before midnight. My driver and I go from hotels to motels, and it seems as if the whole country is in Ilesa this Friday. We do not find any space until we get to Ayeso, the last part of town I would have chosen to stay in because it is so close to your father's house. But I have to sleep somewhere and I take the only vacant room at Beautiful Gate Guest House. I beg the attendant to allow Musa to sleep on the couch in what appears to have been a sitting room before, but now serves as a reception.

I am tired, but I cannot sleep. I step out of my room onto the adjoining balcony and I can see your father's house from here; right across the street, just after the point where the tarred road dips into a valley. It is easy to pick out because, apart from this guesthouse, it is the only house where the lights are on, thanks to a generator. There are several cars parked outside, double-parked on the main street. There are people eating on the balcony; there are people everywhere. Although I cannot see the backyard from where I stand, I can see smoke rising from there. I should be there now, keeping vigil over boiling stew and telling the hired cooks to turn over the sizzling meat before it gets burned, making sure they start cooking the Jollof rice by 5 a.m., yam and stew by 6 a.m., so that everyone can eat before they go to church for the funeral service. It is what wives do; I did it many times, do you remember? Did you even notice how hard I tried?

Why did you invite me for this funeral? How did you even know where I was? I thought you had wiped me off the way a teacher wipes off old notes from a chalkboard with a duster. Then I got that card in the mail and the printed words asked me to be the guest of Akinyele Ajayi. I watch the family house, hoping to recognise somebody, at least one of the people that I used to think of as family in this place that I once called home. But it is too far away. I can see people, but not their faces, and any of the men could be you. There are still canopies outside; I assume they are from the wake that was held this evening. I had no plans to attend that, to listen to you and your siblings tell carefully crafted lies about your dead father in between hymns.

I can imagine the measured words you must have spoken tonight, the platitudes expected from a first son. You would have delivered them well, made some people want to weep. Those who did not know your father would have been tempted to cry their hearts out that the world had lost such a gem at the tender age of ninety. Your mother would have, as always, been proud. Since you would have spoken first, none of your siblings would have matched your oratory skills, none of them could, even if they had a year to prepare. I am on the balcony until the lights go off in your father's house, then I go back into my room and fall asleep at once.

I am awake before 6 a.m. The floor feels cold and chills snake up my legs as I walk to the balcony. It is as though nobody went to bed at your family house. Maybe you closed up the house in Imo and slept here last night. I settle in a plastic chair and watch. I'm in no hurry to get ready because I will not be attending the church service.

The praise singer arrives around 7 with his mini megaphone. He stays on the street and chants, praising first of all Ijesa people, to whom your father belongs. I learned the verses of this *oriki* just before I married you. Your mother taught me every line she knew and I memorised them eagerly. She told me to wake you up in the morning on my knees, chanting the lines of your lineage's praise. I chose instead to cling to your body and whisper the words into your ears, but you did not like to listen to poetry in the mornings or at any time, and it was Sesan who would enjoy my renditions. The chanter is praising your paternal grandmother's family now. They still make my head swell, these words about people who were dead long before we were born.

There are tears in my eyes by the time the chanting finally gets to your father's *oriki*. I do not know if I am crying for myself, you, your father, all the years that have passed or because the praise singer renders the verses so beautifully. There is a woman standing beside the praise chanter—her hands are up in the air. I can see she is weeping, shaking her body until her wrapper slips to the floor. She does not pick it up. My hands are cold on my cheeks as I wipe away my tears.

There is such loud wailing when your father's coffin, white from where I sit, is brought out of the house. The wails reach a crescendo as the pallbearers hoist the coffin to their shoulders. People stand in twos or threes, holding on to each other as though they might collapse under the weight of grief if they do not hold on to somebody. A female voice pierces through the din and reaches me. "My father, is it really over? Are you really leaving us? Won't you wake up? Won't you wave goodbye? My father? My father?"

The pallbearers begin a march towards the hearse; a lone trumpeter leads the way, playing "Shall We Gather at the River." The praise singer, too, continues his chant.

Ma j'okun ma j'ekolo
Ohun ti won ba n je l'orun ni o maa ba
   won je

The little crowd that is gathered in front of your house disperses. Many climb into the parked cars. The cars begin to move slowly, forming a convoy behind the hearse. A pickup van that has a man hanging out of the window with a video camera on his shoulder is the first to gather speed. The hearse follows, its siren announcing your father's final departure from the neighbourhood where he spent most of his adult life. He will not be back here again; after the service, he will be interred in the church cemetery at Ijofi. Several cars follow the hearse, shiny jeeps and SUVs owned by his children and close relatives. I wait until the last car is gone before going back into my room.

I put on my clothes about the time you will be standing by your father's freshly dug grave, surrounded by family and clergy. You will be the first among the children to throw a clump of earth into your father's grave. The wailing will start again and as you all watch the grave diggers begin to fill up the grave with earth, even the men will become tearful. Couples who have not spoken to each other in weeks will hold hands. I was too shocked to cry at my father's funeral, but you had tears in your eyes even though you did

251

not let one of them fall. I held your hand while you sniffed and blinked rapidly.

Akin, who will hold your hand today if you cry silently?

32

The first time Dotun had sex with my wife, I stood in front of the bedroom door and wept. It happened on a Saturday. Funmi was visiting relatives or something. I was supposed to be at the sports club. I thought then that I had the capacity to play tennis or drink beer while my brother tried to get Yejide pregnant. I had it all planned so that by the time I got back home, Dotun would have left our room, Yejide would have put on her clothes, and I could act as if I didn't know what was going on.

But halfway to the club, I turned the car around and drove back home. Hoping I would find them in the sitting room, watching something on the television, sitting on opposite sides of the room. Thinking it was possible that Yejide wasn't as vulnerable as I'd imagined, that Dotun wasn't as persuasive as I'd believed and I would have a chance to tell my brother that I'd changed my mind. I wasn't sure about the plan anymore, could no longer bear the thought of his hands on my wife.

There was nobody in the sitting room.

Could have turned back when I stood in front

of our bedroom door, when it became obvious that it was too late to stop what I'd set into motion. I should have gone downstairs, left the house again. But I found that I couldn't move. I felt like my body was suddenly without bones, about to collapse. So I clung to the stainless-steel door handle with both hands, pressing my forehead against the doorframe. Tears began to slide down my cheeks as I imagined what was happening on the other side of the door.

Until that day, the tears I'd shed as an adult had all been because of Yejide. The first time was when she asked me if I thought she was responsible for her mother's death. *I'm sure my mother would still be alive if she had never conceived me,* she'd said, twisting a braid around her forefinger. I didn't know what to say, but my body responded to the utter despair in her eyes with the sting of tears in mine. She blinked and the despair was gone, just like that. Then she smiled and asked me to forget what she'd just said. *Of course it's not my fault; I didn't create my own head,* she said, letting the braid go. She moved on to another topic while I rubbed my eyes with the back of my hands. She didn't acknowledge my tears and I felt as if I'd just witnessed an argument she was having with herself. I realised that she hadn't looked into my eyes because she thought I would give her answers—she had looked in my direction only because I happened to be there.

Two weeks later, her father was dead. At his graveside, I was shocked by how her stepmothers went out of their way to make sure that Yejide stood without any family member by her side. They all moved from one side of the grave to another so that Yejide and I stood alone like outcasts. When I nudged Yejide and asked that we both follow her siblings and stepmothers, she smiled and told me that they'd moved because of her and if we went to their side, they would all simply move again.

Yejide had mentioned before then that her stepmothers made a sport out of ostracising her. But until that day at the burial, I hadn't thought much about what it must have been like for her to grow up in a family where her only ally was her father. Her father, the man who had told her more than once that the love of his life could have lived forever if only Yejide's head had been smaller when she was an infant, small enough for her mother to push into the world without losing too much blood. The tears I managed to hold back at the funeral were not for Yejide's father—I met the old man just once before he passed on. Tears blurred my vision because of the lonely little girl who had become the woman whose hand I held as she bent over to throw a handful of sand on her father's coffin.

Long before I discussed it with him, I knew Dotun would agree to have sex with my wife. Steeled myself ahead of time and assumed that, when it eventually happened, the only emotion I'd have left would be pity for Yejide. She tried to act the part of a good in-law around my brother, but I knew she despised him and thought his wife was unfortunate to have married him. Once, she'd let it slip that she could hardly believe that we were brothers. She didn't explain what she meant, but I knew she was trying to say she believed I was Jekyll and he was Hyde. I thought I'd pity her for the guilt she'd carry; feel sorry that she had to find comfort in a man she despised. Didn't imagine that Dotun's touch would ever become something she enjoyed. But that Saturday, instead of feeling any emotion for my wife, I wept because I felt humiliated, hopeless, angry. My tears had nothing to do with Yejide. I didn't give a damn about how she felt that day. Rage coiled itself around my throat like a constrictor, made my eyes water, gave me a sharp pain in my chest each time I took a breath.

The tears were gone by the time Dotun stepped out of the room—shirtless, beads of sweat around his collarbone like a melting necklace. All I had left was the rage that was choking me.

"She's in the bathroom," he said as he shut the door behind him. "You said you were going to the club. Brother *mi*, are you OK?"

I turned around then, dashed down the stairs, drove off before Yejide could realise I was back in the house. I spent the rest of the day driving around town, returning home when it was almost midnight.

Yejide was still awake when I entered our bedroom. I remember thinking as she came to me and put her arms around me that it was the first time I wanted to hurt her, to make her feel pain. My hands shook when I touched her hair. I'd always felt I didn't deserve Yejide, and that day as I opened the bedroom windows to let in some fresh air, I knew I would never become the kind of man who deserved to have her.

The next evening, Dotun went back to Yejide upstairs as planned. I drove to Ijesa Sports Club, tried to eat catfish pepper soup. When I got back home, Yejide was in bed, curled up, blubbering about something I couldn't make out. I took off my shirt and singlet, held her while she cried and talked about how she'd been so sure she'd been pregnant that first time. *I felt it kick,* she said. And though all I could think about as I kissed her face was how Dotun had been in that same bed with her earlier that day, I managed to reassure her, told her it was a matter of time before she really conceived.

That was all it took to have Olamide—one weekend. The master plan was to have four children: two boys, two girls. Once every other year, Dotun was supposed to spend a weekend with us, get my wife pregnant, and go back to Lagos. I always assumed I was the instigator, the one who decided when it was time for them to go into a room and make babies. After Rotimi was conceived, I decided that it would be cruel to bring another child into the world when it was possible that he or she would go through the kind of pain Sesan had endured. I told Dotun that our arrangement was over. And I never thought that I would return home one day to find him thrusting into my wife without my permission.

When I walked in on the two of them the rage that had stayed coiled around my throat since that first Saturday stirred again, tightening its hold. My eyes met Yejide's and I felt ashamed. The eyes that had once looked at me as though I was all she had in the world now stared at me with contempt. She glared at me as if I was an insect she would like to crush. She made no move to stop Dotun, just turned her head. I realised that while I'd thought my brother and I would trade places once in a while, truth was that from that first Saturday he'd occupied vistas I'd never even glimpsed.

I waited until Dotun rolled off her and saw me. He leapt off the bed. I took off my jacket, took my time, folded it, then placed it on the bed. There was no ready weapon within reach, no pestle, no sharp knife waiting for me to grab.

I marched towards Dotun, armed with the only weapons I really needed—my raging anger, my clenched fists.

"Bros Akin . . . wait, wait, Bros Akin . . . don't let the devil use you, *Egbon mi* . . . please, don't be . . . wait . . . the devil's tool . . ." Dotun screamed, wrapping a bedsheet around his torso.

I laughed, the sound clawing its way out of me, scratching my throat. "Devil's tool? *Me?* You bastard." I punched his mouth, his nose, his eyes. I felt his skin give way, heard his bones crack and saw blood flow from his nose. The pounding in my head intensified each time I rammed my fist into Dotun's face. He kept backing away from me, until he tripped on the sheet he'd used to cover himself. He fell, hit his head against Yejide's bedside table on his way down, knocking her lamp over. He landed on his back and the bed sheet unwrapped itself from his body.

I knelt over his bare belly and punched—his neck, his chest, the hands that tried to ward me off. There was blood on my hands—his blood, my blood. The blood seeped into the rug on the floor, spreading into a map-like stain that would never wash out.

"I trusted you!" I got off him, kicked his chest until there was a bleeding gash below his nipple. He coughed blood onto the rug. Blood and a tooth; the tooth shone in the small red pool.

He tried to say something, then coughed and spluttered more blood.

It enraged me, the still-moist, limp penis between his legs. I thought of where the penis had just been and a lifetime of rage heated up my head. The images of him with Yejide that I'd spent my waking hours fighting for years, pictures that dragged me down in dreams each time my head hit a pillow, broke loose from the cage of denial I'd constructed for them.

I knelt between Dotun's spread-eagled legs, grabbed his limp penis and twisted it. His scream would have deafened me if I'd heard it, but the sound of my head exploding shut out everything else.

There were soft hands on my shoulders, pulling me back. I kept twisting, twisting.

"For God's sake, Akin. Don't kill him, please." Yejide was on her knees beside me, still naked.

I took my hands off Dotun. "Shut up, you whore."

"Me? Akin, me—a whore? A dog will eat your mouth for saying that." Her voice was angry, not pleading.

I reached for the knocked-over lamp, yanked its cord out of the socket.

"What are you doing?" Yejide's voice was shrill with panic. "Akin, Akin?"

I lifted the lamp with both hands.

Yejide wrapped her hands around my chest,

tried to pull me off Dotun. "Akin? Akinyele, I beg you in the name of God, don't let the devil use you."

Dotun tried to sit up, covering his eyes with his hands. I hit him on the chin with the lamp, knocked him back to the ground. Yejide said something, but all I could hear was the pounding in my head, the sound of glass cracking. I smashed the lampshade against his head, shattered its glass panels and low-watt bulbs against his scalp until he was still.

I got up, cradling what was left of the lamp against my chest.

"You have killed your brother," Yejide whispered behind me. "You've murdered your own mother's son."

And I hoped she was right.

33

During the next couple of weeks, Yejide spent her mornings in the hospital with my brother. She stopped talking to me, would just leave my breakfast on the dining table as though she was leaving food out for a dog, then tie Rotimi to her back and head to the hospital.

I wished Dotun were dead, that he'd never been born.

But this is a lie. What I wished was that I was dead, that I'd never been born. I brought Dotun into our home, invited him, cajoled him, threatened him, did everything I could to convince him. Never imagined that I would ever in seven lifetimes have to see my brother thrusting into my wife, grunting like a pig as he came. As I factored unforeseen circumstances into my plan, I'd left out the things that would ruin it: sickle cell, Dotun losing his job, and all the mess of love and life that only shows up as you go along.

The day after my fight with Dotun, Moomi showed up in my office just before lunchtime. She didn't respond to my greetings, didn't take a seat, she came straight to my side of the desk and leaned over my chair.

"You were both inside me," she cried, slapping

her belly. "The two of you sucked these breasts that are on my chest. Was my breast milk not sweet? Is that the root of wickedness in your heart? Was my breast milk sour? Akin, answer me. Can you not hear me? Are you now deaf?"

She was so sure there was an explanation, that there was something I would say to help her understand what had happened. I could sense that she would take anything I said to her in that moment, anything at all, and shape it to suit herself. Shape it into a reason that explained it all. All she needed was an answer, any answer.

I didn't say a word.

"You want to kill me," she said, grabbing my shirt at the collar with both hands. "Make me understand why my own sons will try to kill each other. Tell me right now as I stand here!"

I could see her heart breaking, but what was I to say? The truth? I knew it would have finished her. This truth.

She left with a promise never to speak to me until I explained why I'd tried to kill her precious son. I knew she would keep her promise. My mother could hate as fiercely as she loved.

I worked until I was almost too tired to drive home. Stumbled into the house when the lights were already out and Yejide was asleep. But Rotimi was still awake and her eyes latched onto me the moment I walked into the dimly lit room. I stood by her cot, listened to her soft babble, let her wrap her little fingers around my thumb. In her eyes, I was brand-new, forgiven, unstained. I waited until she drifted off to sleep before I climbed into bed.

And though I was worn out, I couldn't sleep. I stared at my wife and wondered if the rage pounding in my brains would ever be intense enough to make me smash a lamp into her head. I hated myself because I watched her delicate face until I fell asleep, etching each feature into my mind in case she was not there when I woke up.

During the following weeks, I kept expecting her to leave me. It seemed to me that it was the only thing left to be done. Some nights I traced her lips with a finger and whispered *I'm sorry* into the silent space between us.

I hated myself for this too.

On the day Dotun was to be discharged, Yejide spoke to me for the first time in over a month. She gave me his hospital bill. I wrote a cheque. That evening, she moved out of our bedroom.

"I am staying because of my child. If not, if not, if not, *ehn* . . ." She let the threat hang unspoken, like a dark cloud between us.

"You bloody . . . bloody . . . did my brother behind my back. You are the unfaithful wife." I trembled when I said this, kept my fists in my pockets, fought the urge to plant them in her smug face, because if I started I would never stop.

"You would have preferred it in front of you? Under your careful supervision? You are a cheat, a betrayer and the biggest liar in heaven, hell and on earth." She spat at my feet, entered her new room, slammed the door.

I let the rage loose, punched the closed door until my skin bruised and bled. And even then, I didn't stop. Couldn't stop.

Yejide didn't lock the door. There was no click, no key turning on the other side. It occurred to me that I could just turn the knob and go in, face her. Ask her what she knew, what Dotun had told her about me while they were cavorting. I didn't have to stand alone in the corridor, speaking with my fists to a wooden door that wouldn't answer, lifting my shoulders so I could wipe sweat off my face with my shirtsleeve. Not tears. Sweat.

34

When my father-in-law invited Akin and me to a family meeting, I knew before we arrived in Ayeso that Moomi was the one who must have pushed him to call the so-called emergency meeting. I held Rotimi in front of me like a shield as we entered the sitting room and sat beside each other on a brown couch. The couch was small and for the first time since he'd caught Dotun on top of me, Akin and I sat right next to each other—we were so close I could feel him breathing. Dotun was already there, seated beside his father, when we arrived. I had not seen him since he had been discharged from the hospital.

Moomi was the first to speak: "My sons are here to explain why they fought, why they could not bring whatever disagreement they had to the family to settle. They are here to explain why they want to disgrace our family and make us the topic of gossip in the marketplace."

"No, stop there. You mean to you, Amope. They have disgraced you. The whole world knows my name is a good name in Ijesaland," Akin's father said.

"It is that way now, Baba? Now they are my sons? Useless man, of course they are my sons, since you never spent a kobo on them. I paid the school fees, bought uniforms and when they graduated from the university you just showed up for the pictures. But now again they have become my sons?"

"Are they not your sons? Did you steal them from the hospital?" Akin's father wagged a finger in Moomi's face. "Ha! That is what you are here to tell us, that you stole them from a ward, *abi*?" He laughed at his own joke.

Moomi hissed. "But this is not your fault. It is the children of the orange tree that cause clubs and stones to be thrown at their mother. Foolish children, explain yourselves—explain. Speak the words that are lodged in your mouth." She glared at Akin, then at me, waving her arthritic hands at us like oversized claws.

Dotun cleared his throat. His left hand was still in a sling, there was a bandage around his head and one side of his face was covered in tiny stitches.

"We had an argument about money," Dotun said.

Beside me, Akin's body relaxed with what I imagined was a sigh of relief. I should have been listening and committing the story Dotun was telling to memory. I should have mastered every detail to retell to relatives who were bound to quiz me later on, with expressions of concern, eager for gossip to down with their pounded yam at family gatherings. But by then I no longer

267

cared about what Akin's family thought. I was letting go already, even though I did not know it yet. So I rocked Rotimi and fiddled with her necklace, pressing my thumb against the hard edges of the crucifix that lay beneath her blouse. I did listen when Akin began to speak. I was amazed by how easily he plugged the holes in his brother's story. It was as if they had rehearsed the lies over and over.

"The money was not mine. I borrowed it from the bank. After all I did, after all my sacrifices for him, how could Dotun gamble it away?" Akin said, slapping his knee.

"Brother *mi*, I did not gamble. It was a business that went bad. It was supposed to bring in more than enough money to pay off the loan, but many things went wrong." Dotun did not look in our direction as he spoke, his head was bent down and he seemed to be starring at the crisscross patterns on the blue linoleum that covered the floor.

"It was not a business; if you were not so stupid you would have known they were fraudsters. Wouldn't we all be rich if money doublers really existed?"

"Money is a tiny thing," Akin's father said, tapping Dotun on the shoulder.

Akin and Dotun kept weaving the strands of their lies until their story was as strong as a rope of truth.

"You must not allow money to come between you. You have the same blood in your veins. What example do you want to leave for your children if you allow money to divide you?" my father-in-law said when his sons were quiet.

Moomi snorted and shook her head, but her husband ignored her and kept talking.

"You must reconcile, apologise to each other." The old man leaned forward in his seat and gestured with his hands. "Unity—every family must have unity. Have you forgotten? A single broomstick is useless, but when you put it in a bunch, what does it do?"

"It sweeps the house until it is clean," Akin said.

"So you understand what I have been trying to say?" my father-in-law said.

Dotun touched the side of his face that was half covered with stitches. "I am sorry, Brother *mi*, don't be angry with me. I will find a way to get the money back for you."

Akin coughed. "It was the devil that used me, Dotun. That anger, I don't know where it came from."

"It is over." My father-in-law turned to face Moomi. "Iya Akin, are you at peace now? I told you Yejide had nothing to do with it. She cannot come between them for any reason. How can you even imagine she would be involved in such a thing?"

"All I know," Moomi said, standing up and coming to stand in front of Akin and me. "All I know is this: anything that is done in the deep darkness will one day be talked about in the marketplace."

I looked down at Rotimi and saw that she had fished out the crucifix from beneath her blouse and was now sucking on it. I removed it from her mouth, careful not to hurt her gums.

Moomi leaned towards me. "You can never cover the truth. Just as nobody can cover the sun's rays with his hands, you can never cover the truth."

Whenever I went into the salon, the first thing I did was hand Rotimi over to Iya Bolu. It was Iya Bolu who tied Rotimi to her back if she cried and followed her around the passageway after she started crawling. She was the one who noticed when her first tooth emerged and cheered on the day she clung to the leg of a stool to hoist herself up.

"Why are you behaving like this?" Iya Bolu said, picking Rotimi up when she began to cry.

"Behaving how?" I rinsed out a batch of rollers and put them in a colander.

"You did not even glance at her when I told you that she stood up. Is it not your business?" She patted Rotimi's back and rocked her.

I gave her the feeding bottle into which I had

expressed breast milk in the morning. "Maybe she is hungry."

"You, this woman. I have told you that this child is too old for just breast milk. Why are you behaving as if your ears have been nailed shut? Rotimi, sorry *o jare*, manage her breast milk, don't mind your mother, just manage it this time."

I was grateful for the silence when Rotimi began to suckle from the bottle's teat. The sun was already setting and I had developed an ache around my knees and ankles from standing throughout the day. I reached for my purse and counted out some change for the two girls who had stayed behind to help with cleaning up. After the girls slung their handbags over their shoulders and left, I sat beneath a dryer and lowered the hood. Iya Bolu was still speaking to me, but from under the dryer it sounded as if she was speaking from a far-off place, another room, another world. Her words did not seem so important while I stayed beneath the dryer, they were not things I needed to think about or respond to in any way. I shut my eyes to heighten the effect of being far from everything, of being alone.

"When are you going to make fresh fish and mash for Rotimi? Or even just buy formula and milk?"

"I'm busy," I said, crossing my legs so I could massage my knee.

"Iya Rotimi, fear God-o. You are too busy to buy formula for your baby? If there is something that is bothering you, let us talk about it. Get it off your mind so that you can take care of your child."

"Has she finished eating? We need to get home before it is totally dark."

"Come and snatch the bottle from her now. You are not even listening to what I am saying." She turned to the child. "Rotimi, don't you worry. I will buy some formula for you very soon. Don't mind that woman, she will soon come back to her senses, I am sure."

I yawned.

Dotun came to the salon the next day while I was braiding a little girl's hair. I asked him to take a seat and wait because I never allowed the stylists in training to touch a child's hair. I believed their scalps were too tender to be used for training. When I was done braiding the hair, I took my time rubbing pink oil into the lines in between each braid and waited until the girl skipped out of the salon before I went to sit beside Dotun.

"Would you like something to drink? Coke or Fanta?"

"No," he said and sighed. "I came to say good-bye. I'm leaving Ilesa tomorrow. For Lagos."

"Oh, OK. Did you get a job in Lagos?"

"Something like that."

I did not ask him to elaborate because I really did not care. The extent of my interest after Akin had injured him was to make sure that he lived. I wondered why he had come to me to say goodbye.

"I will miss you," he said.

I looked at his face then—really looked. The bandage around his head had been removed to reveal a large scar where the glossy stitches would never allow hair to grow again. He appeared to have lost some more weight and there was a hopeful smile on his face. I wondered if he expected me to say that I would miss him too.

"Safe journey. You should greet your wife and children for me," I said.

He looked away and touched the scar on his head. "I went to Akin's office this morning. He told his secretary to send me away."

"*Brother* Akin," I said. "You have no right to call him 'Akin,' he is not your mate."

"Wait, Yejide. Me?" He jabbed his chest with a finger. "You are angry with me?"

"Keep your voice down."

He shook his head. "It is not my fault, you know, Yejide. It was all his idea."

"Dotun, you and your brother conspired against me."

"Look, Yejide, I thought you knew." He placed a hand on my knee. "He said he was going to tell you everything."

"You need to go now, Dotun. You can see I'm at work. I don't have time for all this."

"I will miss you." This time he whispered the words and they sounded as if they were meant to convey something he could not say.

I pushed his hand off my knee and stood up. "Have a safe trip tomorrow."

I walked away from him and went to an elderly woman who was hovering around the stylists, but had not taken a seat.

"Good afternoon, *Ma*," I said. "Has nobody attended to you?"

"Oh, they have, my dear. But I told them I would wait for you. I don't want anybody to ruin the scanty hair I have left."

I smiled and led her to a chair. In the corner of my eye, I saw Dotun stop by the door to say hello to Iya Bolu and Rotimi before leaving the salon. I waited as the woman in front of me removed her scarf, and thought about what Dotun had meant by repeating himself. He would miss me? The woman's hair was not scanty at all, but full and long, streaked with white in front. I remembered who she was as I ran my hands through her hair. She was a retired principal who came in to have her hair braided once a month and always insisted on using nothing other than the shea butter that she brought in a plastic container.

"Have I told you?" Iya Bolu had come to stand

274

beside me. "Have I told you about my niece's wedding?"

"No," I said, combing the retired principal's hair.

"It is happening next year-o, my brother's first daughter is getting married. Was it not just yesterday they gave birth to her? *Na wah.*" I could see Iya Bolu's reflection in the mirror. She held Rotimi up and grinned at her. "Before you know it, we'll be dancing at Rotimi's wedding too."

I was sure she had said the same thing about Olamide and Sesan and I was definitely not looking ahead as far as Rotimi's wedding. Hope was a luxury I could no longer afford.

"That is how it always seems-o, children grow up so fast," the retired principal said, smiling. "My youngest daughter got married last year. You know, I can still remember when I discovered I was pregnant with her, now she too will soon be a mother."

"Congratulations, madam," I said, picking up a wooden comb.

"Thank you."

"So when is this wedding?" I asked Iya Bolu.

"Sometime in June maybe, they have not fixed the exact date yet."

"Hope the elections won't affect the preparations," my customer said, bending her head so I could part her hair into four equal parts.

"That's why they are still waiting to fix the exact date. My brother wants to be sure about the exact date the elections will take place."

I scoffed. "Do you think there will be any elections? This Babangida who has postponed the date time and time again?"

"Transition," my customer said. "This is a transition. A transition is a process. It is not a one-off event. There is no need for us to be cynical. There have been setbacks, but I think they are quite understandable."

"Me, I don't think the man is going anywhere. This election story is another fraud. They are just deceiving us, these military people."

"This time he is leaving, I'm telling you. Just remember I said so. At least we have civilian governors now, and the legislators will take office by December. It is a gradual transition, step by step, my dear. That is the only way to ensure lasting change."

I stuck the wooden comb in one half of her hair and began to braid the other half. I had no faith in the so-called gradual transition. My customer was obviously invested in the whole process. She reeled off dates and statistics like someone who spent her days reading newspapers. I nodded as she explained why the federal military government had every right to create and fund the two political parties that existed in the country. She found a way to justify the fact that

276

the government had written the constitution of both parties and designed their emblems.

"Look," she said, "it is not the perfect situation, but once we move into a democracy, things will be different. Let's just get the country into a total democracy first. After we do that, we can get everything else in line."

I let the issue go because I didn't care that much about it. As far as I was concerned, 1993 would come and go and at the end of it we would know if the government was serious about its promise. I had no intention of registering to vote.

"By the end of this year, the government will tell us when the elections will be and my brother will fix a definite date. And you, Iya Rotimi, you must go with me to Bauchi," Iya Bolu said. "Whichever day the wedding is, you must go with me-o."

"Bauchi, *ke*? That is where your brother lives? That is a long journey-o."

"That is why I am telling you now. Start preparing your mind."

"OK, I will think about it," I said. "But I've not agreed to go yet, Iya Bolu. I will keep it in mind anyway."

"You know if you go with me, you can buy gold in Bauchi to sell here. Remember my customer who was asking if you sold jewellery? Now you look at me, *abi*? I know that one will entice you now. I talk about business and your ears stand up.

My brother's wife is into the gold business. She can show you all the places where you can buy, and who knows, maybe Bauchi gold will sell here."

"That is an interesting idea," I said as I rubbed shea butter into my customer's scalp.

35

One Monday afternoon, Linda, my secretary, came into my office and gave me a letter. I usually went through the correspondence in the morning, once I was done reading newspaper headlines, before my daily meeting with the head of operations.

"This just came in, sir," Linda said before I could ask her why the letter hadn't been included in the folder of mail that she made sure was on my desk before I came in each day.

I examined the envelope and recognised the cursive handwriting immediately. Each postage stamp bore "Australia 45c" above the image of a long-tailed rat. I tore open the envelope and pulled out the single sheet it held, spreading it out.

Brother *mi*,

How are you? As you must know from the stamp, I am now in Australia. I arrived here just last week. Please let Moomi know I'm safe.

Let me start by saying thank you for all you did for me after I lost my job. I didn't have the chance to thank you before I left. I want you to know I appreciate all your efforts to help me secure another job and get back on my feet. I am really grateful to you for giving me a roof over my head after I lost all I had.

About everything that happened before I left Nigeria, I want us to forget about it all. We can't keep fighting over this thing, you know. We are brothers, we are blood. A woman can divorce you, family can't. I'm still surprised that you did not even grant me an audience when I came to your office. I can excuse what happened at your house, you were angry so you beat me up. I can forget that, we can both put it behind us and move on. But from the way you turned me away from your office, it appears you want us to start a feud over this issue. Brother *mi*, get this right. You can't fight with me. You can't fight with family.

Is Yejide still with you? I'm sorry if she left, because I know you loved her. At least I think you did. You can't blame me for her leaving. Your marriage already had problems. She is such an understanding woman. She would have listened and understood you, I'm sure of it. I didn't mean to tell her any secrets. I thought you had told her everything, not half-truths. I just assumed that you had told her like you promised.

She is an easy woman to talk to. An easy woman to love.

Anyway, the important thing is that we must forgive each other and move on. As for me, I have already forgiven you.

I will be expecting to hear from you very soon.

With all due respect,
Dotun

I considered throwing the letter in the shredder, but I tore it up instead, into tiny pieces. I wondered if he'd told Yejide that he was leaving the country, if she'd given him money for his flight. The Dotun I knew was broke. I couldn't figure out how he could have managed to travel anywhere without my help.

Dotun's letter destabilised me, but answered the only question I'd wanted to ask him after I'd caught him with my wife. It told me he'd been stupid enough to discuss me with Yejide. I'd been wondering how much she knew and I'd almost concluded that Dotun had already told her the secrets I'd confided in him. It was there in the defiant way she carried herself, the movement into another room, the way her eyes had met mine when I walked in on them. But I'd been hoping that Dotun had kept his big mouth shut. I reasoned that all we'd been through was enough to make Yejide angry, told myself it explained her silence, the contempt that remained in her eyes.

I'd managed to convince myself before Dotun's letter came that she would have confronted me if she'd known, given me a chance to explain myself. Not that I had anything to say—I would probably have told more lies. But only because I still had hope; I always had hope that everything would change and the lies would not matter anymore. I was still seeing a specialist in Lagos University Teaching Hospital, and he had expressed some optimism. I'd taken his cautious comments and run with them, told myself it would be any day now, convinced myself the specialist in LUTH could work miracles. We'd find the right cocktail of medication and all would be well. Hope has always been my opium, the thing I couldn't wean myself off. No matter how bad things got, I found a way to believe that even defeat was a sign that I was bound to win.

In the weeks that followed the arrival of Dotun's letter, I felt as though our house had shrunk. It felt tiny, too small to keep me from running into Yejide. For the first time since she moved into another room, I was happy that I was alone in my bed. I stopped eating the food she left out for me, wondering for a few days if she planned to poison me, to punish me without ever confronting me.

I was too ashamed to force the confrontation I'd dreaded, had wished away since the first time I saw her and decided nothing could keep me from spending the rest of my life with her. I slunk around the house, left for work early, arrived home late. I spent my weekends alone in my room, rethinking every choice, retracing my steps backwards, asking if I really had a choice, if there were things I could have done differently. Before I had fully recovered from Dotun's first letter, the next one arrived.

Brother *mi*,

How are you? And how is Moomi? Are you hearing from Arinola and her husband?

I have a job here now. I am making money. Small small money, but I survive.

I know you got my last letter. Why won't you write? How can I get you to write?

Brother *mi*, let me try and explain things from my side of the story. The first time I had sex with your wife, it was to save your marriage. I still haven't got a thank-you for that, you self-righteous man. I even closed my eyes when she undressed that day. You know that first time, I tried to kiss her, not because I particularly wanted to but because it seemed the thing to do to make it less like rape. We had chaste sex like they do on home videos,

283

with the sheets firmly covering our bodies as though someone was watching. I honestly thought you had told her everything like you promised. And when I discussed it with her the first time, it was only because you were away, and she'd just got the news that Sesan had sickle-cell disease. I felt she needed someone to talk to, that was all. Did I want her? To be honest before you and your Creator, yes. But, I didn't tell her all that to betray you. I thought she already knew. Brother *mi*, that is all I can say.

Ajoke is remarrying. She is marrying a major general. His name is Garuba and he has three wives already. Isn't she stupid, this my ex-wife, marrying a military man just when they are going out of power? She says the children will be coming over here for the holidays. I believe the general will be footing their bills.

WRITE ME. I will be expecting your letter.

With all due respect,
Dotun

P.S. When you write, tell me about the presidential elections. There is no way for me to know what is really going on in Nigeria. I want to know what is going on.

I felt no anger as I fed the second letter to the shredder. The shame I felt left no room for any other thing, not even hope. I was not angry with my brother anymore; already I was realising that all the rage had been an affectation. Something I'd reached for to use as a defence against shame. Anger is easier than shame.

Rotimi saved me from my despair, helped me find my way back to hope. I returned from work one night, in the early hours of the next day actually—it was almost 2 a.m. when I walked into my room and found Rotimi asleep in her cot. At first I thought Yejide had moved back into our room, so I knocked on the bathroom door, opening it slowly when there was no answer, but she was not in there.

I went into the corridor, opened the door to Yejide's new room about halfway, felt some relief when I saw she was there, asleep in bed. I returned to my room, wondering what message Yejide was trying to pass by pushing Rotimi's cot back into what had once been our room. I didn't have enough energy left to think about it all. I stripped down to my boxers, climbed into bed and fell asleep.

Rotimi woke me up at 5 a.m. I stayed in bed, not surprised by the wailing, expecting it to stop without my intervention, as it always had before then. The cries continued, though, sounding angrier and louder until I could hardly believe the sounds were coming from someone so small. I got up, wondering what I would do with her after I picked her up. My first instinct was to take her to Yejide, but I didn't need to do that. Rotimi stopped crying once she was in my arms.

She was quiet but tense, breathing through her mouth, punching the air, blinking rapidly. After she calmed down, shut her mouth and laid her head against my chest, I decided to set her back in the cot. But she started yelling as soon as she left my arms. I picked her up again and she fell silent. She screamed when I tried to lay her on the bed, when I sat down, when I lay on my back with her on my chest. Took me a while to figure out what she wanted: to be in my arms while I was on my feet. She didn't go back to sleep for another hour. Nestling against me, she didn't do much, just yawned and watched my face. I didn't let her go after she fell asleep—there was something comforting about her weight and the warmth of her breath against my chest. It had been a while since I had been that close to another human being. I leaned against a wall, just holding her until Yejide came in around 7, took her from me without a word and left the room.

That day, I got home around 9 p.m. It was the first time I had arrived home before midnight since I'd received Dotun's letter. Yejide was in my room with Rotimi. She stood up when I walked in and handed Rotimi over to me.

"If she cries before eleven, give her some water." She pointed to a bedside table where she'd placed two vacuum flasks and several feeding bottles. "Or some pap, she likes that with milk. There are nappies in the bag on the floor."

I dropped my briefcase so I could hold Rotimi with both hands, surprised that her mother was speaking to me.

"Don't come and disturb me. I want to sleep. I'll come for her in the morning," Yejide said as she left the room.

And so, from that day on, I looked forward to coming home. Yejide didn't bother to explain the increasing number of baby items she was leaving behind in my room, just handed Rotimi over to me as soon as I walked through the door.

Every morning, Rotimi woke me up at 5. Her wails were as punctual as an alarm clock. I would lean against a wall and hold her for about an hour. I watched her face daily, looked into her eyes and felt something like faith, knowing even then that this one would live, she would stay. She was not a playful child; there was already something serious in the way she held her chin. She seldom babbled. Initially, our morning hours were quiet as long as I didn't try to sit down or let her go. And then one morning she looked up at me, one fist beneath her chin as though she was pondering what she was about to say, and said, "Baba." She said it two more times before she went back to sleep, as if she knew that I needed to hear the word again. Each time she said it, it was like an absolution. That simple word lifted the crushing weight of Dotun's letters and all my mistakes just a bit.

I felt as though she'd given me a gift, something almost divine because it was perfectly timed. She'd claimed me as her father. Yes, she was just a child who knew nothing about the workings of the world. But still, she claimed me as her father. I felt compelled to give something of myself back to her, to forge some connection that would last as long as we both lived. I started to whisper stories to her, told her the stories Moomi used to tell Dotun, Arinola and me.

I didn't have any favourites, but there was a story I still remember telling Rotimi very often. Moomi often began each tale with a saying. For this story, she always started by saying: *Olomo lo l'aye*—He who has children owns the world.

In the time of Forever, when most animals walked upright and humans still had their eyes on their knees, Ijapa the tortoise had a wife called Iyannibo.

They loved each other and lived happily together. They only had each other—they did not have a child, not even one solitary child. They begged Eledumare for a child for many years,

288

but none came. Iyannibo cried every day. Every day people ridiculed her everywhere she went, pointing their fingers and laughing behind her back in the market.

Iyannibo wanted a child more than anything else, more than life itself. So one day Ijapa got tired of seeing his wife cry, and he went to a faraway land where there was a powerful Babalawo. He had to cross seven mountains and seven rivers to get to this faraway land. It was a long road, but Ijapa did not mind. This Babalawo was the most powerful one in the world at that time. Ijapa was sure that if there was a solution under heaven, he would find it with the Babalawo.

When Ijapa got to the Babalawo, he begged the Babalawo for help. The Babalawo prepared a meal. He put it in a calabash and asked Ijapa to take it back to his wife. The Babalawo assured Ijapa that once the wife ate the meal she would get pregnant. He warned Ijapa not to taste the meal at all or open the calabash before he got home. Ijapa thanked the Babalawo and left with the meal.

On his way home, Ijapa had to cross the seven mountains and seven rivers again. The meal smelled so delicious, the sun was hot and he was tired. After the third mountain, he stopped beside the third river to rest and drink some water. There was nothing for him to eat, no fruit-bearing

289

trees around, not even grass. Ijapa was starving.

Ijapa decided to take a look at the meal, just one look. He was not going to eat the food at all; he would just look at it. He opened the calabash and saw that it was *asaro*. And it was rich *asaro*; as well as the mashed yam and palm oil, there was fish, meat, vegetables and crayfish.

Ijapa was tempted. His stomach grumbled very loudly. But he thought of his wife's empty arms and closed the calabash. He continued his journey. The sun became hotter, he became hungrier and even more tired. So he stopped after the fifth mountain just beside the fifth river to rest.

Ijapa thought to himself: I will just touch the meal with a finger and feel how the palm oil rubs against it. I can tell if the Babalawo used good quality palm oil that way. I don't want Iyannibo to eat anything that will upset her stomach.

Ijapa touched the *asaro* with just one finger. Just to tell the quality of the palm oil. He rubbed the oil between his hands. It felt right. It feels right, he said to himself, but it might still not taste right. So he took a tiny bit more and tasted it. Immediately, his stomach began to rumble like thunder and he wolfed down the meal in a few minutes. He could not resist or stop himself once that small taste passed the gate of his lips. He smacked his lips after the meal and washed his hands off at the stream.

Ijapa fell into a deep sleep immediately.

When he woke up, three days had passed, but he did not know this. He felt as though he had been sleeping for just an hour. He decided that he would head back to the Babalawo's house. I will just tell him the *asaro* fell and poured away, Ijapa said to himself. I am sure he will make another one for me, he is a kind man.

Ijapa tried to get up and realised it was a struggle. He looked down and, behold, his stomach was big. In fact, it was as big as that of a woman who had been pregnant for nine months.

As fast as he could, he ran back over the five mountains and four rivers that he had crossed. When he got to the Babalawo's house he sang:

Babalawo mo wa bebe
Alugbirin
Babalawo mo wa bebe
Alugbirin
Oni n mama f'owo b'enu
Alugbirin
Oni n mama f'ese b'enu
Alugbirin
Ogun to se fun mi l'ekan
Alugbirin
Mo f'owo b'obe mo fi b'enu
Alugbirin
Mo wa b'oju w'okun
O ri tandi
Alugbirin

291

Babalawo, I've come to beg you
Babalawo, I've come to beg you
You told me not to put my hand in my
  mouth
You told me not to put my feet in my
  mouth
The medicine you made for me the other
  time
I touched it and put my hand in my mouth
Then I looked at my belly
And it was big

Rotimi always fell asleep before I finished the song, so I'd stop telling the story then. I never began the story with Moomi's *Olomo lo l'aye* saying. I'd believed her once, I'd accepted— like the tortoise and his wife—that there was no way to be in the world without an offspring. I had thought that having children who called me Baba would change the very shape of my world, would cleanse me, even wipe away the memory of pushing Funmi down the stairs. And though I told Rotimi the story many times, I no longer believed that having a child was equal to owning the world.

36

Although lightning did strike the same spot twice, I didn't think it would leave destruction in its wake the second time around. I took Rotimi in for her genotype test shortly after her first birthday, then had my worst fears confirmed when I picked up the results on my way back from work a couple of days later. But I was calm by the time I got home, was sure my daughter would survive in spite of the red-lettered SS verdict on the result sheet. Still can't explain where the assurance came from, but it was there, firm as the ground I walked on. Yejide covered her eyes with her hands when I told her the results—other than that she showed no reaction to the news. And when Rotimi had her first sickle-cell crisis, she refused to stay with her in the hospital.

"Me? I should spend the night with her? Akin, I'm exhausted, totally exhausted," Yejide said, just before leaving the ward after Rotimi was admitted. "I need to rest."

I blamed myself for the way she spoke, as though all possibility of joy had been wrung out of her. I watched her trudge out of the ward, wondering if she just needed a good night's sleep or whether her tiredness had morphed into a permanent weariness.

After about two hours, I was allowed to sit with Rotimi. She looked so small, out of place in the hospital bed. She was hooked up to an IV drip. I wondered if it was enough, if the doctors knew what they were doing, using a single drip to battle something that had already snatched a son from us. I sat in a chair beside her bed, keeping my hands on the edge of the mattress, afraid to touch her.

"Mama?" she said after a while, lifting her free hand. "Mama *mi*?"

I cleared my throat and stared at the bedpost. "Your mother is tired, she is sleeping."

I couldn't look into her big brown eyes while I lied. Even with my eyes glued to the bedpost, the lies felt so wrong, like something I needed forgiveness for, forgiveness from a child whose face was a miniature version of Yejide's own. So much so that looking at her felt as if I was looking at Yejide through a minimising glass. Every feature on Rotimi's face belonged to Yejide, except for the nose. Her nose was already flat and wide, exactly like mine. I loved it when people noticed this, when they said, *This child has taken her father's nose.* Her father's nose.

Later that evening, a doctor trailed by students carrying notepads came in to check on Rotimi. I'd wanted to be a doctor once when I was a little child, before my right hand was long enough to touch my left ear, before I was old enough to start school. It was at a time when I didn't even know there were other professions, when I thought it was the only thing that people who went to school could become.

After the others had moved on to another patient, one of the students spoke to me in a hushed tone. "I'm carrying out a research, sir. It's about sickle-cell disease. It will help premarital counselling. I would be glad if you could fill—"

I nodded like an *agama* gone mad, snatched the questionnaire he was holding out to me, eager to get him out of my face. I wondered how many questionnaires Yejide had filled out during the days she'd spent in the hospital with Sesan. The questions were tightly packed on a single page as though the student was trying to save money on photocopying; just trying to read the words gave me a headache.

"Baba *mi*."

"Yes, dear. What?" I welcomed the distraction and put aside the questionnaire.

"Mama *mi*?" she asked, her voice barely audible. She breathed heavily as though saying that one word had sapped all her strength.

I held her hand, looked into her eyes this time. "Your mummy is coming, soon, very soon, but while we wait, let me tell you a story. It's about Ijapa the tortoise and his wife Iyannibo."

I repeated the beginning of the story, about the barren couple and the futile attempts to get pregnant. I described Ijapa's visit to the Babalawo, the pot of stew he couldn't resist, his shameful return to the Babalawo after he had ruined his only solution with his own hands. Rotimi was still awake when I finished the song, so I continued the tale.

When Ijapa got back to the Babalawo, he begged and begged. He rolled and rolled on the floor, begging for forgiveness, pleading for another chance.

"No, I cannot help you," said the Babalawo.

"Help me, not for my sake. Think of Iyannibo, my wife. Help me, no, help my poor wife, help her."

The Babalawo thought of poor Iyannibo. And though Ijapa had done something horrible, had disobeyed instructions, for the sake of poor Iyannibo, the Babalawo had mercy on him. He gave Ijapa a potion to drink. Soon after Ijapa drank it, his stomach was flat again.

The story Moomi told me doesn't stop there. Apparently the tortoise and his wife couldn't just stay as Mr. and Mrs. Tortoise, that wouldn't be enough. It goes on to tell how the tortoise's wife has a baby so that everyone can live happily forever and ever. I didn't bother to tell my daughter that part. It was the lie I'd believed in the beginning. Yejide would have a child and we would be happy forever. The cost didn't matter. It didn't matter how many rivers we had to cross.

At the end of it all was this stretch of happiness that was supposed to begin only after we had children and not a minute before.

Rotimi spent a week in the hospital that first time. I could only take two days off work to sit with her, but I spent the nights in the hospital, sleeping on a wooden chair in front of the ward, dreaming again for the first time in years about Funmi.

Funmi had been on my mind since Rotimi had been diagnosed. It was impossible not to wonder if Olamide and Sesan had died as a form of retribution. Whether, on some universal scale of justice, by some skewed process of karma or *esan*, the children had paid the price for my sin. Whenever I woke up from nightmares about Funmi, I couldn't help but wonder if the dreams were an omen about Rotimi's fate, if three children equalled an adult on the universe's scales of justice.

The thoughts never lasted beyond the dark hours before dawn. As the sun rose and I went in to check on my daughter, I was able to dispel them. This child was going to survive every crisis, be the exception to every rule—live—I was sure of it. If there was indeed a universal hand doling out justice, it would take me instead of the innocent children.

Besides, I'd never intended to kill Funmi.

On the night Funmi died, the night of Olamide's

naming ceremony, all I'd wanted was to make it to my bedroom without tripping on the stairs. Thanks to the bottles of beer I'd downed, the steps swam before my eyes. I held on to the banister as I climbed. Funmi was right behind me, slurring her words.

"So how did Yejide get pregnant?"

I didn't have to think before I answered, "The way people get pregnant."

Funmi laughed. "Do you think I'm a fool? Your lies and the fake nonsense you've been doing in bed, you think I don't know? Is it because I've not decided to expose you?"

I kept walking up the stairs. Whether I was too drunk to respond or I trusted that my silence would be interpreted in a way that favoured me, I can no longer tell for sure.

I do remember that Funmi grabbed my trouser leg from behind, but that didn't bother me.

"Tell me," she said. "Tell me how a penis that has never been hard makes a woman pregnant? And don't tell me again that it only happens when you are with me. I don't believe that anymore."

I've never been sure if Funmi whispered those words or shouted them. But that night it sounded as though the words were being bellowed, it felt as though they were echoing through every room in the house. She'd already let go of my trousers when I turned around to cover her mouth with my hand. And my palm did touch her face,

298

cover her mouth for a fleeting moment before she staggered, fell backwards, and tumbled down the stairs.

When she finally sent for me, Moomi didn't ask me to come and see her at home. She asked me to come to her stall in the market. It was a well-calculated insult. A move meant to remind me that she had never stepped into the shop I bought for her after Dotun left the country.

Moomi had always complained about the market. She hated the ground because it was slippery and muddy during the rainy season, hard and dusty in the dry season. She despised the market women who dumped their trash right into the street, hated the persistent din, the unbearable heat of several people pressing into each other, trying to make it through the narrow streets. She loathed how every day someone's hand, handbag or oversized ass would knock over her wares. How hurrying feet crushed her tomatoes and peppers before she could pick them up and put them back in the tray. But above all, she hated the stench—she never stopped noticing it. Her nostrils never adapted to the disgusting odour of too many things decaying in a single space.

All her life, even as a young bride whose husband refused to give the money for a wooden stall, Moomi had always believed that her place in life was well above a street-side stall in the market. In her heart, she knew her place was with the women who could afford to sell their wares in a shop, protected from the wicked heat of the marketplace. That was why I got her the biggest shop in the most expensive section of the market. Yet, when I visited her in Ayeso and gave her the keys to the shop, she threw them back at me.

When I showed up at her stall, she acted as if she didn't know me, refused to acknowledge my greeting. I sat down on a wooden bench for the next half-hour while she attended to customers.

I knew she was ready to talk to me when she pulled a transparent piece of nylon over her trays of tomato and pepper. She sat on the wooden bench, as far from me as she could possibly sit without sitting on air. She greeted me with the only words she'd deigned to speak to me since she had asked me to cut her legs off if she ever entered my house again. "Where is my son? When is Dotun coming home?"

Even though I'd told her Dotun was safe in Australia, doing very well too, if his letters were to be believed, she acted as if I'd locked him away in a basement, just so I could make her life miserable. I'd learned the hard way that there was no good way to answer her questions. All the answers I'd tried only fanned the flames of her anger. Ignoring her questions was the best thing to do, the easy thing to do.

"Why didn't you tell me to meet you at home? What can we talk about in the market?"

"Why? Akin asks me why. Let me tell you why, I have to come here and sell my goods because I don't want to eat grass and sand. You know that is what people eat when they don't have any money? I thank my God for your sister." She tilted her face to look at the skies. "My Maker, I thank you for Arinola, she always remembers her poor old mother. If I had given birth to just Dotun and this one here, I would have been boiling sand for breakfast now."

I sighed. "Moomi, is this what you have called me here to discuss?"

"And so? If that is what I want to say, are you going to walk out on me? It will not amaze me if you do. My words are meaningless to you now."

"Moomi, what do you want?"

She folded her arms across her chest. "You can perform any magic you want, keep tricking me. You're your father's son and you too can tell enough lies to wake the dead."

"Why do you want to see me?"

"Why are you shouting? Is that how you talk to your mother? Like a child with no home training?"

I took a deep breath. "I'm sorry, *Ma*. Don't be angry, please."

"How is your wife?"

301

"Fine."

"She didn't even send her greetings? So it has come to that now? You know she has not visited me in over a year? And we live in this same town, this same town."

"She has been busy with her work. She too doesn't want to eat grass and sand."

"You think you are funny, *abi*? Anyway, Arinola told me that Rotimi has been admitted to hospital. How is her body now?"

"She has been discharged."

"Hmmm, may God watch over her." She said the words with no passion, as if she were praying for someone she didn't know or care about.

I stared at passersby so I didn't have to look at her. "Amen."

She sniffed, then sighed. I knew I wouldn't like whatever she was about to say. I was familiar with her sniff-and-sigh move, it was an age-old tactic, a move she made to fortify herself when she was about to make demands that I would be reluctant to bend to.

"Why are you looking away?" she said. "Look at me, look at my face. The reason why I have said you should come to see me, even though you might have killed my son for all I know . . ." She sniffed. "Still, if the world sees how your life is starting to look like a madman's property, they will say that is Amope's son whose life is coming apart like an old rag. So I cannot keep silent even if you will say my mouth stinks. I will say my piece. Can you hear me?"

"I'm listening, *Ma.*"

"You see, it seems that your wife is destined to have *Abiku* children. You this boy, don't roll your eyes at me—you think I can't see you? You think I have gone blind?" She smacked the back of my hand. "If you live to be a thousand years, you will not be old enough to look at me like that. When all I am saying is for your own good! When everything I have done since you were born is for your own good!"

"Moomi, what do you want from me now? Please, just finish saying what you are saying."

"There is this girl, you may even know her." She shook her head. "No, she is not your mate at all, you can't know her. She is just out of secondary school. She is a good girl, her eyes are not open yet, you know, like these girls of nowadays."

"And?" I could feel a throbbing in my forehead, like the beginnings of a bad headache.

"God does what pleases Him—who knows, maybe this girl will be able to bear children for you, children who will live. I'm not saying Yejide is a bad person, but you can't fight destiny. And the way things have played out since you married that Yejide woman, I don't think she is destined to have children in this world. She has tried hard-o, even a blind person can see how hard

303

she has tried. But only a few people can win in a fight against their destiny. I have lived long enough to know that."

"You want me to marry this girl that you have found?" I turned away from her. Across the street, a man was gluing election campaign posters to a lamppost.

"Will you not have children in your life? What will you do if this Rotimi dies?"

"Rotimi is going to live." I wasn't trying to convince her. I believed it like it was a fact. The sun rose in the east, four plus four equalled eight, my Rotimi would live.

"See, even if Rotimi lives, just one child? All your life, one single child?"

"You want me to marry another wife, again?" The man across the street stepped away from the lamppost, examined the green poster, nodded, then moved to the next lamppost. The poster he'd put up was green and white, and from where I sat, I could make out "Hope 93."

"It is not by force. If you don't want to marry her, we can arrange something. Just get her pregnant." She slapped the back of one hand into the palm of the other hand. "Wisdom cannot become so scarce in this world to the point where we have to travel to heaven before we find some."

"*Lai lai*, Moomi. Never ever."

"Don't be so quick to say no. I know you are

304

thinking of what happened to Funmi, but . . ."

When she mentioned Funmi's name, I stopped hearing her words. I could only see her mouth move.

She tapped my shoulder. "Akin? Can't you hear me? Won't you say anything?"

I cupped my forehead with one hand, tapped my feet in tune to the throbbing rhythm in my head. "Moomi, as if you have not destroyed my life enough."

Her mouth dropped open. "Akinyele, what nonsense are you saying?"

"Don't involve yourself in this matter anymore, *ema da soro mi mo*, do you hear me?"

"Are you sick? What have I said that—?"

I stood up. "Don't call me for this kind of discussion again. Never again. *Lai lai.*"

"Me? *Abi*, you don't know who you are talking to *ni*? Akin? Akinyele? *Abi*, you are walking away, Akin? Come back here. Akin, I'm still talking to you. Are you not the one I am calling? See this boy. Akinyele!"

I didn't look back.

37

The few times my father told me about his love for my mother, he would end by saying, *Yejide, oro ife bi adanwo ni.* He used the saying as if it were the only part of all he had said that was worth remembering. I got the impression that he believed it was the lesson he had learned from my mother's life and her death, the wisdom that he had to pass on to me: *Yejide, love is like a test.* I never understood exactly what the implication of the saying was supposed to be. I didn't bother to ask him because I suspected that his explanation would involve his usual descriptions of how much my mother had suffered because of me. By the time I was a teenager, I was able to tune out his horrifying descriptions of how much she bled, but I never got over the way he looked at me when he talked about her death, as if he was evaluating me, trying to decide if I was worth what he had lost.

I would hear the saying many times from other people over the years and still never quite know what they meant each time. So love is like a test, but in what sense? To what end? Who was carrying out the test? But I think I did believe that love had immense power to unearth all that was good in us, refine us and reveal to us the better versions of ourselves. And though I knew Akin had played me for a fool, for a while I still believed that he loved me and that the only thing left for him to do was the right thing, the good thing. I thought it was a matter of time before he would look me in the eye and apologise.

So, I waited for him to come to me.

When Dotun had come into our bedroom just after Sesan was diagnosed with sickle-cell disease and told me that he was sorry Akin hadn't found a solution to his impotence, it was obvious that Dotun thought I already knew that half of Akin's trips to Lagos were made because he had to see the urologist at LUTH. The truth was that I knew nothing about the urologist, the drugs that had been prescribed, or the procedures Akin had undergone. But that night, because when life laughs at you, you laugh and pretend you are in on the joke, I nodded along with Dotun and tried to act as if I had been smart enough to figure things out by myself. But it was obvious before he left our room that Dotun too had realised that my marriage had been built around a lie.

In spite of it all, I was convinced that Akin loved me. And because love was supposed to be the test that brought out the best in us, I told myself that my husband would soon come to me and explain himself. I channelled my energy into keeping my son alive, but all the while I was waiting for Akin to come to me.

After he caught me in bed with his brother, I was sure Akin would confront me, apologise, share the struggles he'd managed to keep hidden from me and beg me to stay with him. It was hard to accept that he intended to keep up his deceit for the rest of our lives. Even after I moved out of our bedroom and stopped talking to him, I was sure that I knew who he really was and I believed that man was still there beneath all the deception and pretence. The man I thought I knew was not the kind of person who would have let me go to my grave while still deceiving me.

At some point during the weeks before Rotimi's first sickle-cell crisis, I came to accept that Akin would have spent the rest of our lives lying to me if he had found a way to get away with it. As I drove away from Wesley Guild Hospital after Rotimi was admitted there for the first time, I wondered how Akin could have asked me to stay with her in the ward. Did he not see that I was tired of all those doctors offering bad news, good news, grim silences, reassurances, and a hand on the shoulder to deliver more good news, bad news? Through Olamide and Sesan to Rotimi, I had been dangled from the edge of a precipice and I was now so weary that I wanted to be dropped.

By the time she was discharged and they came home together, I looked at Akin differently. I did not see him as someone who had changed, but as a man I had never known. I doubted the love I had once been so sure of and concluded that he had married me because he thought I was gullible.

A week before the presidential elections, I decided it was time to confront him. He was with Rotimi in the sitting room, watching the two candidates debate with each other on television. I saw no reason to wait until the end of the debate before starting the conversation; after all, I had spent almost three years waiting for him to come to me. On some level, I felt I had to strike when he did not expect it and give him no room to prevaricate. I sat in an armchair directly opposite him because it was a vantage point. I wanted to watch the emotions play out on his face and judge his reactions to my ambush.

"So, Akin, is it true that you can't . . . that you can't . . . Are you impotent?"

I wish I could say he respected me enough to answer my question directly when I finally confronted him. He smiled and leaned back in his chair until he was staring at the ceiling. He did not say anything for a long time.

I waited, watching as Rotimi climbed into his lap. On the television, the moderator was talking about the impact of the IMF's structural adjustment policy on Nigerian society.

"When did Dotun tell you?" Akin finally asked, pulling Rotimi closer to himself.

"Just before he told me that you asked him to seduce me."

There was no steam in our words as we spoke—no passion, no heat. We could have been discussing the rain that had fallen all morning. As Akin crossed and uncrossed his legs, I thought about the road we had walked until we arrived at the point where we sat opposite each other in our sitting room and discussed his impotence for the first time without displaying much emotion.

I thought about Funmi. I remembered how Akin had been so sure I wasn't pregnant, even before the doctors told me I had pseudocyesis.

Akin pinched his nose. "What are you going to do now?"

I almost smiled. Not much had changed about him. It was almost comforting to see that he was still avoiding the truth by responding to queries with his own questions.

"You have not answered my question," I said. "Akin, is it true?"

He covered his face with both hands as though he could not bear my gaze. I was not moved because I was consumed with a desire to hear him confess.

"Akinyele, why are you covering your face? Look at me and answer my question."

I felt no pity for him as he slid his hands from his face and wrapped them around his neck as though he wanted to strangle himself. How could

I? After all, he had looked me in the eye during the first year of our marriage when he said each penis was different, told me that some got hard, that others never did. He had said it casually, slipped it into the conversation so it sounded like one of the things men told their virginal wives about sex. I was amazed by the way he did not even need to tell lies in order to deceive me.

"Yejide, why do you want me to tell you what you already know?"

What did I know? I knew that I was once as invested in his lies as he was, probably more than he was—I imagine he at least admitted the truth to himself. I could not do that until Dotun had spoken the words. Akin was supposed to be the love of my life. Before I had children, he was my salvation from being alone in the world; I could not allow him to be flawed. So I bit my tongue when customers talked about sex and I let him hold my hand when he told the doctor our sex life was *absolutely normal.* I told myself I was respecting my husband. I convinced myself that my silence meant I was a good wife. But the biggest lies are often the ones we tell ourselves. I bit my tongue because I did not want to ask questions. I did not ask questions because I did not want to know the answers. It was convenient to believe my husband was trustworthy; sometimes faith is easier than doubt.

"I'm sorry," he said, patting Rotimi's head.

I knew then that he would not answer my question directly, not even if I held a machete to his throat.

"Did you fool Funmi too?" I asked.

He shook his head. "She was not like you."

I sighed. "You mean she was not foolish?"

"I only mean she was not a virgin."

I had nothing left to say to him, so I stood up and left the room. And he did not even bother to ask me to keep his secret—he already knew I would.

The preelection excitement that had gripped the country caught up with me in spite of myself. In the days that led up to the elections, I found myself humming along to campaign jingles. Iya Bolu had convinced me to register to vote. And I felt an unfamiliar sense of power as the elections approached.

Iya Bolu was at our house by 7 a.m. on the Saturday that we went to the polls. She could hardly sit still and kept asking me to hurry up so we would arrive at the polling station before 8. Akin had already left for Roundabout to vote: he had registered there since it was close to his office. Around 8:30, I tied Rotimi to my back and we set out.

By the time Iya Bolu and I got to the polling station, hundreds of people were already there. After we cast our votes, we sat in the shade of a mango tree and discussed her niece's upcoming wedding while we waited for the station's results to be announced. The ceremony was two weeks away, but we planned to leave for Bauchi some days before the wedding was to be held. Iya Bolu wanted to be on the ground to assist her brother's family with preparations for the event.

When the station's results were announced by an electoral official, whose spectacles covered half of his face, there was a round of applause and a number of people shouted "Congratulations, Nigeria." I was caught up in the momentary euphoria and shook hands with strangers as though we had survived a long and arduous journey together.

The day I left for Bauchi, I dressed Rotimi up in a sleeveless purple dress while Akin fiddled with the car downstairs. He was on annual leave and had decided to go to Lagos for a couple of days. I did not ask him why he wanted to be in Lagos— I did not want to know. Rotimi's dress was something Akin had bought because he thought I would be throwing her a party on her birthday. Of course there was no party, but Rotimi liked the dress and every time she wore it she would slide her palms over the lacy bodice and smile.

It took longer than usual to dress her that morning; she was cranky because I woke her up early so we could leave the house before 6 a.m.

313

After I convinced her to put on her shoes, I sat her on the dressing table and applied compact powder to my face. When I was done, I applied a light coating of talcum powder to her forehead, and she held her face perfectly still as I rubbed it over her skin. Then I sat on a stool and coated my lips with pink lipstick. While I peered into the mirror to make sure I did not have lipstick stains on my teeth, Rotimi leaned forward and pressed a thumb against my upper lip. I watched as she took her hand towards her mouth, expecting her to suck on the thumb, but instead she traced her lower lip, imitating the way I'd worked the lipstick.

"You are a clever one, aren't you?" I said.

She touched my mouth to get more lipstick, her finger soft against my lower lip, its pressure feather-light. When she was done smearing her thumb against her lips, I placed her on my knee so she could look in the mirror, but she barely glanced at it. She twisted until she was facing me, then she tilted her head this way and that beneath my gaze, as though I was the only mirror that mattered to her.

"You are the fairest of them all," I said to the one child whom I had never told stories. My stories and songs felt useless in the face of the disease she was battling, so I never bothered with them. I did not want to tell her tales, I wanted to heal her, save her. And as she pressed her lips

314

together the way I'd done moments before, I wanted to clutch her to myself until she somehow went back into my womb, from where she could reemerge with a new genotype, forever free from the constant threat of pain and disease.

It wasn't until Rotimi squealed that I realised I was gripping her shoulders and panting. I let go. This was why I did not allow myself to be alone with her too often—because of the thoughts that pushed me over the precipice into a bottomless pit where I flailed as I fell. I fought the sudden urge to lay my head on the dressing table and weep. I took a deep breath and arranged the gold necklace around my daughter's neck.

I held Rotimi on my knees as we drove to the estate where we used to live to pick up Iya Bolu. She was waiting on the porch with her travelling bag.

"Can you see your former house?" she said as she settled in the car. "The new family that moved in has destroyed it. Can you see the way the paint is coming off? They haven't even bothered to repaint it. And the man, he is a randy dog, I tell you."

Akin drove to Omi Asoro to pick up Linda, his secretary. She was also travelling to Lagos that morning and Akin had offered to give her a ride. When we arrived at Linda's house, she poked her head through a window and said she would be out within five minutes. While we waited, Akin fiddled with the car's radio, trying to get a station where the news was on. It was nine days after the elections and no winner had been announced yet.

"You are looking for updates on this election matter?" Iya Bolu said to Akin. "Like play, like play, it's almost two weeks now. It's another Monday already. How can the court give an order to stop the release of the results? Why?"

"Don't mind them. The court has no business with this issue and that judge knew that, only the presidential election tribunal has the jurisdiction."

"*Abi*, these soldiers don't want to leave power, *ni*?"

"But I know the military will still hand over," Akin said. "So much money has been spent on this transition. Are we going to throw it all down the drain?"

"God should just have mercy on us," Iya Bolu sighed. "*Abi*, our children are going to grow up under military government?"

I sneezed when Linda got into the car. It was as if she had emptied two bottles of whatever perfume she was wearing that morning. Akin switched off the air-conditioning and wound down his window.

I handed Rotimi over to Linda when we arrived at the motor park.

"Are you not bringing Rotimi with you?" Iya

316

Bolu said, slamming the car door shut and readjusting her wrapper.

I shook my head and waited while Akin opened the boot. He pulled out my travelling bag and led the way to the wooden shed where buses were parked. There were seven passengers waiting in the bus that was heading for Bauchi.

Akin gave my bag to the bus driver and then walked around the bus. He examined the tires and peered at the steering wheel, pedals and gearshift. It was something he always did whenever he dropped me off at motor parks. I had found it amusing when we were dating, but that morning I wondered what his real motives were. I now viewed his simplest actions with suspicion, wondering if some grand deception was motivating them.

"Linda and I will be on our way now," he said as I climbed into the bus.

"Have a safe trip," I said, shifting so Iya Bolu could settle in beside me. Akin and I were civil when we were in public together; sometimes we even made an effort to appear friendly.

"I will call you later tonight," he said. "Iya Bolu, you said it's OK to call your brother's house after seven p.m.?"

"Yes, there is no problem. Just tell their maid who you want to speak to."

"All right then, have a safe journey."

38

"Will madam be joining you later, sir?" The receptionist's eyes judged me incapable of taking care of Rotimi without a woman's assistance.

"Can you get room service to send a bottle of wine to our room?" I said. I'd spent hours in traffic after I got into Lagos around noon, and managed to arrive in time for the appointment with my urologist at LUTH—only to be informed that he'd taken ill and wouldn't be back at work until Thursday. I was in no mood to humour the receptionist with a response.

He nodded and picked up the phone.

I changed Rotimi's nappy after we got into our room. As I soaked the soiled one in the bathroom sink, I made a mental note to ask Yejide if it was time to potty-train her.

I didn't go down to the restaurant for dinner, but had some rice brought to the room instead. Rotimi didn't want to be fed. She kept trying to wrestle the spoon from my hands. Before I surrendered it to her, she'd thrown a piece of meat on the floor in anger. I switched on the television after room service cleaned up the mess Rotimi had made, paced the floor and argued with the television about what the hell was going on in the country. On the bed Rotimi laughed, clapping as though I was putting on a show for her. After an hour of flipping through channels, hoping for some update from the military government about the elections, I switched off the set, feeling agitated.

Before Dotun lost his job, any time I was in Lagos, I stayed at his place in Surulere. As I watched Rotimi pull off her doll's arm in the hotel room, I wished I was back there with him, disagreeing over the current state of the nation. I knew he'd have justified the military government's refusal to release the election results; he was the kind of idiot who announced to anyone who cared to listen that the military was the best thing that had happened to the country. I missed him.

It was impossible not to think about him while I was in Lagos. We'd attended the University of Lagos together, shared a flat off campus during my final year. It was during that year that I told him I'd never had an erection. At first he laughed, but realising I was serious he scratched the back of his head and told me not to worry because it would happen when I met the right girl. And because he was Dotun, while we waited for the right woman to show up he paraded a series of girls through our flat during the day and dragged me to red light districts on Allen Avenue at night. He was the one who, even after I started treatment at a private clinic in Ikeja during my final semester at university, bought herbs and miracle drinks that purged me but did not harden my penis. Thanks to him, I must have watched every pornographic video that was available in Nigeria. I watched it all: men and women, men and men, women and women—nothing worked.

As I thought about my brother, I considered calling up his wife, Ajoke, to ask if I could visit their children while I was in town. I didn't intend to ever respond to Dotun's letter, but as Rotimi pulled my nose and laughed each time I yelped, I could no longer deny that I owed him something in spite of his affair with Yejide.

I called Bauchi instead, spoke with the house-maid who told me Iya Bolu and my wife had already gone to sleep.

On Tuesday morning, I bought a newspaper, searched its pages for news about when the election results would be released. The pages were filled with wild speculation, several theories and angry op-eds, but little information. There was no statement from the federal military government. It was becoming evident that the bogus court injunction that stayed further release of electoral results was serving their purpose in some way. High courts in Ibadan and Lagos had already issued counter-judgments and ordered the national electoral commission to release the rest of the results. I didn't believe the bizarre drama that was playing out indicated that the military intended to hold on to power indefinitely. For some reason, I thought they were simply trying to push back the handover date by a few months and were delaying the result to achieve that.

I remember thinking, as I folded up the newspaper, that the situation would be resolved within a few weeks at the most. I assumed the military knew that it had become unpopular and would head back to the barracks before the year ran out. If someone had told me that morning that Nigeria would spend six more years under military dictatorship, I would have laughed.

After breakfast, I placed another call to Bauchi and spoke with Iya Bolu. She raised her voice when she told me Yejide was in the bathroom at the moment, giving me the impression that my wife was right there, but just didn't want to speak to me. I wanted to talk to her. I'd assumed that because she was away she would want to talk, if only to hear how Rotimi was doing. I was planning to slip in a line about what I was doing in Lagos. I thought I was ready to discuss my condition with her, felt it would help that I wouldn't have to look at her, figured she couldn't walk out on me. The worst she could do was drop the phone. As I told Iya Bolu that I would call back before the end of the day, I felt I was ready to tell Yejide anything, even about my desperate visit to a traditional herbalist.

I had travelled to Ilara-Mokin to consult Baba Suke during a period I still consider as one of the worst I've lived through. At the time, Yejide was rubbishing all medical evidence to the contrary as she proclaimed to the world that she was pregnant.

I'd assumed that all herbalists were old men. But Baba Suke was young; he was probably in his twenties. He gave me a tar-black concoction to drink and charged five naira.

As I drove back to Ilesa, a movement started just above my groin. I parked by the roadside, wondering if the slow rumbling, the tightening and relaxing of my stomach muscles, meant the potion was working.

It was sudden. And until the stench filled the car, I couldn't bear to believe it. I didn't have a cure—just diarrhoea like I'd never had before. I sat dazed, the watery stool soaking through my jeans while cars sped by. The next month, I travelled to Lagos to see Dotun and didn't say a word about Baba Suke as I begged him to come to Ilesa and get Yejide pregnant.

When I called Bauchi in the afternoon, the maid said Iya Bolu and Yejide had gone out. Even when Iya Bolu told me in the evening that Yejide was once again in the bathroom, I told myself that the fact that she stayed with me after confronting me meant something. Although she

322

still wasn't speaking to me and often walked out of the room if I tried to talk to her, I was grateful that she had remained in the house. My secret was out and we were still under the same roof. That had to count for something. I planned to sit her down when we were back in Ilesa, ask her if we could begin again on fresh terms.

On Wednesday I woke up to the rumour that the presidential elections had been annulled. I don't think I'd heard the word "annul" used except in reference to marriage before that day. I'd definitely never heard a hotel waiter use it before then. By evening, the rumour had become news and a small crowd had gathered in the street, protesting without placards, burning tires. A man stood in the middle of the road, holding his hands aloft like wings while other men set up barricades with large tree branches, scraps of metal, nails and broken bottles.

I turned away from the window to face my daughter. "This is impossible," I said, "impossible. These soldiers must be joking. Who do they think they are?"

She mimicked the word "impossible," then threw her rattle in the air.

That night, I insisted on waiting on the phone until Yejide got out of the bathroom she seemed to be living in since she'd got to Bauchi.

"So?" she said when she came on the line.

"Are you all right? People are really reacting to this annulment news here. Are things peaceful at your end?"

"Yes."

"I just wanted to make sure you are fine. People were blocking the streets in Ikeja today, looks like they'll be back tomorrow. I don't think I'll be able to get out and see my urologist tomorrow."

I tapped the phone's rotary dial, hoping she'd noticed that I'd mentioned what I was doing in Lagos, wishing she'd acknowledge the last sentence with something—a sigh, a question, a hiss. I would have been grateful for any reaction.

"Are you there?" I asked after a while.

"Anything else?" she said.

"Well, Rotimi is doing fine—she just fell asleep."

"Good night."

The next morning, I woke up just before 8 and was surprised to find that Rotimi was still sound asleep. Since we'd arrived in Lagos, she'd taken to waking me up by kissing my chin while she drummed on my cheeks. Outside, a crowd was gathering—chanting, waving placards. Before noon, there were thousands of people on the street; the air was thick with fumes as several tires were set ablaze. There was no point trying to get to the hospital.

Rotimi didn't eat any of the beans I ordered for lunch, so I ordered some rice. She didn't eat any of that either. When she climbed off my knee and lay on the floor, I knelt beside her, promising ice cream if she ate some food. But she didn't try to sit up, smile or try to negotiate. She closed her eyes, then covered them with her left arm. I placed a palm against her forehead: it felt warm, like the beginnings of a fever. I lifted her off the floor, placed her on the bed. I had packed paracetamol syrup for the trip, along with other drugs, but because she shivered when I let her go, I decided it might be best to get her to a hospital straight away.

I went to a window and looked out into the street, wondering if the crowd would let me drive through if I just explained my daughter's health condition. That was when I saw the soldiers. I was still at the window when the first gunshot was fired into the crowd. I fell on my face, crawled to the bed and pulled my daughter to the floor. Her eyes were shut and she was screaming. At first I thought it was the sound of the gunshots that was startling her, but when I touched her forehead it felt as though there was a furnace right under her skin.

39

As we got ready to sleep on our first night in Bauchi, Iya Bolu gave me a little lecture about how I needed to sit up and take care of Rotimi. She was in front of the dressing mirror, rubbing lotion into her neck and peering at a pimple that sat on her nose.

"I have to tell you the truth, Iya Rotimi. This thing you are doing is not right. What did that child do to you? I've never seen you play with her, not once. Think of her Creator before you treat her like that now. See the way you carried her on your knees, far far from your body. It is not good-o. Is it because of this sickler thing? Ah, we can't always tell how tomorrow will be by looking at today. Your own job as her mother is to take care of her. Leave it to God to decide if she will live or die. Don't kill her in your mind yet. Don't do that."

"Before you call the snail a weakling, tie your house to your back and carry it around for a week," I said. I found it strange that Iya Bolu, who had never watched any of her children stop breathing, thought she could tell me how to live my life. "Besides, when your daughters were her age, did you not leave them alone to crawl all over the passageway?"

She frowned and rubbed night lotion into her face. "You think you can shut me up by insulting me. All I know is that you need to stop punishing Rotimi for the death of . . . the others."

"Their names are Olamide and Sesan. And I'm not insulting you. *Abi*, you did not leave them in the passageway?"

Iya Bolu rose up and went to sit on her bed. "At least I fed them when they were hungry and held them when they cried. Iya Rotimi, I'm not trying to poke your wound with a stick. I'm just saying, she cannot have any other mother and, for now, she is the only child you have."

I was not punishing Rotimi for anything. I simply did not believe that she would live long enough to remember anything I did or did not do. I believed it was a matter of time before she went the way of my other children and I was readying myself, adjusting myself to being without a child. Whenever I thought about it, all I hoped was that she would not suffer too much. I did not hold her too close because I was protecting myself from her. I had lost pieces of myself to Sesan and Olamide and I held myself back from Rotimi because I wanted to have something left when she was gone.

"This one that you asked the maid to lie to your husband that we were already asleep, are you fighting with him?"

"Even the tongue and the teeth cannot cohabit without fighting."

"Iya Rotimi, all these proverbs. Good night *o jare*." She turned her back to me and pulled the covers over her head.

On Thursday, I was alone with the maid in the house. Iya Bolu's brother and his wife had left for work and Iya Bolu had gone to the market to do some shopping for her children. The bride-to-be, a lecturer at the University of Jos, was expected to arrive that evening. I was reading an old newspaper when the maid came to the room and told me that I had a call from Lagos.

"I've told you to tell him I'm busy."

"He said he must speak to you, madam. He said your baby is sick."

I put down the newspaper and went into the sitting room.

"Yejide," Akin said after I picked up the phone. "Rotimi lost consciousness."

I fell back into a chair. Before that day, I thought I was prepared, distant enough in emotion and location to take the news that Rotimi was dead or dying. But what do we know about ourselves? Do we ever really know what we will do in any situation until the situation presents itself? Since the day she was born, I had been getting myself ready for the worst but a lifetime was not enough to prepare me for the dizziness that hit me.

"You have to get her to the hospital," I said.

"They are shooting in the streets, Yejide. The soldiers are here. They are shooting, shooting people. She just stopped screaming all of a sudden. Then I . . . then I tried to wake her up, but she has not responded. But she is still breathing, she is still breathing."

"You have to get her to a hospital."

"Is there anything you know that I can do? Is there anything I can do now? Yejide? Yejide? Are you there? What am I supposed to do now?"

"You have to get her to a hospital."

"Say something else. I'm sure they've killed people already; we could get shot. Is there anything I can do? Yejide? Do you know anything? Did they teach you any emergency procedure for Sesan? Yejide?"

I could see what was left of Rotimi's life unfolding before me.

"I am not coming back to you."

"What are you saying?"

"I am not coming back to Ilesa. I am not coming back to you."

"What are you saying? Look, I need to go. I will call you tonight to let you know if . . . if . . . to let you know."

I sat in the strange sitting room, holding the receiver to my ear long after the line had gone dead. A good mother would wait for the inevitable phone call, go back to Ilesa and receive visitors, accept condolence messages as chief mourner, play her role as Rotimi's mother even though she was gone. After I had done all that, only after that could I leave my husband. But I was tired and there was nothing left in Ilesa for me. The salon was there, but it was not enough to take me back into the same city where Akin lived. I could not bear the thought of driving past Wesley Guild Hospital one more time or seeing children dressed in the same school uniform Sesan had worn when he was alive. So I did what I really wanted to do.

I drank two glasses of water and then went into the room I was sharing with Iya Bolu. I took only my handbag. All the things I needed were in it: my chequebook, a pen, a notebook, all the cash I had taken to Bauchi, and my only photo of my mother. I left a note on Iya Bolu's bed. I was sure her sister-in-law would read it and explain to her that I was not coming back.

I went into the street and flagged down a taxi that was going to the motor park. Tears clouded my vision as I got into the car and I almost stumbled. I admitted to myself then that I had failed and Rotimi too had taken a part of me. As I got out of the taxi and wiped my tears away so that I could see the signs indicating where each bus was heading, I knew that I would never forget Rotimi, I would never be able to erase her the way I wished I could.

I boarded a bus that was heading to Jos. Jos because I had heard it was the most beautiful city in Nigeria and I had always wanted to go there. It would take a while for me to realise that each of my children had given me as much as they took. My memories of them, bittersweet and constant, were as powerful as a physical presence. And because of that, as a bus bore me into the heart of a city I did not know, while my last child was dying in Lagos and the country was unravelling, I was not afraid because I was not alone.

PART FOUR

40

I am here. My hands tremble as I adjust my wrapper and my heart thumps against my throat, but I'm here, and I'm not leaving until I see you.

The guests have turned up in their hundreds and the canopies are the very expensive types with air-conditioning—your father has died well. This secondary school field has been transformed. There are banners bearing your father's photo, policemen to send miscreants away and strung-up lights to keep the party going into the night. Any man whose children can pull off this kind of carnival to honour him when he is gone has died a successful death. But I am not here because of his death; I have come because of the child I left behind, the one whose passing I did not want to watch.

I wanted to come back many times, just to ask you about her final moments. I could no longer afford the luxury of hope, so I shut out the idea that somehow she might have made it. And any time I considered coming back to you, it was so that I could ask if she did not suffer too much pain.

More than once, I packed a weekend bag and told my driver to get ready for a trip to Ilesa. But on the days I was supposed to leave Jos, I was always frozen in place, unable to get out of bed, certain that any movement would shatter me into a million tiny pieces. I spent those days in bed, weeping without sobbing, letting tears trickle down the sides of my face until they tickled my ear, because I did not have the energy to lift my hands to catch them. After a decade, I stopped planning those trips and for five years I did not pack a weekend bag or tell my driver to prepare for a trip down south.

I am ready now, ready to hear about her last moments and to know where she was buried. There is no point denying that the worst has happened to me more than once, and not seeing their graves does not change the fact that I have outlived the ones who should have stood on freshly dug earth and thrown the first handfuls of sand on my coffin. Akin, I no longer care about honouring tradition: I must see my daughter's grave.

Under the canopies, everything is yellow and green. Green tablecloths, yellow satin covers with green bows for the chairs. I sit down on the first seat I can find under a canopy that has your name on it; there are over a thousand guests here. You must have spent a lot of money, but it is not showing as well as it should. Everyone at this table is complaining, no one has been served anything. Not even a bottle of water.

"But the canopy is very fine and they've decorated the chairs so well." I still jump to your defence, as though this is my family, as though I am not a prodigal here.

The man next to me scoffs. "We are supposed to eat the tablecloths? I have food in my house. If they knew they didn't have the money to feed us, why invite so many people? Must they throw a big party? Is it by force?"

"I'm sure the servers will get to us soon." I stand up and go to another table. After I sit, I am restless; I drum my fingers against my knee and search the crowd for a head that looks like yours. Your cap will be off by now; caps make your head sweat. I am looking out for a bare head.

"Testing, testing, microphone. One, two, one, two. Testing, testing, one, two, one, two," someone says over the public address system.

I see you now; you are standing a table away. My eyes make contact with your lips; the lower one is still pink. You do not see me; your eyes scan the crowd and you greet your guests absentmindedly. You are looking for somebody. You pass by my table. I push my nails into my palms so I won't reach out to touch you. I no longer feel as brave as I did when I decided to come, and I want to cling to the small comforts of ignorance. Maybe I am not ready to know how my daughter died after all. Maybe I do not need to know.

"Baba Rotimi, the banker, see how he is walking, money is walking," a woman at my table says, slapping a palm on her thigh. Her gaze follows you.

I'm startled that they still call you by Rotimi's name and I hope no one uses it to your face. Only the cruel would remind you of our loss this way.

"Is his brother here? The only two sons of their mother, I hear they don't even greet each other?" the other woman at the table asks.

"Of course he is here too. Is it not also his father who has died? Is it not? They will have to settle their quarrel for their dead father's sake at least," the first woman says.

"You know they say it was his wife that caused problems between the two of them? Imagine some wicked women, they don't want their husband's people around them at all—wicked women."

So, this is how our story is told? I am the wicked one and you are the saint. I stand up and walk round and round the canopy until I find you standing in front of a table laden with drinks.

There's a teenage girl next to you. She looks like me but she has your nose. I blink and she is still there, standing by your side. I move closer, and my mouth slides open. I have thought of this meeting happening in so many ways, but I

338

never imagined that your arm would be around her shoulders, never let myself think she would be smiling up at you.

How could you not have let me know?

My eyes meet hers first; she stares at me the way people stare at intruders, as though I am someone she has never seen before. There are so many words bubbling up in my chest, they take all the space for my air and I can hardly breathe. You turn sideways and our eyes meet. I look from your face to hers and feel as though I might faint. This is a battle I thought I had lost and suddenly it appears I have won—not just the battle, but the war.

She has my mother's eyes, her long neck and the thin slash of her lips. I want to touch her, but I am afraid she might recoil or even disappear. As I take a deep breath, she reaches up to touch the crucifix that dangles from her gold necklace.

I step closer. "Is this my daughter? Akinyele, is this my daughter?"

41

Yejide, every day since I sent you an invitation to this funeral, I have worried about how this moment would play out. Timi has told me several times that it will all be all right. But what does she know? Only enough to think there is still a chance that the three of us will become a happy family. I should know better—do know better—but with you, I can never let go of hope.

"Who is this?" you keep saying, pointing to Timi but looking at me. "Is this Rotimi? Akin, who is this?"

She prefers to be called Timi, says she is her own person, not a monument to siblings she never knew. I agree. She plans to change her name officially, but wants to discuss it with you first. She has always believed that we would find you, yet has backed out of every plan we've made to get in touch since we got your address. We booked flights that we never boarded. I wrote letters that she tore up. She wrote letters and tore them up.

What if Mum doesn't want me? she'd ask as we left the airport, as she threw shreds of carefully crafted letters in the bin. I'd tell her that you loved her, would never have left if you knew she was alive, that you would want her now. Just once, she said: *Even in spite of my sickle-cell issues? See, I've got this friend at uni and his father left their family because of his SCD, he couldn't bear it. You can tell me if that's why Mum left. I can take it.* That one time, I assured her that you'd never let her out of your sight when you were with us, told her the day you left for Bauchi was the first time you'd left the house without her in your arms. It's only fair to tell her good things about you.

She was the one who decided that we should send you an invitation after my father died. She picked the courier company; I sent the invitation. Since then we've waited and worried, and now here you are, just within our reach.

Now she touches my arm, leans close and whispers, "It's her, isn't it?"

You are staring at her, looking as though you are about to collapse. Some party guests are giving us sidelong glances, craning their necks in our direction.

I hold Timi's hand. "Yejide, please come with us."

I'm not sure whose hand is sweating, Timi's or mine. You walk behind us. Timi keeps turning to look at you, brows furrowed as though she thinks you will not be there when she looks back. We walk until the sound of music is faint and I can hear your heels clicking against the stony ground.

Before us, there is a freshly painted block of classrooms.

When we are inside one of the rooms, I clear my throat. "Yes, this is Rotimi," I say. "But we call her Timi now."

"Oh my God! Please, I need to sit down."

Timi and I watch you sit on a wooden desk. You bend over, hold your head. Timi's grip tightens until my hand begins to feel numb.

"We found you last year," Timi says. "Bolu, you remember her, right? She is studying for a master's degree at UniJos. She came to buy gold from your store—she recognised you."

You look up at Timi with your mouth slightly open. I can hear you breathing.

"It's all right if you want to leave. I . . . I just wanted to . . . I just wanted to see you. That's all."

But that is not all she wants. That is not all I want either. She wants you to hold her, to tell her you didn't forget about her, even when you thought you'd never see her again. She wants you to stay.

"Rotimi," you say, standing up.

"Timi," her voice quavers. "Everyone calls me Timi."

"My child, *omo mi.*"

Timi lets go of my hand as you step towards her.

You touch her face as though you expect to

342

catch tears, but her cheeks are dry, just like yours. She lets her hands hang free by her sides, waits until you pull her into a hug. Then she places her arms around you ever so carefully, as if she thinks she could break you.

"Please, Rotimi. Timi," you say. "Can you please wait outside? Please? I need to talk to Akin."

"OK," she says. Then after a while, she smiles and adds, "You've got to let me go before I can go."

She pulls out of your embrace and leaves the room. Her back is straight, her chin held high, like yours. She moves away from this building, stands with her side to us, shakes wrinkles out of her yellow dress.

"You told me she lost consciousness." Your back is to me but I can tell that your focus is on the place where Timi stands.

"She did. But eventually I walked to a clinic. Had to lift her up in the air like a flag while I was on the road so that the soldiers wouldn't shoot. They wouldn't let me take a car, even when they saw she was unconscious."

You turn towards me, search my face. I will not blame you if you don't believe me, but this is the truth as it happened. You frown, lean against a wall, turn your face towards the open door. You are silent for what feels like hours. And the only sound between us is the faint music from the

343

party. I should find words to break the silence, but all I can think of is how beautiful you are to me, after all this time, and I know that is not what you want to hear. I decide to wait for your questions before I say any of the words I have rehearsed in front of the mirror you used when we shared the same room.

"What did you tell her about me? About why I left?"

"I told her that I'd said she was dead when I called you. So, as far as she is concerned, when you disappeared, you did so thinking you had lost another child."

You begin to walk away, towards the door, towards Timi. Suddenly you stop and turn to me.

"Did you tell her about us and Dotun? About—?"

"Does she need to know?"

You purse your lips and nod. "How has it been—with her health?"

"She is brave."

You raise your voice, like you expect me to disagree. "I need to be with her tonight."

"Of course," I say. "I've prepared a room for you at home. We can leave right now if you want to."

You stare at me as if I've just given you a knife and asked you to stab yourself. "No, I can't come to your place."

Your last two words are all it takes for me to swallow all the foolish words I've prepared. *I want you to live with me. We can be companions. I have missed you. If you want to keep lovers, just be discreet about it. We can start again, on new terms.*

"What I mean is, if Rotimi, Timi doesn't mind, I will take her with me back to the hotel so she can spend the night with me. We'll come to your place tomorrow and then you and I can discuss how this will work."

"Of course," I say.

"All right then." You turn round, loosen and retie your wrapper as you walk through the door. You go to Timi, hold her hand; put your forehead against hers. She nods as you speak to her. You put an arm around her shoulders and lead her out of my sight.

42

I hold my daughter's hands, slide my thumbs over her palms, touch the insides of her wrists and feel her pulse. This is not a dream. My daughter is here, standing before me with her back to the classroom. Her feet are clad in gold sandals, her toenails painted green. The scalloped hem of her yellow dress brushes against her knees, a crucifix hangs from her gold necklace, her lips are coated in pink gloss and her eyes are lined with kohl. She *is* here. I step forward, put my forehead against hers and feel her breath on my face. Her head-tie crackles against my scarf.

"Rotimi . . . Timi, Timi." This is all I can say.

I count her fingers, running my right thumb and forefinger along their lengths and stifling the urge to go on my knees and count her toes. I am Thomas, seeking tactile proof of what my eyes have seen before giving in to joy. My daughter blinks back tears and smiles.

I touch the crucifix. "Is this the—?"

"Dad said you gave it to me." She clears her throat. "I wear it a lot."

I do not hold back my own tears as I think of all the years my daughter has spent as a motherless child. I want to hold her face in my hands until she lets the tears flow. I want to hug her tight and tell her she will feel better if she cries, but I realise that I don't know if she will. I don't even know if she tied this beautiful *gele* all by herself or needed someone else to help her spread out the edges. The child I left behind is now a young woman I recognise but do not know. A fresh stream of tears wells up in my eyes, this time for me and all the years I lived as a childless mother while someone else held my daughter's hand on her first day of school, while someone else showed her how to line her eyes perfectly with kohl.

"I am so sorry. If I had known you were alive . . . if I had known, I swear I would have come back. I would have come. I would have come for you."

"You're here." She wipes away my tears with her hands. "You're here now."

Her words wash over me, an absolution for the lost years.

"Moomi," she whispers.

I glance behind me, expecting to see my mother-in-law. "Your grandmother? Where is she?"

My daughter laughs—and the wonderful sound brings a smile to my face. I want her laughter to ring on until the end of time.

"Mum, I've been waiting to say that for like forever. You're my own Moomi. I don't call Grandma that." She touches the crucifix and shrugs. "Nobody understands, it's just my weird thing."

"I understand." I understand how a word others use every day can become something whispered in the dark to soothe a wound that just won't heal. I remember thinking I would never hear it spoken without unravelling a little, wondering if I would ever get to say it in the light. So I recognise the gift in this simple pronouncement, the promise of a beginning in this one word.

"Will you please say it again, call me that again?" I ask, grateful that my child will not have to settle for a substitute.

My daughter draws me into her arms. "Moomi." Her voice is soft and tremulous.

I shut my eyes as one receiving a benediction. Inside me something unfurls, joy spreads through my being, unfamiliar yet unquestioned, and I know that this too is a beginning, a promise of wonders to come.

Acknowledgments

As always, I am grateful to my mother for her steadfast love and faith in me.

To my amazing sister, JolaaJesu, who somehow finds the time to read everything I write, thank you for standing with me. *O ra n'ukan ro.*

I am grateful to Clare Alexander and Kathy Robbins, whose enthusiasm and diligence made this U.S. edition possible.

Ellah Allfrey, Louisa Joyner, Jennifer Jackson and Joanna Dingley, thank you so much for making this a better novel.

To the Knopf team—Zakiya Harris, Katie Burns, Katie Schoder, Nicholas Latimer and everyone else—thank you for your commitment to this novel.

Paula Cocozza, Rory Gleeson, Jacqueline Landey and Suzanne Ushie, thanks for invaluable feedback, kind words and insightful criticism.

Dami Ajayi, jolly papa, thank you for always believing I could do this.

Emmanuel Iduma, brother-man, I am grateful for your faith in this novel.

I am especially grateful to you, Professor Chima Anyadike. Thank you for granting me access to your impressive library, being a splendid teacher and believing in my writing. Dr. Bisi Anyadike, thank you for celebrating with me every time I succeed.

I remain indebted to the staff of Ledig House, Hedgebrook and Threads for the time and space the residencies there provided.

At different times, the kindness of Professor Ebun Adejuyigbe and Dr. A. R. Adetunji made it possible for me to keep writing; I am grateful.

Arthur Anyaduba, Abubakar Adam Ibrahim and Laniyi Fayemi, thank you for reading bits and pieces of this book.

And of course, thank you to Yejide and Akin Ajayi, who chose to stay with me for as long as I needed them.

A Note About the Author

Ayobami Adebayo's stories have appeared in a number of magazines and anthologies, and one was highly commended in the 2009 Commonwealth Short Story Competition. She holds BA and MA degrees in literature in English from Obafemi Awolowo University, Ife, and has worked as an editor for *Saraba Magazine* since 2009. She also has an MA in creative writing from the University of East Anglia, where she was awarded an international bursary for creative writing. She has received fellowships and residencies from Ledig House, Sinthian Cultural Centre, Hedgebrook, Ox-Bow School of Art, Ebedi Hills and the Siena Art Institute. She was born in Lagos, Nigeria.

Center Point Large Print
600 Brooks Road / PO Box 1
Thorndike, ME 04986-0001 USA

(207) 568-3717

US & Canada:
1 800 929-9108
www.centerpointlargeprint.com